CRICKETS

By Chester Alfonso

ISBN
978-1-962868-28-0 (Paperback)
978-1-962868-29-7 (eBook)
978-1-962868-27-3 (Hardcover)

TABLE OF CONTENTS

ACKNOWLEDGEMENT

Much thanks and appreciation to the folks at Twenty20 Literary Group. Your guidance, encouragement, and patience kept my fingers moving and my creative juices flowing. Special thanks to my agent, Rizza Taylor. Her constant input, smile, and belief aided me immeasurably. Looking forward, Twenty20 Literary Group, Rizza, and I, to our next collaboration.

What kind'a job you do? Where you work at? Buy me a drink of that Scotch whisky. The one on the second shelf.

You don't look like you do what you say you do. This some good shit. I could drink this shit till I fall out. Thanks for buying it for me. You got one of them mischievous smiles. Don't know if I can trust you. You married or what? Got any babies? What about diseases? You ain't sick, is you? Be sweet and buy me another one? Sal, bring me another one. Make it a double. This fine looking, sweet gentleman is buying.

Ain't no telling when that no-good bastard gonna walk through the door. Sonofabitch, 'cording to what MaryAnn just told me on the phone, is out at that low down whore house drinkin' shine and messin' with them girls young enough to be his granddaughter. One of these days he gonna tumble over dead from just thinkin' 'bout what them sorry bitched be doing.

This one, like all the others, is for Judy, Jacqueline, Mason and Griffin. I love you more than you'll ever imagine.

I still love Marvin Gaye's music. Lord, that boy sure could sing. I remember Marvin Gaye's his style. I still love listening to "What's Going On," and "Inner City Blues" and "Mercy, Mercy Me." But, hard as I try, I can't remember the day Marvin died. Can't remember what I was doing when Marvin's daddy shot him dead. Can't remember where I was going when Marvin's mother broke down and cried at his funeral. Still, I love Marvin's music, but I never did love Marvin's addiction to all that dope.

INTRODUCTION

Got me a passport. Went through ATL customs. Flew to the Netherlands. Checked into a clean Amsterdam hotel. Walked the streets. Had coffee in quaint cafes and coffee shops. Kept looking. Kept observing. Kept writing. Kept inventing, reinventing phrases, while telling stories that are waist-deep in imagination and knee-deep in truth.

Back in Selma, during the late-thirties and on through the mid-fifties, sitting and listening to the old folks rehash their past, speak about their present, and look skyward for a better future. My mind was glued to every word, every sigh, laughter, hope, and groan.

Maybe that's why I love telling my stories the way I tell them. Telling about things that most people never believe happened or need to be reminded of. That's why I write the way I do. That's why I walk European and Asian streets.

Some of these writings are about the terrible situations people, without much help, must survive. Certain things bother, pound on my mind and wreak havoc throughout my entire body. These are things I should have tried to avoid. But sometimes I can't stop myself from getting bothered and upset about the nastiness and ugliness folks delve and wallow in like they be downright crazy.

Through these words, I want you to see, feel, smell and touch where I've been and what I've experienced. I hope these writings paint pictures for you the way I want them to.

Take Care,
Chester Alfonso

NEGROES AND THEIR HALF-WHITE, HALF-BLACK PRESIDENT: THE BEFORE & THE AFTER - (UPDATED)

Statements by ten African Americans concerning the election of Barack Hussein Obama, America's first Half-Black, Half-White President…

Sauntesa Johnson, January 2009

Shit, I knowed he was gonna win.
God being good as God is,
He done finally give us a new day.
And a brand-new way.
A sho-nuff prophet,
He done give us.
Done give us another path,
A better path that ain't so crooked
And ain't so filled with evil.
One of them glory paths just
For us Black folks to travel on.
Even folks who don't like 'em,
Like these hateful and evil White devils,
Couldn't stop the power of the Lord.
Couldn't stop what was ordained
 By the Almighty.
You see when the Lord declares
Somethin' then whatever He
Declares is gonna be.
God, long time ago,

Looked down on Barack's
White Momma
And Barack's Black daddy
And told'em they was gonna
Have them a miracle child.
Once they had their miracle child
They was gonna breakup from each other
And go their own separate ways
'Cause their deed done been done.
They will have made,
With the power of God,
One of them miracle babies.
They named him after his,
Black-to-the-bone, African daddy:
Barack Hussein Obama.
What I'm tellin' everybody is that
God done blessed this man.
In a few days he gonna be
The most powerful man
In the whole wide world.
These crackers, these po white folks,
These racist, these lynchers,
And these night-riders,
With all their shenanigans,
And with all their big money,
With all their lying newspapers,
And their back-stabbing
Television stations, ain't had
The power to overcome God's will.
First time I heard Barack words
Coming outta his mouth,
I knowed he was bound for
Glorious things. Hallelujah things.
Beautiful things. Godly things.
Righteous things. Things that is

Gonna make this fucked up
World tremble. Especially this
Sho-nuff fucked up
United States of America;
I'm talkin' bout the goddamned,
U.S. of A.
Whenever he stood on them stages
And made a speech, I would just sit
And listen and smile, squeeze my
Hands and pray one of my serious prayers.
That man, every time he opened his mouth,
He took me to a special place.
A place like I ain't ever before thought existed.
Whenever I watched television and
They showed him walking –
The way he strutted with all his stuff
And wit his brains and his good looks -
I would get so nervous and proud like
I ain't never been so nervous and
Proud since the day I was born.
I had to stop whatever I be doing
And take a deep breath,
Go get me a glass of cooled water
From the frigerator and fan myself.
I could tell by the way he talked
That he had worked hard,
Sho nuff real hard,
For ain't no tellin' how long,
To get where he be.
Where he deserves to be.
Where he belongs to be.
I ain't never watched so
Much of that CNN
And them other news channels like
I watched when he,

With his pretty and sexy ass,
Was whipping the hell outta
All them White folks.
Had to stop watchin'
My daytime soap shows.
Had to turn-off Wheel of Fortune,
Maury and Jerry Springer.
I was tickled to death when he
Told that smartass bitch, Hillary,
Where she could take her big
Thighs and made-up face.
Barack's daddy, you know,
Was one of them real Africans
Who came to America on his own.
Not on some slave boat.
Came to be educated and not to
Work on anybody's fuckin' plantation.
He dead but what I been told by Bessie,
The girl who fixes my hair,
That man, Barack's daddy,
Was some sorta African king,
Or somethin' like a king,
Back in his African country.
They say he was smart,
Just like Barack,
But he was way blacker.
Yep, that African man
Who was the daddy of
The soon to be president,
Was sho nuff black.
He was a midnight-black, Black man.
Too black for my taste but,
Like I said, he was smart as hell.
Now, Barack, he be high-yellow
'Cause his Momma was

One of them White girls from
One of them places where they
All the time gets lot of snow
And storms. Kansas, I believe it is.
So, when that African man,
With all the baby-making juice,
Them African men be carrying,
Tapped that girl's booty and shot
His load into her, anybody, who
Knowed anythang, could'a told'em
A baby was gonna be coming
They way mighty soon.
But, you know what's so
Sad 'bout it all: that Black African
Bastard, even smart as he was,
Did what most'a these trifling
Black men do, whether they be
From Africa or some place in Texas,
He said: "Fuck it. I'm outta here,
I ain't gonna spend my time helping
To raise no baby."
So, this African man walked out
On his White wife and his
New baby, Barack.
How come Black men all the time,
No matter where they from,
Do shit like that?
Why they always leave the
Momma and the baby to fend
For themselves?
But, this White girl was strong.
She was smart.
Smart as that Black African man,
Barack's Daddy.
Even if she didn't have common sense,

She had whole bunch'a book sense.
So, she kept right on with her
College education.
Got herself a new man and little
Barack, a new daddy. A step-daddy.
Taking Barack wit'er, she up
And followed that man back
To where he lived.
To one of them po countries with
Bunches of them damn Muslims;
Where ain't too many of the people
Got a pot to piss in.

Barack's Momma and
Her new husband,
And Barack's new step-daddy,
They had a child together.
Then, for no-telling-why,
They broke-up.

See, that smart girl from Kansas,
Had gone and met another no-good,
Ain't-worth-a-good-goddamn man.
Another educated shyster
Who was kind' a dark-skinned,
Almost black.
Break-up didn't last too long fo they
Got the divorce papers signed.
Before long, his second daddy,
His step-daddy, that is, not long after
Git'n divorced from Barack's Momma,
Up and died.
Just like Barack's real daddy
Had up and died.
Us po blacks all the time be saying,

"God don't like ugly" and "Shit happens."

Little Barack.
Boy, so young, seeing all the
Disturbin' thangs going
On 'round 'em;
Hell, he had to notice the shit,
Had to see it.
The bad going-ons had to
Bother the child.
It's a wonder, ain't it,
That he turned out to be
As precious and smart as he is.

But, when God got his eyes on supin,
That supin's gonna be taken care of.
And, God was looking real
Close at Barack. God was sayin':
"I'm gonna make this boy into supin
Everybody under the sun will come
To 'preciate, love and wanna always
Be around."

Before long this Blessed Child,
With his Momma in bad health
And on her death bed,
Kept on receiving the
Helping Hand of God.
He went to one of them colleges
in Los Angeles.
Then, he went on up there to
That fancy school in New York
And then went to the same school
That them rich Kennedy boys went to.
But, Barack, is smarter than any of them

Kennedys or any of them other White folks.
Graduated, yes, he did, with a law degree.
Was the smartest one in his class, too.
Made the best grades. Got the highest honors.

Before anybody's spit could hit the ground,
Barack was getting' ready to walk down
That street all the presidents walk down:
Pennsylvania Avenue, in Washington, D. C.
Him and his pretty, long-legged Black wife
And they two cute daughters.

I done already gone to Target and
Bought me a real pretty outfit.
Stopped by the drug store
And got me some Tylenol.
Wants to make sure when
All the excitement starts
I will have something to take
To calm my nerves.

I'm'a get up early on
That January morning.
Then, I'm'a fall on my knees
And thank the Lord for
All He's done for all us po black folks.

I'm'a take a long, hot shower.
Put on my new clothes.
Put my medicine on the table
Next to my easy chair.
Turn on the television at
Five in the morning and enjoy
The best day I will ever
Have in my life.

Sauntesa Johnson, October 2012

I done just 'bout gave up.
I been through so much in this here life.
So many trials and tribulations.
So many ups and downs.
These last few years done been
Pure Holy Hell for me.

I had so much love and prayed
So hard for President Obama.
I believed the *Hope* and *Change*
He talked about, was gonna happen.
I prayed harder for Barack than I
Ever thought I could pray for anybody.
I prayed for him to be the best president
This country and the world ever beheld.
I wanted him to lift up us Black folks
And carry us, if not over the finish line,
At least close to the finish line.

Now, I'm halfway disappointed
At what he didn't get done for the
People who gave him nearly all
The votes they could muster.

One thing I do 'preciate that
He did was that health care
Bill he got passed and signed.
You see two years ago, I was so
Worked-up over what Barack was saying
And what he said he was gonna do,
I ended up having a stroke.
Had to go to the hospital.
Stayed there for two whole weeks.

Don't know what would have
Come of me if that health care thing
Wasn't there for me to use.

But, to tell the truth,
I ain't too pleased
'Bout some of that other junk Barack
Spent his time on.
During President Obama's years –
Sometimes I call him Barack -
Other times I call him President Obama,
I never use his middle name.
Anyway, Black folks continued to suffer
More'n anybody else in America,
Other than them pitiful Natives - the Indians.

The President was, every-other day,
Talking 'bout how he was gonna do
This and do that for the gays and the
Lesbians and them transsexuals.
He would then go on and on 'bout
How all the Muslims was alright.
Then the next day he would send them
Drones and bombers over where the
Muslims live and kill a bunch of'em.
Didn't make no sense to me
What he was doin'.

What he wasn't doin' was talking
Serious and actin' serious
'Bout issues in the Black communities.
The communities, both times,
That came out and voted for him
Like we ain't ever voted for anybody
In the history of America.

The communities, like the one I live in,
Is suffering just as bad as they was
Before he got to the White House.
Some of us done even ended up worst off.

Taylor Lipton, April 2008
The color or the pigmentation
Of a person's skin does not matter.
Their gender, religion, and sexual
Preferences don't matter, either.
None of that bullshit matters to me.
Not one iota. Not one damn bit.

What I look at is ability. Character.
Fortitude. Compassion. Determination.
How smart the person is.
Where they stand on social issues.
I want to know if they are willing
To do what's right for the country.
Integrity. Spirituality. Wholesomeness.
Whether they have an open mind.
These are the things I use when
Most of the times I vote for the person
I think should be president.

Now, don't get me wrong,
I'm tickled as can be that a
Black man is way ahead in the polls.
I'm happy he has overcome all
The racism, prejudice, hatred,
And bigotry he's had to face.
Like I said, color don't mean a thing
Unless it is used in the proper context.

You see, you gotta understand what's going on.

Blacks only make up a little over thirteen
Percent of the U.S. population;
Yet, we are on the threshold of having
A Black man running the country
And becoming the leader
Of the Free World.
That alone tells you how far
This country has come.

It's been a long and tough struggle, though.
Heck, there were the
Pains of Montgomery, Birmingham,
Nashville; Jackson, Mississippi;
Albany, Georgia; Boston, Chicago, Memphis.
I still remember being sad and mad
About Emmett Till and how
White folks beat him to death
And threw him off that
Bridge into a swamp.
Yes, sir, I still think about
Them three youngsters:
Goodman, Chaney, and Schwerner;
One Black, two White.
I remember all of those things like
It was yesterday.

You cannot rid the mind of all the
lynchings, house burnings,
Police brutalities, and Blacks
Being put in jail for no reason.
I'm saying all of this to remind
Myself and everybody else just
How far we've come.

Lots of White people say

Obama ain't qualified.
Says he does not have the experience.
Says he has not held any powerful
elected office. Says he's too young.
No great voting record.
Talk about him not being vetted enough.
That's what White folks are saying,
Especially the ones supporting Hillary Clinton.
Speaking of the Clintons,
I never liked them.
They remind me of White-trash
That done gone and got educated.

I mean here was Bill Clinton,
President of the United States,
Getting blow jobs in the same
place he conducted the country's
Business and in the same place
His wife and young daughter lived.

Ain't no telling who else,
Besides Monica, was giving it up
For that morally corrupt, sweet-talker.
And, these days he's running
Around telling everybody to trust
What him and his wife be saying
And not to pay attention to what
Senator Obama is talking about.

Hell, if Hillary had any strength,
She would have left that no good
Sonofabitch, Bill, long time ago.

While I might not be the least
Bit racist, my wife, Denise,

Is a downright, non-apologetic, racist.
She hates White people.
Can't stand to be around them too long.

And, don't mention any White
Person from the South.
And, she ain't even from
That part of the country.
Never even been down South
And refuses to go.

Ask her why she supports
Obama and she'll tell you
Without skipping a beat that
She supports him because he is Black.
I have to remind her that
He is Half-White and Half-Black.

I keep telling her he was raised by a
White mother and his White grandparents.
Weren't any black folks reading
Him books, teaching him mathematics,
Science, geography, history, religion,
And how to play games.

I have to always remind her that
He didn't receive an oral history
Or hear old-time stories from the
Mouths of a bunch of Blacks.
When he was growing up,
What he heard came from the
Mouths of his White mother,
White grandmother, White granddaddy,
And his Indonesian step-daddy.

Now, some of us know
About the Kenyan man,
His biological daddy,
And the Indonesian man,
His step-daddy,
And that other Indonesian man,
His nanny – a transvestite who
Dressed-up in female clothes
And pretended to be a woman.
Wonder how much influence
These three men had
On Barack's young mind.

Most of his forming took place
In Hawaii and Indonesia
Back then, in Hawaii, there were
Only a handful of Black people.

But, getting back to politics.
Senator Obama will be a great
President if he is given a chance.

First, though, he's got to get
Beyond the Clinton machine
And whoever the republicans
Choose to head their ticket.
Just hope the secret service and
Law enforcement people pay
Close attention and keep a
Watchful eye out for all the
Right wing racist and other crazies
Who will be plotting to do him
Some gravely harm.

Like I keep telling all my
Friends and anybody else

I talk to, I'm not prejudice.
Not even a little bit.
Skin color don't mean
A thing to me.
But, anybody with any objectivity,
Gotta admit that this is one Black
Man that is better than any White
Man or White woman to
Ever enter American politics.
That is, except for, maybe, Lincoln.

Taylor Lipton, December 2016

Looks like the Obama years
Are about to come to an end.
Two times I supported and
Voted for this man to be president.
Now as we approach the final days,
I must say I have mixed feelings
About his presidency.

I will never regret how excited
I was voting for him.
I will always be proud and
Happy to say I helped elect America's
First African American president.
I will one day tell my grandchildren
And, hopefully, my great-grandchildren
About the Black man with the
Funny name who ran for president and won.
I'll tell them how intelligent he was.
What a smooth talker he was.
How he held the black masses
Spellbound and made liberal
White folks fall in love with'em.

I'll explain how he, with the help
Of a democratic-led congress, pushed
Through the *Affordable Care Act* that was
Later called "Obama Care."

I'll tell them that the *Black Lives Matter*
Movement became prominent while
The first Black president was in office.
 I'll also tell them how his administration
Was responsible for the killing
Of Osama bin Laden, the mastermind
Behind the September 11, 2001
Bombing of New York City's
Twin Towers and the Pentagon.

I'll tell 'em how President Obama
Was respected almost everywhere
In the world.
I'll even explain how he won the
Nobel Peace Prize even before he
Did anything to really earn it.

What I want this current and
Future bunch of Black youngsters
To understand is that we, us Blacks,
Made history and it's up to
Them to keep following in our footsteps.

Bertha Jo Wather, February 2009

I done already wrote up a list of the things
I want President Obama to do to help
Us black folks.
I started writing late that Tuesday night,
Right after he had kicked
John McCain's White ass.

I tried to think of all the things
We Black people been missing,
Been needing, been wanting,
Been promised and been denied.

I came up with this here list of twenty-five
Things I know if I ask him,
President Obama is gonna make
Sure us Black folks gonna be getting.
And, he's gonna make sure we get it
before his first two years are over.

Hell, we gave 'im ninety-six
Percent of our votes.
We campaigned hard and
Long and loud for'em.
I handed-out flyers and
Leaflets up and down First Street,
All the way over to Prude Avenue,
Back up to Fourth Street,
Crossed over to Tremont
And then back again to First Street.
Every other day I was walking the streets.
No mater rain, snow, hot, cold —
I walked the streets giving people flyers
And them green, red, and black leaflets
With Barack's picture and name on' em.
That's how come I know he's gonna do
Most of the things I be wantin' him to do.
Not just for me but for all the Black folks
In this country he's gonna be in charge of.

Being as active as I been being,
I made up a list of all the things
I want him to do once he sits

Down behind his new desk.

Here it is, my list of the twenty-five
Things he ought'a do to help the
Ones who put 'im in office.
I mailed a copy to the people who
Was always sendin' out them letters
Askin' us for money to support Barack.
I'm keeping one copy of my list
In a box under my bed.
The third copy I taped to the
Side of my refrigerator.
Here is the list I sent, and I'll bet
My life that Barack is gonna do what
I'm askin' him to do. This here is my list:
1. Make us Black folks have safer streets
in our Black neighborhoods.
2. Get crack, the crack dealers,
and other drugs and dealers, too,
off our streets, along with the
prostitutes and they pimps.
3. Make it easier for Black folks
to get a decent house.
How much these houses
be costing is way
too much for the average Black
man or Black woman.
We ain't got that kind'a money.
The price of these houses is too
expensive, even for most White people.
4. Create a heap more jobs for us Black folks.
We need to work so we can get enough money
to buy things we need.
We can't even shop at any of the good
stores in any of the good malls 'cause

we ain't got no damn money,
cause we ain't got no decent jobs.
5. Get us better schools and teachers
in our Black neighborhoods.
Our black schools got the sorriest,
dumbest, and most ignorant teachers t
hat ever walked into a schoolhouse.
The ones we got need to be fired
and replaced with some that know
how to teach our children.
Also, need to teach these Black children
how to act and behave.
They rather be cussing and fighting than learning.
6. Stop the police from treating us Blacks so bad.
Even though things supposed to
be better between Black folks and the law,
they still the same or worse.
Barack, you gotta do something about this
before there be a lot of burning and looting
like it was when Watts got burned down after
they beat Rodney King like he was some kind
of beat-me-to-death doll.
7. Make it easier for Black folks to get a car.
We tired of looking at all these
raggedy cars with all that smelly smoke
coming outta broke tail pipes.
They all the times breaking down
and being left on the street.
Please make it so Ford and General Motors
and Chrysler will allow Black folks to buy
cars at a cheaper price than what White folks pay.
Being the President of the United States of America,
this ought to be easy to do. Just call 'em on the
phone and talk to them the way you must'a
heard gang members talking to each other

when you was a community organizer in Chicago.
Yep, call 'em on the phone and scare the bastards
into doin' what needs to be done so
we can get cheaper cars.
8. Get us more doctors in our Black neighborhoods.
If you get sick down here where all the Black
folks live and you need a doctor,
you be out of luck.
Mr. President, we need some hospitals,
too, down here in the Black folk's neighborhoods.
And, make the doctors and the hospitals
stop charging Black folks so much.
9. Give us more money to buy food.
Tell the people in charge of the EMT
cards to add more money to the amount.
We can't live off'a what the government
be giving us.
10. Have a big picnic, in front of the
White House, every Fourth of July.
Better yet, make it every June 19th.
You ought'a have a real blowout of
a celebration for Black folks and our
invited White and Mexican friends.
11. Stop acting like you White and start
acting like you a real, strong Black man.
Please quit all that proper talking and
skinning and grinning up to White folks.
Start acting and talking like you be one of us.
And, act like you proud of it, too.
Cuss-out a few of them Crackers.
Talk about they mommas. You know,
play the Dozens wit'em.
12. Build us some new government-run
housing projects.
The ones they build in the 60s, 70s, 80s and 90s

is all tore up and falling down.
Those of us without work need some
more decent and pretty places to live.
These sixty-, forty-, thirty-year old
government-run housing projects
done been destroyed and ain't safe no more.
Make sure, Mr. President, you tell the
building people to get their asses to
the Black neighborhoods and start
building us some new projects.
And, tell 'em, Barack, that the new
apartments need to be furnished
with free electricity, gas, water,
washing machines, dryers, refrigerators, stoves,
air conditioned, 65-inch televisions and free cable.

Thank you, Mr. President Obama, for reading my letter. I know you
gonna do what's right for Black folks. We will be watchin' and praying.

We love you, Mr. President Obama.

Your hardest working and most dedicated supporter,
Miss Bertha Jo Wather,

Bertha Jo Wather, Summer 2012

I'm through with politics and these fuckin' politicians.
Through with voting.
As a matter of fact, voting can kiss my black ass.
I'm through being made a fool of.
I put everything I had and everything I wish I had,
in the basket for Barack Obama.
Did it 'cause he be black.
That black man made me do things that
I never knowed I had the gumption to do.

Back when he was running the first time,
I spent most of my waking hours going 'round,
Door-to-door, preaching, handing out flyers, doing
Whatever I thought it would take to make this Black
Man President of the United States of America.
I was in love with Barack Obama. Yes, I was.
I cussed out anybody who said he was
Not gonna be a great president.

The first thing he did that disappointed
Me was choosing all them White folks
To be up around him, in his Cabinet.
But, the thing that really pissed me off
Was when he picked that lying and
Deceitful bitch, Hillary Clinton,
To be Secretary of State.
And, if he hadn't selected Eric Holder
For the Attorney General position,
There wouldn't have been
Any blacks in his Cabinet.
That made me madder than one of
Them rabid dogs hungry for some meat.

Back when he first got elected president,
I wrote a long list of twelve things,
Back in February 2009,
It was, asking him to do for Black people.
Twelve things that would help Black people.
And, I sent him the list, certified mail,
And begged him to do what
I was asking him to do.
I never heard a word 'bout what I sent him.
Nobody responded. Nobody replied.
No phone calls. Nothing.
Not a word from the people I worked

So hard to get elected.
Also, if they did get the list,
I don't suppose they read it because
The only thing they did was the
Health care thing and they didn't do
it for Black people, they did it for the rich people.

I'm fed up. Nope, I ain't doing
A damn thing this time.
That Mormon fellow, I hear,
Just might beat Barack.
I hope, though, what I'm hearing ain't true.
I still want Barack to win
A second time around,
Just like he did the first time.
But, you know what, I ain't liftin'
A finger to support 'im.
I'm so disappointed in what done
Happened these first four years
I'm just gonna sit this one out.
To hell with it. Let the Mormon man win.

Reverend Darrell DeWitt Hallows, November 2, 2008

Praise the Lord. Let, everybody say,
Praise the Lord! Hallelujah! Hallelujah!
God, Almighty. Jesus! Jesus! Jesus!
I feel really good this morning.
I've been feeling good all week long.
Yes, Sir. Yes, Ma'am. Feeling good all over.
Feeling good through-and-through!
Yaw'll hear what I'm saying?
I feel like shouting this morning.
I feel like running through the aisles of
This church with my arms raised

And my eyes lifted up to the Great Kingdom.
Lifted up to the Mighty Kingdom.
The place where our Savior sits on His throne
And controls all that walks upon His Earth.
Yes, Sir. Yes, Ma'am, this is one of the best
Mornings we, as a people, have had
In a mighty long time.
Do yaw'll hear me?
Are your ears open to what I'm talking about?
Do you know what I'm talking about?
Are you experiencing what I'm experiencing?
Are you feeling, this morning, what I'm feeling?

You see, church, God, from on high has spoken.
The King of Kings has rendered His verdict.
The One who is mightier than the most-mighty.
Mightier than the Wall Street money folk.
Mightier than all the generals and their armies.
Mightier than every terrorist walking the face of
This Earth and ready to kill those they don't like.

Yes! Listen to me, I'm talking about our God
And His strength and His wisdom.
And, His foresight. And His helping hand.
And His guidance. And His salvation.
I'm talking about the One responsible for
Parting the Red Sea so Moses could lead
The children of Israel out of Egypt and into
The Promise Land.
God, Almighty, I feel like shouting.

This morning, we are gonna look
at the Book of Exodus, the 14th Chapter.
God, please help us, this morning.
We are gonna examine the words of Moses.

How this man, God, Almighty, help me here;
How this man, with the name of Moses,
Who having been anointed by the Almighty,
Went to the Red Sea, somewhere between
Africa and Asia, and stretched out his
Hands over that wide sea of water.
And, lo and behold a path was opened right
Through the middle of that sea of water,
Named the Red Sea. Moses told the Israelites
To walk on the dry path to the other side.
Told them not to worry about the waters
Coming onto them and drowning them.

You see, God, by way of Moses,
Was leading His people to freedom.
And, the Israelites were able to walk
Away from Egyptian slavery into something
Everybody ought to have: Freedom.

Can I get an Amen, in here?
Will somebody please say, Amen?
Say it again. Say it loud like you mean it.

Several months ago, while watching
My television, I heard this man by the name
Of Barack Hussein Obama. A man having
The same skin color as Moses.
I heard Mister Barack Hussein Obama speak.
He voice sounded like I imagine Moses'
Might'a sounded. Like John the Baptist's
Might'a sounded. Like Shadrach, Meshach
 And Abednego voices might'a sounded.

Then I saw Obama walk and strut across
That stage, the way, I imagine, Moses

Walked and strutted on the banks of the
Red Sea before stretching out his arms.

And, when I saw all of this, happening
Right before America's eyes, before the eyes
Of the world, I knew salvation had arrived.
The parting of the modern-day Red Sea
Was about to take place.

Now, listen to me.
Please, yaw'll, hear what I'm about to tell you:
There have been those, in this country of ours,
Who have done everything and are still
Doing any and everything to try and destroy
This Black man, our Moses. They have told lies.
They have schemed. They have plotted.
They have done things we know
They always do and love doing to us.
And, they ain't through doing their evilness.
You just wait and see.

There are the folks that have always
Been trying to keep us down.
These same folks have shifted to another
Gear in order to stop Senator Obama from
Becoming president of these United States.

You and I have witness all type concoction,
Conniving, conspiring, trickery, shenanigans
And plots to try and ruin our Moses before
He ever reaches the White House.
Yaw'll know I'm telling the truth.
Yaw'll need to let me hear you say, Amen.

But, this is what we gonna do:

We are going to follow the scripture.
We gonna do what Jesus said in
Luke, Chapter 6, when He talked
About giving and helping those who
Are against you. And, Lord knows,
There are those demons here in America
Who are against Barack, against this
Wonderful Black man. These folks are not
To be hated. We must love 'em, pray for'em
And forgive'em for what they have been
Doing and will continue doing.

This is what God wants us to do.
And, if we follow the words of our
Savior, everything will be alright.

Our Moses has arrived.
His name is Barack Hussein Obama.
He has stretched out his hands,
And like the children of Israel,
Who walked on dry land through the Red Sea,
We, too, are about to place our feet on dry land.

Now, I shouldn't have to remind you
What to do on Tuesday –
That's the day after tomorrow.
I want each and every one of you
To get up early so you can go to your
Polling place and vote.

If you need a ride, all you gotta do
Is call our hotline.
The ushers are passing out flyers
With all the telephone numbers and
Names that you can contact for

A ride and a free meal.
That's right if you vote.
We gonna let you get a free
Somethin' to eat at either Chick-fil-A,
Popeye's, Bojangles, or DeeDee Barbeque.
That's one of the other.
You ain't gonna get a free
Meal at all three. Can I get an Amen?

Now if you need to miss a day of work, then
Go right ahead and miss that day of work.
If you can't take off, then remember the
Polls don't close until 8 o'clock Tuesday night.
Deacon Rudolph and Sister Matthews are in
Charge of this operation. If you have any
Problems or questions, then,
You should call either one of them;
And they'll take care of you.

Remember this: listen to me now,
You gotta have a picture ID when you
Go to the polling station.
This can be your driver's licenses
Or the free photo ID you got from
The Department of Safety
And Homeland Security.
Yaw'll can also use the same ID
You use when you buy
Your Jim Beam. Say, Amen.

If you failed to get your free ID
Or you don't have a driver's licenses,
Then see Deacon Rudolph or Sister Matthews
And he or she will help you.

This is gonna be a historical occasion.
We have been praying to our God for
Something like this to happen.
Now that it has, we can't sit on
The sidelines and talk about having
A headache, a backache, a stomachache,
A tooth ache or how our sore knees have
All of a sudden started to act real crazy.
We can't complain about our feet hurting,
Or how we ain't got something nice to wear.

No matter what you think your problem is,
Put it aside and vote on Tuesday for the
Person who most resembles us.

Now, let us bow our heads and pray.

Reverend Darrell DeWitt Hallows, July 5, 2016

How is everybody feeling this
Sunday morning after getting your
Bellies filled with ribs, fried chicken,
Catfish, salads, pies, pork-n-beans
And all them sodas that we had yesterday
Out at Warner Park, where we celebrated
The 4th of July, this
Country's Independence Day?

I hope yaw'll in a good mood.
Hope you didn't have to take too much
Pepto-Bismol or whatever we take when
We have a stomachache from eating too much.

Today, I'm not gonna keep yaw'll in here too long.
Despite the outstanding air-conditioning system,

We have, this is still July,
And we are still in Tennessee.
As a matter of fact, I'm gonna just
Break some news to yaw'll.
I'm gonna let you in on a little secret
I've been holding onto for a few months.
This is something I think we need to look
At before the next democrat
And republican conventions.
We need to examine which road
We plan to go down.

Now, I realize that for most of us
We have already decided.
After all, President Obama has been campaigning
For Senator Hillary Clinton.
That is, Secretary of State, Hillary Clinton.
We remember when she used-to-be
First Lady Hillary Clinton,
Bill Clinton's wife. President Obama
Been going 'round saying she is the
Best thing since sliced bread, okra,
Watermelon, and a good night's sleep.
Well, my secret is:
I'm not sure this time around. I mean,

Barack has done so little for us Black folks;
I'm thinking that if Hillary follows
In President Obama's footsteps,
We, as a people, will be farther, and farther,
And farther behind than we ever
Thought we would be.

The other night I got on my computer
And started looking at what the Obama

Administration has done for us Black folks
And I came away very disappointed.
Now if you happen to support the
Planned Parenthood folks and all the abortions
They perform, then you'll say he has helped us.
If you happen to support gay rights at the expense
Of full-support for the traditional
Male-female relationship, then you'll say
He has been a great president.
If you think he has done as much for
Black folks as he has done for
Illegal immigrants coming into this country
And taking jobs from Black folks, then you'll
Think he has been a great president.

I looked at the data that are provided by the
People he put in place,
And I found Black poverty,
That's the number of really poor Black folks,
Has remained in the same shameful place
Or have gotten worse.
I see in President Obama's hometown,
Chicago, Black youngsters are killing
Other Black youngsters each and every day.

Yaw'll know I'm right but yaw'll
Ain't gonna give me any Amens
Because the democratic party has
Convinced us that they know
What's best for us.

This time around, after seven years of Barack,
I'm not sure anymore. I'm not sure if we can
Stomach another democrat in the White House.

Rollin DePriest, Ph.D., Spring of 2009

The history of the blacks in America
Is long and tragic.
We all know this.
There is little if any debate about this.
That tragedy lingers like a huge
Dose of partly-digested castor oil:
Whenever you belch you can
Experiencing its bitter taste.

Because of continual agitation,
Going back to slavery,
Blacks in America have progressed,
Ever so slowly, to where we are today.
We have constantly reminded
The world of White America's
Dastard behavior, deeds, and
Anti-Christian acts regarding
Its treatment of Black Americans.

Blacks have been America's relentless
Gadflies; cajoling, pestering, probing,
Persuading, criticizing, and protesting those
In power to bring about positive change.

With the election of a man of color,
I'm afraid we will cease being this
Country's most persistent gadfly.
We will stop or reduce our protestation.
We will become silent
As we harbor our agonies.

Because we celebrate a Black man taking
Power and because we have an
Overwhelming desire to prove to

White folks that a Black person
Can govern America as well as or
Better than any White person,
We will muzzle our voices of criticism.
No matter how terrible things
Become during Barack Obama's tenure,
We will be reduced to muted, tolerant,
And inactive political bystanders.

We will go out of our way to protect
President Obama and his administration
Even if that means leaving our own
Selves without protection.

Black institutions, Black groups,
Black societies, and influential Black
Leaders have already come together,
In a united front, to protect the Black
President from real or perceived negative
Comments or actions.

Our rallying cry, when all else fails,
Is to accuse his White critics of being
Bigots, racist, right-wingers and haters.
It will be easy, but foolhardy, to cite bigotry
And racism as the White critics' primary and
Motivating factor should they examine too
Closely *our* Black president.

White racism surely may be a factor,
However, the primary factor, I believe,
Is the deep dislike and distrust most
Black Americans have concerning Whites.
One must understand, Blacks don't
Dislike and distrust all White people,

Just "White Americans."
Not Canadians. Not French. Not Brits.

Black people carry the scars of the ugly
And inhumane history of slavery and
Its aftermath, in our genes.

This history and its aftermath,
Steadfastly come to the fore
Whenever there is conflict or
Competition between Black and White.
This history erects a defense mechanism
That prevents Blacks from faulting,
Negatively judging, or punishing
Their fellow Blacks.
The can be said of American Whites.

This is especially true of any
Black American who has defeated
A White American at
The White American's own game,
Using the White American's rules.
This is why nearly all prominent,
Intellectually gifted, hardworking, poor,
Unemployed, religious, nonreligious
And every other kind of Black American,
Will give Obama their overwhelming support.

This has nothing to do with Obama's
Abilities but everything to do with the
History of how badly people of African
Decent, have been treated in this country
And their thirst for revenge.

And, African Americans,
Without pause or shame, will
Eagerly characterize everyone "racist"
Who disagrees with their points of view.
This is rather ironic because African
Americans are some of the most racist
And dogmatic persons in the world.

In political discussions with my
White colleagues, I'm often asked
My feelings concerning Barack Obama
And if I think he will be one of the
Greatest presidents in America's history.
I usually tell them I don't know but
That I will be pulling for him to be more
Successful than his predecessor.

Sometimes I'm asked by close friends
How much money or time I've
Donated to Obama's campaign.
My response is: A lot.
To be truthful, I've donated neither
Money nor time to the Obama campaign.

Many, if not the majority of African Americans,
See Obama as one of God's Angels
Who have been placed in America to
Expunge all that is wrong and all
The sufferings that have been heaped
Upon the lives of Blacks here in America.
They see him as the Savior that God
Has placed among them so as to make
All that ails African Americans vanish.
They and their liberal cohorts see
The Obama phenomenon as some kind
Of *great cause. A great cause* that

Will resonate worldwide and penetrate
Every heart it touches.

In his book *The Temper of Our Time*,
Eric Hoffer wrote:
Every great cause begins as a movement,
becomes a business, and eventually
degenerates into a racket.

I hope the Barack Obama movement,
Which is already a business,
Does not become a "racket."

Rollin De Priest, Ph.D., Spring of 2011

The first years of the Obama Presidency:
What a blown opportunity.
Obama could have chosen numerous,
Highly-qualified, and gifted Blacks
To fill his cabinet.
Rather, he chose those
Dictated to him by White political
Elites and ruling-class oligarchs.
One only needs to look at his
Selection of Hillary Clinton.
Need I say, Tim Geithner, Robert Gates,
Bill Richardson, Kathleen Sebelius,
Shawn Donovan, Arnie Duncan,
And Tom Vilsack?

I wonder how much input, if any,
the pathetic and impotent
Congressional Black Caucus,
Had in shaping Obama's decision
To go with such an
Overwhelming White cabinet.

Sure, there was Eric Holder,
As the Attorney General,
But most Blacks contend that
Was not enough.
After receiving monumental support
From every segment
Of the African American community,
How could Blacks have been given
Only one cabinet position?
What a pity. What a shame.
This, in itself, was an affront to
Those Blacks who walked,
Prayed, campaigned, and fought
For Barack Obama's election.

Lastly, here we are in the Spring of 2011,
And Barak Obama, with two chances
To nominate an African American for a
Seat on the United States Supreme Court,
Failed to do so.

With his reelection, he'll more than
Likely have an opportunity to make
One or two more nominations.
If so, I will wager that he will
Not nominate a Black person.

Of the many instances when
African Americans have been
Disappointed by those they helped
to elect, Barack Obama must rank
Near the top.

**Helen Littlefield, U.S. State Department Employee,
October 2008**
I've been with the Department of State
For fifteen years.
I've been posted in South Africa,
New Zealand, Bermuda, and Nigeria.
I'm now back in Washington.
My husband, who also works
For the Department of State,
And I, are republicans.

Next month when we vote,
We will not vote for Barack Obama,
But should he be elected he will
Receive our full support in carrying
Out this country's missions.

Until this presidential election,
I did not know how difficult it
Is for some Blacks to be open-minded
Regarding race and politics.

Because we chose to discuss
The upcoming general election
And not hide the fact that we
Are registered republicans,
My husband and I have been called
Vicious names, ridiculed, threatened,
Insulted and ostracized by people we
Thought were our friends.

Simply because we said we had
To think through who we would
Support for president, we have been
Labeled sellouts and stupid.

To be honest, initially, we were
Thinking of voting for Senator Obama.
We were impressed with his education,
Ability to deliver a message, his
Seriousness, and his rapport with
All types of Americans.
Then, in the midst of all the good
Vibes being cast, his campaign started
Engaging in race:
Calling those who disagreed
With him racists, bigots and uninformed.
At that point we decided to thoroughly
Examine his voting record and his
Background by using the Department's
Database and other search engines.
We spent two weekends going
Over as much as possible.
After our exhausting searches,
We concluded that we could never
Support Barack Obama.

Whenever his name was mentioned
And we failed to show enthusiasm,
Our associates became upset.
Finally, we said we were still undecided.
From that day onward, we have faced the
Wrath of our Black colleagues and many

Liberal, non-Blacks.
We are not the only ones suffering
This ostracism and criticism.

Many Blacks, with the courage to
Support the republican candidate,
Have been called vicious names,

Have been mocked, and dismissed as silly,
Or referred to in the most horrible,
Vile and demeaning language.

So, when my husband and I go to
The polls, the Tuesday after the first
Monday, in November, we will be
Voting for Senator John McCain..

**Helen Littlefield, U.S. State Department Employee,
Late November 2016**

My husband and I still vote republican.
Naturally, we are still African Americans.
Since the start of the Obama Administration
And with the appointment and confirmation
Of Mrs. Clinton, as the Secretary of State,
Who is our boss, much has changed.
Secretary Clinton has had a tremendous
Impact on our lives and the lives of many
Members within the Department.
First off, she had no leadership skills
When it came to running a massive
Organization like, State.
As a substitute for her lack
Of leadership skills, she acted
As if she was constantly auditioning
To be the next president.
The Department was rampant with
Rumors that the Secretary, and her
Most trusted aides, who were
Not State employees,
Were seriously violating
All type protocol, legal and otherwise;
Most of which were ignored or swept under

The rug by the Obama White House,
The Department's Inspector General,
Long-time State Department
Seasoned diplomats and
State Department legal officers.
But, also the press.

Everyone knew nothing could
Get to Secretary Clinton without passing
Through two of her fiercest protectors,
And I do mean "fiercest protectors,"
In the strongest sense.
I'm referring to none
Other than Cheryl Mills and Huma Abedin.

I constantly thank God for giving me
The wisdom to have seen Mrs. Clinton
For what she is and how harmful she is
To this country. I just hope Mr. Trump
Will prove to be a better president
Than was President Obama.

Leon Davis, October 2008

I been cutting hair ever
Since I been old enough
To hold on to a pair of
Scissors and some clippers.
Folks been coming in
Here for years to get a
Haircut and a good, clean shave.
I was shaving faces before
I even started high school.
I've always had a steady hand
and an agreeable disposition.

I always been good to my woman,
Trena, and all our children,
God bless they souls.
All in all, I've been a pretty good man.
Mostly, I've been what
You call, "Even-Keel."
Nothing ever makes me
Too sad or too happy.
But, I gotta tell ya,

I am one happy fellow these days.
I'm tempted to run up and down
These here streets hollering and
Shouting at every White man
And White woman I see.
I wanna to tell 'em how we done
Up and put a Black man at the
Top of the democrat ticket.

Yes, Sir, I want to scream
At the top of my voice,
Telling these Crackers how we
Gonna put Barack Obama in
The White House and it ain't
A damn thing they can do
To stop it from happening.

The other day Big Red was
In here talking all kinds of trash.
Had everybody laughing and acting crazy.
He talked so long I had to tell him
To take a break and let somebody
Else say a word or two.
But, what Red was saying was the truth.
He said that he better not

Hear 'bout some , no-count,
Lazy-ass brother or sister complaining
'Bout they ain't gonna vote.
Red said he gonna drive 'round,
Burning his own gas,
And gather up every Negro
He can find, that ain't voted,
And take they sorry ass
To the voting place.

Lucas Dunn was sitting
Over next to the window
And smiling like he was the
Happiest man on in the world.
Red asked Lucas
If he planned to vote.
Lucas shuffled his feet,
Rolled his eyes and stopped smiling.
He told Red he would vote if Red
Picked him up at his house
And drove him to the polling place.
Red told Lucas he would be
At Lucas' house at 8 o'clock
On Tuesday morning.
Told Lucas he better be up
And ready and he better have
His Driver's License in his pocket.

Then, Red went on to talk
About how now ain't
The time for us Blacks to
Get tired, to get weary.
Told us 'bout the Jews
And how they come out of
Egypt to the Promise Land.

Said Obama gonna be our Moses.
Said that's how God done arranged
What's about to take place.
Red said Obama is gonna do things
For us that will make us forget
About all the bigotry, segregation,
And racism we've had to overcome.
That we are gonna be able to walk
Into a whole a new day, a new land,
A new beginning, and with a
Whole bunch of new pride.
Red talked 'bout Doctor King
And what he did 'fo he was killed but,
Red said, what Barack was doin'
Is ten times better than what King did.
I tell 'ya, everybody in my shop
Was up and shouting, running'
Round and high-fivin' and
Carrying on like they be crazy.
People walking by,
Looking through the window,
Saw how happy we were,
Came in and started celebrating, too.
They started acting
Like we were acting.
Finally, everybody calmed down.
Somebody, I forget who it was,
Offered up a prayer.

Leon Davis, November 2012

I sho wish Red was here to
Tell us 'bout what's gonna
Happen this comin' Tuesday.
I can see him walkin' and talkin'

Bout that Mormon man who gonna
try to get Barack out of office.
I can hear him tellin' us how
We better get off our behinds
And get to our voting stations
So we can get President Obama reelected.
But, as we all know, Red had,
'Cording to his wife, Sally,
A heart attack while they were
On vacation in Myrtle Beach.
So, I'm gonna try and take his place.
I'm gonna put a sign on the
Shop's door and tell everybody
I'm closed all day Tuesday due to
The reelection of President Obama.
I'm even gonna go 'round and pick
People up who claim they have
No way getting to where
They need to be to vote.
Heck, we gotta prove to the world
That Barack ain't somebody
That is a one-time thang.
We gotta show the world that
We still love our Black president.

Leonard Gladden, Colonel, U.S. Air Force, December 2008

More often than not, significant events
Occur without significant warning.
They appear, seemingly, out of nowhere.
Back in 2004, on July 27,
When Barack Obama gave the keynote speech
At the Democrat National Convention,
I was a Major, deployed to Iraq.
It was almost 6 A.M., July 28, 2004, in Baghdad.

Every television in the chow hall
Was tuned to the convention.

When Senator Obama started to speech,
There was complete silence.
This young, Black, well-spoken,
U.S. Senator, from Illinois,
Coon captivated the convention
And most of the viewing
And listening audiences.
I remember his words acknowledging
The heritage of his diversity when he
Spoke about his White,
Mid-western mother,
And her parents who had
Dedicated so much
Time helping to raise him.
I particularly remember these words
That still resonate with me:
Tonight, is a particular honor for me because,
let's face it, my presence on this stage is pretty unlikely.
My father was a foreign student, born and raised
 in a small village in Kenya. He grew up herding goats,
went to school in a tin-roof shack.
His father, my grandfather,
was a cook, a domestic servant.

Tears came to my eyes when
The entire mess hall stood and
Cheered when he said:
"- - - there's not a liberal America
and a conservative America —
there's the United States of America.
There's not a black America
and white America and Latino America

and Asian America;
there's the United States of America."

I decided, right then,
That if this guy ever ran for president,
I would support him.
I've kept that promise.
As the new president,
He has inherited nothing
But trouble and problems.
I believe him when he says
He will get us out of Iraq.
I believe him when he says
He will support the military.
I believe him when he says he
Will fix our messed-up economy.
I believe him when he says he
Will bring jobs back to America.
I believe him when he says he
Will have the most diverse cabinet
Of any president.

In six months, I'll be retiring.
I already have a job lined up with
One of the contractors, in Qatar,
Providing operational support to Iraq,
Afghanistan and other of our strategic areas.
I never believed America would
Put a Black person in the Oval Office.
I was wrong.
God Bless the United States of America.

Leonard Gladden, Colonel, U.S. Air Force, December 2015

Two times I gladly supported
And voted for President Obama.
His eight years are nearly over,
And I must admit, I will miss him greatly.
I wish there was some way for him to serve
An additional four or eight years.
Heck, as far as I'm concerned,
He could be "President for Life."
Would not bother me at all.
That's what I think of this man
And the way he has run this country.
Some complain about
His cabinet appointments
And his insistence on drones a
As the primary weapon in Iraq and Afghanistan.
But, none of these things bothered me at all.
I have no complaints.

Thomas Levon Douglas, December 2008

I remember when black folks couldn't vote.
Whites called us "Colored,"
Or "Nigger" when they wanted to,
Back during them times.
If they wanted to, they called us "Boy,"
"Gal," or anything they could
Think of to make sure we understood
They were a higher class
Of folks than we were.

When I went to vote, back in the
Forties and fifties,
down here in "Lynch-a-Nigger County,"

The White person standing at
The voter registration window -
Usually some dried-out,
Pitiful White woman -
Would give me something to read,
Then ask me crazy questions,
But not about what I had just read.
They did this to make sure
I did not qualify to vote.
Questions like:
How many grains of sugar is
In a five-pound bag of sugar?
And, where did the last state
Senator from Alabama
Attend kindergarten and
What was the name of his church?
And, how many words are
In the Constitution of the
United States of America,
That start with the letter "B"?
None of the questions they
Asked could be answered
By reading what they had
A few minutes before given me to read.

In "Lynch-a-Nigger County,"
They also had a poll tax.
This meant I had to pay
My hard-earned money,
Outta my own pockets,
In order to exercise
My constitutional right of voting.
Black folks coming out of
Some White folk's house
As a cook or maid, or from picking cotton,

Or off of some sugar cane plantation,
Or from other very low-paying jobs,
Did not have the money
To pay this poll tax.
Till this day, I don't believe White folks
Had to take a literacy test or pay
Any money before they voted.

I say all of this to let you know
That I am not ashamed to admit
What I did in order to help
President Obama win:
I used the names of eleven dead folks
And made sure they
Voted for President Obama.
These dead people were all good,
Christians and respectable members
Of the community.
Because of segregation, Jim Crow,
And the evilness of these
Low-down White folks,
These eleven people,
When alive, didn't get to
Vote like all citizens have
A constitutional right to.
Them that did, most of'em,
Didn't vote until after the late-1960s.

So, using a technique we black folks
Talked about and planned,
I went through the rolls of all the dead
People and friends, I knew.
Then, I registered them, and then,
I voted for them.
It wasn't hard because,

Starting 'round 1998,
The folks in charge of the registrations
And so-on, were as black as coal.
And, they knew how important
It was to get Barack Obama elected.

Yes, Sir, I am proud of what I did.
I was just making up for all the years us
Black folks had been
Cheated outta our rights.
I'm not the only one who did this.
Lots of Black folks, all over the county
And state, did the same thing.

Thomas Levon Douglas, December 2012

What I did the first
Time President Obama ran,
I did this time, too.
They say,
"Don't mess with it, if it ain't broke."
Only this time
I was a little more nervous 'cause
He was running against that
Rich Mormon fellow, Romney.
So, to make sure
I supported President Obama,
This time more'n I did the last time,
I had more'n a hundred dead folks voting.
It worked, too.
After all he got reelected
And that's the only thing that count.
This great man is the
Second coming of Abe Lincoln.
He's better than Kennedy and

Lyndon Johnson put together.
Ain't never been no
President like Barack Obama.
I pray every night for
His and his family's safety.
I know there are so many people
Who want to see him dead and gone
But that ain't gonna happen
As long as the Lord got his arms
Wrapped 'round Barack.

Gary Turnnert, Activist, January 2009

I'm Part-Black, Part-something-Else,
Which is obvious to most folks.
Well, let me be say,
I'm not a hundred percent Black.
I am, however, a hundred percent Black
In every other regard.
I've marched for civil rights,
Abortion rights and gay rights.
The first time I met Barack Obama
Was back in the mid-80's,
While I was teaching at
Chicago State University and living
In Chicago's Roseland community.
I would see him doing his
Community organizing thing
And hanging with the *together*
Brothers and sisters at all the right spots.
The first time I met him
Was on one of those hellaciously cold
Winter nights Chicago is known for.
This remarkably attractive woman
And he were at this jazz joint

Not far from the CSU campus.
They were smoking weed
And in a heated discussion
About Chicago politics.
Barack noticed my listening
And invited me to join them, which I did.
From that night onward,
I've been a believer and supporter
of Barack Obama.
The man is not only brilliant;
He is intelligent, as well.
He also has a passion for common folks
And those who have been beaten down,
Stepped upon and forgotten.
He knew I was gay
And it didn't bother him at all.
Back then being gay was not as
Easy and acceptable as it is today.
Barack never gave the slightest
Indication that I was not part of his inner circle.
He embraced my partner
And me as if we were straight.
As a matter of fact, Barack flirted
With my partner: several times
Squeezing his thighs and running
His hand over my partner's hard penis.

I love this man. I love his politics.
I love his family.
And, I love what he is
Going to do for this country.

Gary Turnnert, Activist, **January 2011**

I am one of the happiest people
In America. In the world.
Obama has surpassed even my
Wildest hopes and dreams.
He is the first president to openly
Support gays, lesbians, and trans.
Just look at the two persons he
Nominated for the Supreme Court.

Oh, Lord:

Ain't no telling when it all went the way it be goin lately. Lordy, it's been tough. Been rough. Ain't nobody who ain't been through the tough and the rough, like we now having, gonna know what I be talkin 'bout.

Oh, Lord:

Jentella, girl, you need to watch what you be wearin' them tight dresses, with no underwear, and how you be movin' your big behind when you walk. All these no good, ain't-got-no job, broke-ass, men - the married ones and the single ones — be watchin' you like one of them hungry dogs be watchin' a juicy neck bone.

Oh, Lord:

Last fall it was hot one day and cold the next. In the winter it got sho nuff hot, like it was summertime. Then when the springtime arrived it got kind of chilly. When summertime started it rained and there was flooding out near the new Kia plant. That high water kept lots of people from going to their decent-paying jobs that the Japanese had made possible. That girl, from 'round the corner who went off to that college, Jackson State, over in Mississippi, said all this funny weather is happening because of something called, "Climate Change."

We understand now why the black man cannot take pleasure in his insularity.
Frantz Fanon, *Black Skin, White Masks*

AFRICA: SO BAD, SO SAD

1

They sit in their remote villages.
Some rest in isolated corners on pallets.
Some sit, not in villages but in ravaged towns.
Some sit in rundown townships,
Or in big, infested cities.
In international arrival zones, despondent and bleak,
They await rich or prosperous foreigners to visit.
They keep looking at stars, the ones always moving;
The ones that mesmerize who stare.
Put them in a trance.
They have discussions concerning the many and most
Miserable things that will surely bring more misery.
They wipe away their sweat, while summoning
Sadder visions of harrowing futures visiting
These places – large, small, isolated, war-torn,
Ravaged – contaminated with the world's
Worst kinds of sufferings the
Maker of everlasting Ruination
And Malformation ever created.

2

Small children having used their
Allotted number of tears,
No longer cry and the
Begging poor can no longer
Remember where the stomach is located.

The skinny but powerful soldier-lords,
Tote the dusty rifles,
Causing them to act like supreme rulers
Of these remote villages, isolated hamlets,
Ravaged towns, rundown townships, big cities,
And international arrival zones where they always
Await the coming of another rich foreigner.
The *Maker of everlasting Ruination and Malformation*
Has made it so.

3

No matter where the plot of land,
There is always the presence of the
Disease everybody is aware of.
Even the tiniest of children knows about
The disease that goes by the funny name
Nobody can properly spell or pronounce.
So, everybody calls the disease:
The HIV/AIDS.
This is the affliction that was left by *Satan*
During one of his holiday visits to the Congo.
Sitting in a dance club in Kisangani,
In the Tshopo Province of what was
Once Stanleyville but is now Kisangani.
Kisangani men look at Kisangani women.
But, because of the hard to spell and
Pronounce disease Satan left behind,
Kisangani men are afraid to lay with
Kisangani women, no matter how pretty.
Kisangani women are too afraid to lay
With Kisangani men,
No matter how handsome.
Everybody knows that the Tshopo Province
Has too many babies that have come from

Kisangani wombs, that are sick
With the HIV/AIDS.
Therefore, the Kisangani men and the
Kisangani women are afraid to have sex
With one another. But, they do have sex.
Afterall, this is Africa.
This is the Democratic Republic of Congo.
African wives speaking Gogo, Fulani,
Chishona, Tonga, Yeni, Lomwe,
Monokutuba, Ta Bedawie, Lozi,
Ewe, Acoli, Nyakyusa, and Bemba –
Many wives, many children got
Some kind of disease everybody be
Afraid of and prays never to get.
If it ain't the HIV/AIDS,
Then it is the terrible,
Debilitating, and destructive diarrhea,
The dengue, and the always not far away:
Cholera, tuberculosis and malaria
That *Satan* also decreed while casting pain
Upon Black people
On the continent of Africa.
The African diseases wipes
Away villages, hamlets,
And even Africa's largest
And most thriving cities.
The diseases are so powerful
They even wipe away
The belief in superior gods
And prominent witch doctors,
And dismantles religious doctrines
Once extolled by Christian missionaries.

4

Sweden: Life expectancy: 83.65 years.
Infant Mortality Rate:
2.15 out of 1,000 live births.

5

Arikiyka, like many more,
Suffers from one of the dreaded disease.
Damn thing messes with Arikiyka's immune system.
Destroys Arikiyka's body-systems' ability to fight
Against all them other bad diseases.
Them other life ending diseases
That creep into Arikiyka's body.
Makes it so her body cannot combat the colds,
The fevers and the other, smaller, diseases.

6

Japan: Life expectancy: 84.95 years.
Infant Mortality Rate:
1.82 out of 1,000 live births.

7

Africa home to more than one billion folks.
Got fifty-four, maybe more, maybe less, countries.
Got nearly two thousand, maybe more, languages.
The poorest of all continents, with the poorest,
Most destitute folks on planet Earth.

8

Used to be Swaziland, now Eswatini,
 Life expectancy: 57.71 years.
Infant Mortality Rate:
37.42 out of 1,000 live births.
Only the fool will compare Eswatini's numbers
With those of Sweden, with those of Japan.

9

Desperate and miserable,
These Black African folks.
So many, too many, of these
Black Africans folks.
Always, they be needy.
Always, they be hungry.
All the time they be sickly.

10

On this continent, called Africa,
There is always heaps of killings
And maiming going on.
Poor Black Africans killing and maiming
Other poor Black Africans.
Killings and maiming go by the terrible names:
Fratricide, genocide, atrocity, ethnic cleansing,
Stupidity, inhumanity, barbarism, carnage,
Ignorance, shame.
Brother Man killing Brother Man
And Sister Woman.
Sister Woman killing Sister Woman
And Brother Man.
Maiming each other. Smiling 'bout it.

Romanticizing it. Rejoicing while doing it.
Showing not a bit of remorse about it.

11

Angola: Life expectancy: 63.24 years.
Infant Mortality Rate:
48.34 out of 1,000 live births.
Only the fool will compare Angola numbers
With those of Sweden, with those of Japan.

12

Kill the brother. Kill the sister.
Kill the neighbor. It doesn't matter as long as
Blacks Africans be killing other Black Africans.
Killing and grinning. Killing and swaggering.
Massacring each other and chanting.
Celebrating like they done gone crazy
From too much of that African crack cocaine.

13

The unbelievable, the unimaginable,
The unremarkable always takes place
On the continent called Africa.
Seventh-World and Eighth-World people
Walking around with the automatic weapons.
Toting their once-shiny,
Blood-stained machetes.
Wearing oversized soldier britches.
Wanting no land, no clean water.
But, wanting the bright diamond.
But, wanting the Marlboro cigarette.

Maybe it is the greed for the diamond
Or the greed for the Marlboro cigarette
That causes the blood-stained machete
Toting Black African teenager to abide by the
"Kill-every-Black-African-you-see" policy.
But, it could be the writer of the policy
Knew it could be in the Africans' blood.

14

Zambia: Life expectancy: 62.96 years.
Infant Mortality Rate:
41.66 out of 1,000 live births.
Only the fool will compare
Zambia's numbers
With those of Sweden,
With those of Japan.

15

Young girls, young mothers, nearby aunts,
Old grandmas all the time being raped;
All afraid of the Female Genital Mutilation
Procedure that messes with the clitoral gland.

Older, ashy men, rotting-teeth men.
Jet-black-skin men, nasty-breath men,
Crawling across the African sand
Where there be no vegetation in sight.

16

Lesotho: Life expectancy: 54.91 years.
Infant Mortality Rate:
69.88 out of 1,000 live births.
Only the fool will compare Lesotho's numbers

With those of Sweden,
With those of Japan.

17

Over there sits the Central African Republic,
With Sudan to the east, Congo and the
Democratic Republic of the Congo to the south,
Chad and North Sudan to the north,
and Cameroon To the west –
All resembling battlefields that were
Once covered with in dried blood,
Hordes of buzzards and other scavengers.
Unknown, left behind debris
Resembling figures that maybe once possessed
Human bones and once felt the human pain.
With lack of affection, they slowly stroll through
Bangui's Marche Central, their eyes constantly
Searching for the rare European face.
They are fierce-looking 20-year-olds,
And 14-years-old grimacing children,
Covered in Central African Republic
Red dust and filled with the need to destroy.

They parade about like glorified but ignored
Peacocks, wearing t-shirts with logos saying:
Lakers, Nike, Cavaliers, NYC, Puma, I Love Paris.

18

In the Central African Republic, in Sudan, in Congo,
In the Democratic Republic of the Congo, in Benin,
In North Sudan, and in Cameroon there be
Black People always awaiting the quick death.

19

In these places where the Sun scorches deserts.
And where the Sun prohibits too much movement;
Causing these deserts to be inhabited by the very poor.
Still there be mines filled with gold; acres and
Acres of pastures and fields full of uranium;;
And as far as you can see diamonds and bauxite.
All in the deserts and on the continent
We know as the poorest of all the continents.

20

Sierra Leone: Life expectancy: 60.79 years.
Infant Mortality Rate:
80.1 out of 1,000 live births.
Only the fool will compare Sierra Leone's
Numbers with those of Sweden,
With those of Japan.

21

Between the oil fields,
Gold caves, diamond pastures -
Undernourishment consumes
The Black African body;
Leaving no fat in between the Black African's
Skin and the Black African's white bones.

22

At some remote squatting place, in Malawi,
Jaafar, a boy with never an aspiration, tries
To rest on soiled pile of rubbish.
Twenty-two flies play games on Jaafar's face.
They crawl into Jaafar's mouth. Into Jaafar's eyes.

Jaafar will soon have dysentery and go blind.
Jaafar, then, will go begging, as a blind child,
As a skinny boy who always poop on himself.
On the streets of Lilongwe, and even Nkhotakota,
Jaafar's blind, spindly and stinking body will stand
In front of Lilongwe and Nkhotakota whore houses
Beseeching, in his most sorrowful Chichewa, the
Whores and the whores' customers for whatever
They may give a blind, smelling of poop,
Malawian boy who in a few months will be dead.

23

Mozambique: Life expectancy: 62.37 years.
Infant Mortality Rate:
52.77 out of 1,000 live births.
Only the fool will compare
Mozambique numbers
With those of Sweden,
With those of Japan.

24

Miles away from Niger's Arlit uranium site
Sits a woman, sits a man; neither
No more than 40-years-old,
But already in their twilight years.
Dazed-like, the woman, the man, crouch,
Looking skyward, hoping for some good,
White man's humanitarian food drop.

They speak Tebu and Fulfulde that are laced
With centuries of inherited-torment,
Well-practiced affliction, and little hope.
Some passing-by straggler says the next drop

Might be tomorrow, next week.
Might be never.

25

Liberia: Life expectancy: 62.04 years.
Infant Mortality Rate:
58.15 out of 1,000 live births.
Only the fool will
Compare Liberia's numbers
With those of Sweden,
With those of Japan.

26

The African *Language King,* speaks in Fon,
Setswana, Chichewa, Kikuyu, Bambara,
Swahili, Kinyarwanda
And nineteen-hundred and ninety-nine other
Languages strangers will never understand.

The Language King says:
This is Africa.
God ain't ever coming back to Africa.
Says:
The last time God visited this place
He left us bunches of Chromite, Cobalt,
and Manganese Ore.
He gave us Africans more goodies than
He gave anyone else.
I remember when He swooped across all of Africa
And spread upon, what was to become our
Fifty-four nations, Uranium, Bauxite, Platinum,
Titanium, and Cobalt. Gave us Gold, Diamonds,
Copper, Uranium, Aluminum.

Gave us, God, yes God, gave us Black Africans
Most of the best of the best stuff.
He gave us tall mountains and beautiful mountains.
Gave us wide and long rivers and seas, and oceans.
The rivers, seas and oceans, and sands and deserts.
He went back to His kingdom after leaving us with
Lake Abbe, and Tundavala Gap, and the
Beautiful Victoria Falls, and the magical Sossusvlei.

God filled our waters with the best of fish –
All kinds of fish.
And, for the fish to live in, He gave us Africans
The Nile, Lake Albert, the Congo River, Lake Kiva,
Lake Tanganyika, the Zambezi, and Lake Malawi.

Amidst our land, God placed the Elephant,
And the Giraffe, Lion, Chimpanzee, Camel,
And the Zebra, Gorilla, Leopard, and many,
Many more of His precious animals.
God, in His wisdom,
Gave us Africans every element and type of life
Any people would need to prosper, to grow,
To succeed. But, we Black Africans,
Decided to prove God wrong. Mock God.
Play with God.

God has not forgotten how we Africans sold our
African men and our African women to Europeans
So that our men and our women could be made slaves.
Could be made to die before reaching a safe destination.
African men and African women forced to give up their
Native languages, their religions, and their customs.

This is why God ain't ever coming back to Africa.
Make no difference how much we pray and beg Him.

God is fed-up with us Black Africans.

27

There is this place: Sudan.
A place where life has always been afraid to live.
Where decency, long ago, ran away and hid.
Where *loving thy Neighbor* is the worst kind of crime.
Where killings by Black Africans
Of other Black Africans is
A laughing matter and an honor.
Where crucifixion is legal.
Where female genital mutilation is permitted.
Where stoning a young girl until she dies is alright.
Where slavery and the practice of slavery still exist.
And, there in Sudan,
Is that place named, *Darfur.*
Darfur, that piece of land
Even Mephistopheles has said
He is too afraid to visit.
Darfur, a piece of soil and
A Black people that even
God is ashamed He created.
But, before Sudan there were
The genocides and the slaughtering
Of Black Africans by other Black Africans.
And, there were ethic cleansings
Of Black Africans by other Black Africans.
There were Uganda, Rwanda, Liberia,
Angola, Somalia, Nigeria, Burundi, where
Millions upon millions of Black Africans
Killed millions upon millions
Other Black Africans.

28

Weapons? There will always be weapons,
A village chief, in Libreville, Gabon,
Says, in both French and Mpongwe,
Not for hunting game but for the hunting and
Killing of other Black Africans.
Spend more time, we Africans do, with the gun,
Than we do with the plough, the hoe
The trowel and the banana-cutter,
Than we do taking care of the crops.

Yes, we Black Africans prefer the gun over the hoe.
More time with the bullet, than we do harvesting
The corn field and cutting bananas from the tree.

29

Djibouti: Life expectancy: 63.71 years.
Infant Mortality Rate:
47.18 out of 1,000 live births.
Only the fool will compare
Djibouti's numbers
With those of Sweden,
With those of Japan.

30

In a shack outside the city of Maiduguri,
In the Borno State of Nigeria,
On a warm night,
A poor Black African finger,
Belonging to a poor Black African child,
No more than thirteen years
Out of his Momma's belly,

Squeezes a foreign-made trigger
That fires a foreign-made gun
That sends a foreign bullet.
Then, the Black African child watches
As his Black Hausa cousin,
His Black Igbo uncle,
His Black Yoruba neighbor,
His used-to-be Black playmate
Lay dead, in their blood,
As his Boko Haram comrades look
On without showing the slightest emotion.

31

The Christian will always blame the Muslim,
Who they always proclaim, must die.
Saying it is the Allah fanatic Muslim
Who are too crazed to be Christian;
The Allah crazies are the ones who must die.
They are the ones who don't
Believe in our White Jesus,
The White son of a White man
Who died on that Cross.
Therefore, they have got to be eliminated.
We, Christians must always be willing to
Kill somebody who is
Black, African, and Muslim.
Kill anybody who is Muslim.
Slaughter the Muslims for fun. For game.
For the Muslims' American cigarettes.

32

Malawi: Life expectancy: 63.67 years.
Infant Mortality Rate:
29.02 out of 1,000 live births.
Only the fool will compare
Malawi's numbers
With those of Sweden,
With those of Japan.

33

Now, the Allah believers, the Muslims,
Because they are being massacred,
Must slaughter the Christ believers,
Must slaughter the Buddha, Judaism and
The believers of other irrelevant religions.

The Muslim's mantra is the same mantra
Held by the Jesus lovers:
We must kill somebody who is Black and African.
Must kill anybody who holds to a different religion.

They, the waiting-to-be-dead Muslims,
Believe in a Black Allah,
Not in a White Jesus.
So, the Black Jesus believers is urged to kill
Those who believe in a Black Allah.
And, the crazed, Black non-Jesus believers,
Who are the Allah believers, killed the
White Jesus believers.
And, they were all Black.
And, all were African.

34

Central African Republic:
Life expectancy: 55.48 years.
Infant Mortality Rate:
77.5 out of 1,000 live births.
Only the fool will compare
Central African Republic's numbers
With those of Sweden,
With those of Japan.

35

Poor Africans in Morocco, in Tunisia,
Djibouti, Kenya, Eswatini, Libya, Togo,
Botswana, Angola, Benin, Cameroon,
Equatorial Guinea, Nigeria, Niger, Chad,
Sierra Leon, Guinea-Bissau, Mali, Tanzania,
Rwanda, Egypt, Zimbabwe, Eritrea,
Ethiopia, Burundi, Gabon, Ghana,
Mauritania, Malawi, Namibia –
All sleep with their constant companions:
Wretchedness. Hopelessness. Disheartenment.

Walk, these Africans do, all the time,
With growling bellies, aching limbs,
And slowly depleted and abandoned pipedreams
Of someday, before too long, escaping
To Europe's cold and luminous streets.

36

Niger: Life expectancy: 62.93 years.
Infant Mortality Rate:
45.61 out of 1,000 live births.
Only the fool will

Compare Niger's numbers
With those of Sweden,
With those of Japan.

37

Something different; can be felt it in the soul.
Could be wrong; maybe the same as before,
Coming out of RAF Mildenhall, on the next
United States Air Force C-17 aircraft
Carrying eighteen 463L pallets loaded with
Goodies from Tyson, Perdue, and Monsanto.

Something different, maybe the same as before,
Could be coming, though, on the next bullet.
Maybe, something different, maybe the same,
Might be riding on the wings of the next hungry,
Malaria-carrying mosquito, or in the belly
Of the atrocious and deadly Tsetse fly.

38

Chad: Life expectancy: 53.68 years.
Infant Mortality Rate:
67.4 out of 1,000 live births.
Only the fool will
Compare Chad's numbers
With those of Sweden,
With those of Japan.

39

France 24 Television runs a three-part report
On the many odious happenings lurking
In the African skies, beneath the waters,
And on top of the African soil.

France 24 Television says it will examine
Some of the many calamities predicted
To before long, swoop onto most of
The hapless Black African peoples.

A Frenchman who works at the
Renault Truck Plant, in Lyon,
Wants to know why he should
Care about Blacks in African.
Says he doesn't know any Blacks.
Not even the ones working in the
Renault Truck Plant, here in Lyon.
He grunts loudly and says he doesn't
Care shit about the African bastards.

40

Guinea-Bissau:
Life expectancy: 60.56 years.
Infant Mortality Rate:
51.4 out of 1,000 live births.
Only the fool will compare
Guinea-Bissau numbers
With those of Sweden,
With those of Japan.

41

In a shabby Winnipeg strip club,
On Ellice Avenue,
A young dancer, from Steinbach, Manitoba,
A small town 'bout thirty-five miles
Southeast of Winnipeg,
Gyrates her obese body.
She removes her bra.

She removes her panties;
Reveals rolls of fat and other hideous things.
The three male customers
And the female bartender,
Pay her no never-mind.
They are too busy discussing how badly
The Winnipeg Jets are performing.
The Steinbach, Manitoba stripper,
Who claims to be a descendent of the
Anishinaabeg Nation, having displayed
Her obese body, with rolls of fat,
And other things not worth looking at,
Now, sits in a back room and watches a local
CBC television program and yawns after seeing
Fifteen minutes of suffering Africans:
Africa, what the fuck is that?
I don't know nothin' 'bout no fuckin'
Nigeria, no Fuckin' Liberia.
I ain't got no love for them Black sonofabitches.

42

Nigeria: Life expectancy: 53.87 years.
Infant Mortality Rate:
72.24 out of 1,000 live births.
Only the fool will
Compare Nigeria's numbers
With those of Sweden,
With those of Japan.

43

Hey! the Black African man, barks:
You buy this African ring, this African carving,
This African hand-made rug, my mother made?

On the streets of Liege, Delft, Bern, Rome,
Frankfurt, Nice, and Vienna,
The Black Africans try selling their wares.

The Black African man stares at Europeans.
He sits cross-legged on a thin blanket
At the Piazza di Santa Maria Novella, Firenze;
Or close to the Ponte di Mezzo,
Near the Leaning Tower of Pisa.

Black and perspiring, he can also be
Seen near the Vatican, the Louvre –
And close to Madrid's Museo del Prado.

44

Cote d'Ivoire:
Life expectancy: 60.11 years.
Infant Mortality Rate:
57.88 out of 1,000 live births.
Only the fool will compare
Cote d'Ivoire's numbers
With those of Sweden,
With those of Japan.

45

His blood-shot eyes pleading, haunting;
Saying he is from Niger, Eritrea, Congo,
Gabon, Somalia, Madagascar, Sudan.

In Tbilisi, Georgia, a young girl –
Blond, innocent-looking,
Naïve and sweet. Mostly, curious.
She is a Georgian teenager.

She stops, steps forward.
She looks in the Black African man's eyes.
She gives the Black African, 15 lari.
He hands her a wooden cross.

She accidentally touches
The African man's hand.
She feels the hard scales, the calluses.
Then, she sees the four scars cut into
The African man's black face.

46

Somalia: Life expectancy: 57.35 years.
Infant Mortality Rate:
72.72 out of 1,000 live births.
Only the fool will
Compare Somalia's numbers
With those of Sweden,
With those of Japan.

47

The smartly dressed,
Sophisticated, middle-aged housewife,
Strolls through Athens's Monastiraki Flea Market,
Looking with disgust; wondering, why are *they*
In her magnificent and glorious Athens.
Why are their poor,
Black asses here in Greece?
What liberal politician allowed
Them into our most civilized country?
We have too many of our own
Problems to allow this type
People to enter and live in *our*

Most historic and cultured Greece.
They should be rounded-up
And shipped back to
Their filthy homelands.
Back to their jungles and diseases.

48

Ethiopia: Life expectancy: 66.65 years.
Infant Mortality Rate:
35.37 out of 1,000 live births.
Only the fool will compare
Ethiopia's numbers
With those of Sweden,
With those of Japan.

49

The *want-to-be, pretend-to-be,* high-class
Romanian housewife looks with disdain
At the poor, Black African man.
The Romanian housewife is not intimidated.
The poor Black African man is not intimidated.
Neither looks away from the other.
Then, he smiles; possessing,
It seems, the world's
Whitest teeth and the most
Ingratiating look of calm.

The *want-to-be, pretend-to-be,* high-class
Romanian housewife is always on the move.
Always on the lookout.
She has visited Kenya
Madagascar, and Cape Town,
Where she stays, always, at the best
Five-star hotels and resorts.

50

Rwanda: Life expectancy: 67.35 years.
Infant Mortality Rate:
30.27 out of 1,000 live births.
Only the fool will
Compare Rwanda's numbers
With those of Sweden,
With those of Japan.

51

In Africa, the Bucharest housewife,
With anemic-looking, very pale skin,
Always lounge by the pools or along
The hotels' private beaches
Where she proudly, without concern,
Expose her too-white Romanian body.

The boy-servants, the man-servants,
The hired help – all so-dark-skinned,
So damn muscular, brings her fruit juices,
Glasses of Starr African Rum
And suntan lotions.

And, later, those "so-dark-skinned"
Boys and men, with all those muscles
And their big smiles
Without failure, tear her apart.
Makes her have quadruple orgasms.

52

Namibia: Life expectancy: 59.53 years.
Infant Mortality Rate:
30.14 out of 1,000 live births.

Only the fool will
Compare Namibia's numbers
With those of Sweden,
With those of Japan.

53

Those Black African boys –
The ones the Bucharest woman always see
When she visits Africa –
Look like these Black boys
Who these days stroll
About Romanian streets and parks.

And, always, these Black Africans,
Are all the time selling something:
Even their bodies. Even their souls.

The Black African man:
His teeth so very white,
His stomach flat, with muscles
Breaking through the tight,
Brightly colored shirt.
Why the hell is he always smiling?
Why does he seem so goddamn happy?

54

Mali: Life expectancy: 60.03 years.
Infant Mortality Rate:
58.77 out of 1,000 live births.
Only the fool will
Compare Mali's numbers
With those of Sweden,
With those of Japan.

55

The Slovakian housewife fantasizes
And becomes wet between the legs.
The Black African's stare –
His intrinsic savagery,
His wildness; surely, his desire to punish
All that is White, causes her
To have wild and frenetic imaginations.
His smell. Goodness, what is that smell?

She recalls the pains and pleasures
That one African gave her
During her visit to Lisbon.
She still wakes in the middle of nights
And play with herself and is thankful
He did not give her a dreaded disease.

56

Botswana: Life expectancy: 66.05 years.
Infant Mortality Rate:
306.08 out of 1,000 live births.
Only the fool will
Compare Botswana's numbers
With those of Sweden,
With those of Japan.

57

Submerged in total Blackness,
He sits like a panther eyeing a
A prey knowing it is to be captured.
His bright, white teeth.
His red, thick tongue and broad lips.

His huge feet. His penetrating stare.
His fingers look like they are 15 inches long.
A wild animal, a savage, a beast.
A "Thing" that is frightening-to-look-at.
A "Beast," a "Thing," allowed to run
Wild through the streets of civilized
Europe with intentions, to be sure,
Of mutilating helpless and
Submissive, European White women.

The European White woman,
Still standing, looks down.
She is enraptured by the
Crossed-legged panther
Who seductively moves his long,
Red tongue across his thick lips,
While entwining his elongated fingers.

58

Sudan: Life expectancy: 64.10 years.
Infant Mortality Rate:
39.92 out of 1,000 live births.
Only the fool will
Compare Sudan's numbers
With those of Sweden,
With those of Japan.

59

The European
White woman always in heat.
Always envisioning. Always imagining.
Always overflowing with cravings.
Her head, when she looks away, turns too fast.

Her stomachs always churning because of what
That strong, Black African boy,
The one in Kenya,
Once did to her, years ago,
While her husband
Was in meetings, at soccer
Or cricket matches,
Or with a cheap Black African whore.

60

United Republic of Tanzania:
Life expectancy: 67.60 years.
Infant Mortality Rate:
34.72 out of 1,000 live births.
Only the fool will
Compare Tanzania's numbers
With those of Sweden,
With those of Japan.

61

The middle-class European woman
Asks the preying panther
For his mobile-phone number just in case
She might want to purchase something
Else he has for sale.

62

Burundi: Life expectancy: 62.50 years.
Infant Mortality Rate:
38.64 out of 1,000 live births.
Only the fool will
Compare Burundi's numbers

With those of Sweden,
With those of Japan.

63

He is from Congo or Botswana
Or Chad, Guinea, Tanzania, or Mali.
Doesn't matter. He is Black. He is African.

The European White woman nearly faints.
He makes her scream out his Ugandan name,
His Mali name, his Tanzanian name,
His Botswana name, his Gabon name.
Makes sure she will have forever nightmares
About black panthers running wild
Over her White, begging-to-be-pleased, body.

64

Uganda: Life expectancy: 63.84 years.
Infant Mortality Rate:
31.86 out of 1,000 live births.
Only the fool will
Compare Uganda's numbers
With those of Sweden,
With those of Japan.

65

The Black African,
Even with the Diamond, the Bauxite,
The Manganese, the Uranium, Silver,
Gypsum, Phosphates, Chromium,
Copper, and the Petroleum; is always
Wrapped in the arms of the
Worst kinds of poverty and misery.

With all of this
The majority of Black Africans have nothing.
Despite the mountains, rivers, seas, oceans.
And, with all types of animals.
Despite being surrounded by
Nature's greatest gifts,
So many Black African
nearly starve to death, while waiting
To escape to a non-African country.

All the time the Black African becomes
The supplicant, the beggar, the mendicant
Who is always groveling at the White man's
Feet for The white man's crumbs.
Then, by the millions,
The Black African still dies hungry.
Still, by the hundreds of millions,
The Black African dies poor.

66

Burkina Faso:
Life expectancy: 60.57 years.
Infant Mortality Rate:
52.82 out of 1,000 live births.
Only the fool will compare
Burkina Faso's numbers
With those of Sweden,
With those of Japan.

67

In Strasbourg, the Black African sits
On a stool outside Cathedral Notre Dame,
Trying to persuade tourists to pay a few euros

For a badly drawn picture of a
Sad-looking Black child, looking sadder
Than any child anyone in
Strasbourg has ever seen.

Or, maybe the Black African stands
Alone in Luxembourg,
Near the Luxembourg Train Station,
Waiting to catch the Paris Express.
He is constantly being watched,
As a curiosity item, as he goes up to
White Europeans and begs:
Please, I just arrived from Kampala.
Please help me.

68

Cameroon: Life expectancy: 61.92 years.
Infant Mortality Rate:
48.34 out of 1,000 live births.
Only the fool will compare
Cameroon's numbers
With those of Sweden,
With those of Japan.

69

These men. These women.
These Black Africans
Covering the face of the planet.
Always with their gracious smiles
And the pleasant personalities.
Never a stray word. Never angry.
Always, they are, when away from Africa,
And around Whites, the most polite,

Most loveable, charismatic people alive.

However, they, like everybody else,
Are always wanting something they
Think they don't have but desperately
Need.

70

Democratic Republic of the Congo:
Life expectancy: 60.63 years.
Infant Mortality Rate:
63.79 out of 1,000 live births.
Only the fool will compare the
Democratic Republic of Congo's numbers
With those of Sweden, with those of Japan.

71

In Prague's wintry and freezing weather,
A Black African man can be seen
Standing on Melantrichova Street,
Hands in his pockets, lurking outside
Of the Prague Sex Machines Museum.

Or, with cap on crooked, thinking of
Tanzania and his hometown, Dodoma;
Cigarette, made from hashish,
Glued to his black lips.
The Black African man, from
Dodoma, Tanzania, slowly walks through
Amsterdam's Zeedijk, on Warmoesstraat.

Sammy, the African with long braids,
Employs his unique talent as a
Jazz violinist at Bruges 't Zwart Huis.

He is from Togo. He is fluent in French.
He now speaks Flemish and Dutch,
But not as well as Ewe,
His childhood language.

He came to Antwerp to study chemistry
At the University of Antwerp.
He misses Togo and especially, Lomé.

72

Benin: Life expectancy: 60.45 years.
Infant Mortality Rate:
56.54 out of 1,000 live births.
Only the fool will
Compare Benin's numbers
With those of Sweden,
With those of Japan.

73

Even in, Ljubljana, in Larnaca,
In Sundsvall, and Gdansk –
Places you think you will not
Find the Black Africans - they are there.
They have pursued White settlers and
White non-settlers back to the settlers' lands.

They have followed their African minerals
Back to the places the White man calls home.
Back to the rich cities of Europe: Ghent,
Montmartre, and La Sorbonne, the Hague,
The Le Bois de Boulogne and Jardin de Touileries.

The Black African's nose picks-up and follows
The scent of the stolen bauxite, manganese,

Uranium, silver, and gypsum.
He has tracked the stolen phosphate,
Chromium, copper, and petroleum.
He sees how others have benefitted
From his continent's God given resources.

The Black African has hitch-hiked his
Nearly starved, Black African body
To Milan's Corso Buenos Aires,
And Rome's Trieste district,
And Florence's Via Ricasoli.

The Black African, having illegally
Entered Sweden, looks in amazement,
In astonishment at the hordes of blond-haired
People strolling about Stockholm's
Norrmalm and Östermalm, neighborhoods.

74

Mauritania: Life expectancy: 65.48 years.
Infant Mortality Rate:
49.02 out of 1,000 live births.
Only the fool will compare
Mauritania's numbers
With those of Sweden,
With those of Japan.

75

The Black African man always comes begging.
He is a poor man, from a poor continent
But he is smiling. Always gracious.
The *want-to-be, pretend-to-be high-class,*
Middle-aged, European housewife
Looks directly into the poor

Black African man's eyes.
He smiles. She smiles. They do not look away.
She invites him into her European home.
Showing his white teeth, he smiles,
Then he slowly and gracefully enters.
They drink a sour beverage
And eat sliced sausage, with strawberries.
He tells her about his long journey
From Kibeho, in Rwanda
To the beautiful Budapest.

76

Burundi: Life expectancy: 62.60 years.
Infant Mortality Rate:
38.64 out of 1,000 live births.
Only the fool will compare
Burundi's numbers
With those of Sweden,
With those of Japan.

Let's away with study/ Folly's sweet./
Treasure all the pleasure/
Of our youth: Time enough for age/
To think on truth./ So short a day,/
And life so quickly hasting,
And in study wasting/ Youth that would be gay!
Carmina Buranda

And lest, when I come again,
my God will humble me among you,
and that I shall bewail many which
have sinned already and have not
repented of the uncleanness, fornication,
and lasciviousness which they have committed.
2 Corinthians 12:21

WHAT DO THEY SAY?

My name is Falasade.
That's one of them African names.
My Mama's friend, Luvenia, named me this name.

I'm seventeen.
Knows I look more grown than my age.
That just be the way I be made.
Ain't my fault if I be lookin' so good.
Been lookin' good and sexy, everybody says,
Ever since the day I be born.

I ain't graduated from school. Yet.
Things turnout like they 'spose to, though,
I'm gonna go back.
Could be, when I goes back, it'll be at the
Upward Progress Community School.
That's where most'a my friends go.
Anyways, like I said, my name is Falasade.
Falasade Foluke Evans.
I stays with my Momma, Ernestine,
And my Grandma Ella.
Ain't never knowed my daddy.
Heard 'bout'em, though.
Anyhow, staying in the same house wit us is
My other two sisters and my brother.
One'a my sisters is named, Infinity.
The other one is, Lexus.
My brother, is named Chevy.
I be the oldest. Then come Lexus. Then, Chevy.

And, then comes, Infinity.
Besides all of us, two of my own
Crumb-snatchers be in here wit us.
See, I, sometimes back, a while ago, got messed-up.
The first time, 'cause I ain't paid no
'Tention to what be goin' on.
Second time, I was just a stupid fool.
First time – years ago – when I just turned fifteen.
Thought I knowed everythang.
Second time was 'bout twelve months ago.
My Momma near 'bout had a heart attack.
She was bitchin' like she be the one knocked-up.
Tried her best to make me say who I did it wit.
Grandma Ella told her to calm down.
Told Momma I was doin' the same thang she done
When she was even younger than fifteen.
All quick Momma got sho-nuff quiet.
Didn't say not a nother word. Not one.
My oldest is named Pepsi Delight.
Named her that 'cause I
Loves me some cold, Pepsi Cola.
The new one, I named him Escalade.
Named him that 'cause I think that's
Where I might'a got pregnant wit 'em
On the back seat of Harvey Lewis' Escalade.
I'm bettin' Harvey be who Escalade's daddy is
But I ain't askin' that sorry ass, dope-taking,
Dope-dealing, motherfucker for shit.
Not for a goddamn thang.
I ain't sure 'bout who Pepsi Delight's daddy be.
See, when I was damn-near-fourteen,
Goin' on fifteen, I was kinda wild and fast.
I was always screwing 'round with 'a whole
Bunch of trifling, no-good motherfuckers.
If I ever get pregnant one more time,

I done already decided I'm'a gonna git rid of it.
Ain't gonna have it. Ain't gonna change no mo diapers.
Gonna take my ass down to one of them clinics
Them folks run. What'cha call it?
Parent Planning Clinic, or some weird, fuckin' name.
Get me one of them free abortions.
I don't want no more of these damn babies.
I'm sick and tired of 'em and all they cryin' and shit.
Done already told Momma and Grandma Ella.
They be alright wit'it. So, I's be good to go.

What do they say when the babies are born
And the mothers nearly die while the fathers
Are far away telling their sweet lies to other
Little schoolgirls, who, having receptive ears,
Listen as the camouflage untruths these boys speak
Are filled with false, repeated pretty words
And counterfeit feelings?

Receptive schoolgirls who have learned,
Way too early,
How to best spread their thin legs and
How to maturely
Rotate, up-and-down,
Their narrow, youthful hips.
And, who, have somehow,
Grown accustomed to
Feeling huge penises pushing,
Prying, slicing, being forced into
Their used-to-be small cunts
That are now being opened
Wider and wider and made deeper,
Causing them to utter strange,
Incomprehensible, schoolgirls' sounds.

Young girls who have become addicted
To the sensation of feeling big cocks delving
Inch-by-inch-by-inch into them;
Destroying their adolescence until the
Strange juices they've been dreaming
Of discharging and receiving,
Erupt and mix with ignorant passion
And the flowing sweat of their juvenility.

And, rising above them, looking
Down upon them, resting on them,
Panting, smiling, eyes nearly closed,
Covered in transudation and disregard –
Are the cocky, teenaged,
Never had a job, teenage boys,
Who can hardly wait to brag about their conquest;
Anxious to boast how they can become producers
Of babies without becoming parents of babies.

Young girls, school-aged,
So desperately in need of kind words.
Teenagers hoping this is the love
They've always prayed for.
Wanting minuscule bits of tenderness,
Microscopic bits of compassion,
And a few sweet, funny, kind,
And nonjudgmental words.

First- and second-year of high school girls,
In their early years, who a few months later
Will be placed on somebody else's bed.
Bewildered girls. Confused girls. Scared girls.
Unknowing girls. In tears girls.
Girls who will experience excruciating
Pain as whimpering life, destined for

Government aid programs,
Comes screaming,
From their youthful bellies.

Pause:

Too many Lost Wanderers
On the other side of wherever they don't want to be
Still don't know who their daddies are.

Lost Wanderers in too many unknown towns,
Villages, and too many tiny rooms to remember,
Keep on seeking answers to what
Happened at too many unpleasant times.

Lost Wanderers always trying to find
Humanitarian solutions that just might end several
Millenniums of human suffering.

What do they say when the babies crawl
Over cold Minneapolis floors that
Are filled with cracks
And hundreds of hungry roaches,
Scores of desperate rats search for crumbs?
The upcoming decades of pain
Waiting to be carved forever into
The former schoolgirls lives.
Schoolgirls who refused to listen
To mature and concerned mother.
And, who are still children themselves
But who have, in the midst of their
Childhood, become unwed mothers?

What do they say to the unwed mothers who
Have not reached the age of fifteen

Who peep through snow-smudged windows,
Hoping they may see used-to-be schoolmates
And once-upon-a-time good friends?
Hoping to see young girls who
Might just remind them how
Wonderful it used to be when they were still virgins,
Not yet pregnant, and not yet with any sobbing baby.
Watching other teenage girls carrying their
Schoolbooks and fidgeting with their cell phones
While talking to the same boys
The new 15-year-old mothers used to know,
Used to talk to.

Now, the new, too-young-to-work,
Unwed mothers look through their
Snow-smudged windows, as these boys –
These impregnators without a conscious;
These never-apologetic boys who are forever
Dreaded by the girls' mothers, and fathers,
Should the girls have such a thing
As a two-parent home.
These classless, soon to be behind-bars boys,
Smirk and smile their sinister smiles,
As they reach and feel the
Never-had-sex girls' tiny breasts,
Then, squeeze the just-finishing
Middle-school girls'-
Just-starting-to-take-shape, asses.

Giggling little girls sticking out their
Too-young-for-a-real-bra, chests.
Slowly changing their stances, the way they've
Seen girls do on BET, MTV and YouTube.
Giggling little girls posing with glossy
Lipstick covering their lips and Wal-Mart and

Target costume jewelry hanging 'round their necks.
Grinning, pigtailed, first-year-biology girls,
Doing their best to become desirable,
To appear ready for one of the misbehaving boys.
Trying their best to act Beyonce-like.

And these underage children
Who are now little mothers,
With their sad eyes, and with
Their paths blocked and their
Dreams broken, watch Jerry Springer
As their malnourished babies sleep on
Pallets placed on cold, need-to-be-swept
Floors or soiled, unmade beds.

Surely, these young mothers
Will, as they grow older, think back
And remember a time –
During their youthful and playful years -
When these same boys, or boys like them,
Told them – these young, unemployed,
Dependent-on-the-government, mothers,
That they were the most beautiful,
Most precious things God ever made.
Told them they would always love them,
Protect them, cherish them,
And would always support them
And whatever children they may have.

These boys, these hijackers
Of innocence and early dreams,
Always repeat their
Well-practiced and precise lies.
Lies the naïve schoolgirls –
Who had just entered their teens –

Were then and now too eager to believe,
Embrace, and never doubt.

Pause:

Come together and let us start wailing
For the children who have strayed
Into the forest of pain, the garden of discouragement,
The houses of dependency,
The city of rejection, the state of eternal misery,
And the country of worriment.

And what about the disappointed mothers
And fathers of the teenage unwed mommas,
Of the have-not-graduated-high-school mommas?
What about the grandmothers and grandfathers
Of the newly arrived babies, who, by osmosis,
Most of them, everyone knows,
Will become the real mothers
And the real daddies of these
Unprotected single-parent children.

The teenage girls' mothers, fathers,
Grandmothers, and grandfathers
Will be the ones bathing the newborns,
Feeding the newborns, nursing
The newborns, rocking the newborns,
Singing soft songs to the newborns.
They will be the ones telling the newborns
Tales 'bout the older days
When schoolgirls were not so sassy
And schoolboys were not so mannish.
They will be the ones having to raise
Their never married granddaughters' babies.

What do they say to the tiny,
Beseeching-looking children
Who are five-, six-, seven-years-old,
With no remaining,
Known parent and no grandparent,
Or no Grandparent
Worthy of being a grandparent;
Five-, six-, seven-years-old boys and girls
With dirt, lice and sorrow clinging to
Their hungry and confused bodies.
Their minds void of wonderment, of dreams,
Of curiosity and of whatever it is tiny and
Beseeching-looking five-, six-, seven-years-old
Boys and girls should take for granted?

These children, with no loving and caring
Grown folks protecting them from starvation,
From homelessness, are often seen searching
Through the cafes' garbage and the piles of dump –
Looking for discarded food: a thrown away burger,
A partly eaten roll, an unfinished soda, a half-rotten
Piece of fruit, as flies rest on their thin,
Emaciated bodies, where sores have broken-out
And pus sits in tiny holes: one here, two there,
On their slender legs, on their thin arms, while older,
Better-off, religious people walk by; slowing, pausing,
Shaking their heads, and saying, ever so softly:
Lord, ain't that a shame,
Then turning quickly to see if
Anyone close by has heard;
Might complain and consider
Such words insensitive,
Mean spirited, uncaring –
Only to meet the big, round, sad, piercing
Eyes of the children standing and

Staring like damaged and discarded rag dolls.
Looking like something worthy of commentary,
But are too grotesque to be approached, to be helped,
To be apologize to.

And, somewhere are the children, the lucky ones,
Whose bellies stick-out from stale, molded bread,
Rationed enriched rice, black-eyed peas, and too
Much lead-contaminated water that will sometimes
Contain tablespoons of sugar or ALAGA Syrup.
Bread, rice, peas, sweeten-water
Given by distant relatives or foster home
Providers; folks who angrily look around
Their small, overcrowded,
Two-rooms, and see somebody's else children -
Nearly starving children, with their sad faces
Communicating: *Please, let us eat. I'm hungry.*

Distant relatives or foster home people: some skinny,
Some obese, some caring, some not giving a damn,
Others abusive and meanspirited.
Most with high blood pressure, diabetes,
A bad heart who offers profanities each time
The *"where-do-all-these-damn-children-come-from,"*
Children sit for supper, with their sadness as
Their everyday companion, *and*, with their eyes
Looking downward as if searching
For a quick Miracle.

Then, there are those few seconds of reverence
When folded hands are placed together and point
Towards the sky, as they mouth, in unison,
The suppertime's Bible verse:
*God is good. God is great and we thank Him
For this food,*

By His hands we all are fed;
Thank You, Lord for our daily bread.
Amen.

What do they say when the
Children, riding the yellow school buses,
Go off to the city and county schools,
Carrying no books, no crayons, no pencils,
No expectations, no joys and no lunches?

Then, sitting in schools with broken windows,
Little heat, and draconian rules;
Where angry children, before them, like them,
Have thrown rocks and other objects
Because they, like these new arrivals,
Were fearful of their unfamiliar environment.
Afraid of learning, of knowing, of doing, of being,
Of asking, of answering, of wondering, of hoping.
And, these recent children,
Having never heard proper English
Or who have never correctly
Pronounced too many words,
And who are barely able to count to ten,
Or recite their full names. Even afraid to smile.

These children, born of the teenage,
Unwed and scared mothers,
Are now constantly encased in hidden fear,
As teachers from over the other way,
And from distant suburbs who
Earn minimum schoolteachers' wages -
Just enough to properly survive on -
Hurry the children through
Periods 1, Period 2, and Period 3.
Schoolteachers, lucky enough to be teaching,

Who long ago stopped trying to relate, console,
To teach, to make *these children* understand.
To discipline, to wipe away the
Children's escaped tears and snot.

All the time the children, with their aching
And empty stomachs, listen for the lunch bell,
So they can be marched, silently,
Like small, robotic soldiers
Down hallways to an antiseptic-smelling cafeteria
To eat midday, high-in-calories, government meals
Provided by elected people they have never seen,
Have never heard of, but someday, for little reason,
Will come to hate.

Children so in need
Of some type nourishments
Who in their haste, their running,
Their anxiousness,
Spill their milk and juice, drop their hotdogs,
Potato chips onto a floor scrubbed every
Tuesday and Thursday night by an
Old, limping, and lonely custodian,
Then crying when a fat cook,
The vice principle, and other impassionate
Administrators yell, scream, and tell them –
The still hungry children -
Their lunch period has been canceled.

Pause:

Falasade Foluke Evans.
That's a name coming from Nigeria.
Bet you didn't know that, did'ya?
All the time them teachers –

Starting with kindergarten –
Didn't know how to say my name.
Made me laugh. Right in their faces.
Anyways, my youngest – Escalade,
Well he went and got himself all sick.
Be coughing and crying all night-long.
Grandma Ella took all three of us:
Me, Pepsi Delight and Escalade out to
The county hospital's emergency room.
That's where I sho nuff just about showed my ass.
Escalade coughin' and cryin' and this "wanna be
A movie star" bitch-of-a-nurse,
Or whatever the fuck she be,
Kept cuttin' her eyes at Escalade,
Like she wanted him to stop cryin', to stop achin'.
Finally, I got off my ass, walked over to the bitch
And told her to stop lookin' at Escalade
And us like we be po, welfare motherfuckin' trash.
Right away I could see the "wanna be a movie star"
Bitch-of-a-nurse, getting' scared, getting' all nervous;
Thinking she 'bout to get her ass destroyed.
Givin' me one of her phony smiles.
Next thing we knowed, a fast-walkin'
Doctor come running up to us, sayin' real-doctor-like,
He be ready to see Escalade.
Hour later we outta there with all kinda
Free medicine and other free shit.
The doctor, with his sneaky ass, kept lookin' at me like
He was burnin' to git
Some'a what I gave Escalade's Daddy.
Wantin' some of the stuff I be born wit
And knows how to use.
'Cause just checkin' me out, he could tell
I could fuck his doctor-ass to death if I wanted to.
And, he be grinnin', be lookin' and be wishing for

Some of my precious, hot stuff, really bad. I could tell.
I just smiled at his doctor-ass;
Knowin' if he got hold'a me,
I'd fuck his dick off and wear out
His pussy lickin' tongue.
I'd put some moves on his ass he ain't
Never thought 'bout havin'.

Pause:

She sang in the First Lutheran Church choir.
Her voice everyone always boasted
Was better than the other choir members:
Expressing clarity, compassion, and truthfulness.
She was a stout girl, not fat, just stout;
Sorta like lots of girls in the Ottumwa area.

The pastor, the auxiliary club members,
The high school principal, teachers,
Community leaders; all the right Ottumwa folks,
Knew she was one of the nicest girls to be raised
In their part of Iowa, in a long time.

It was Mrs. Dupree, the choir director,
Who glimpsed it first.
Noticed how her singing had changed,
How she was not as attentive.
Was not carrying the notes with
The same sincerity and clarity.
Mrs. Dupree detected wavering
Whenever she sang the high notes.
Then, the high school's librarian had
To wake her up a few times.

Lawrence Vickers, who worked at Walgreens,

The one on 4th Street,
Thought he saw her riding and smiling
In Billie Dent's pickup truck.
Thought he saw them kissing, one night.
Maybe, even doing more than kissing at
The far end of the drug store's parking lot,
Out where the big dumpster used to be.

Her parents, with only a few choices,
Sent her out to Montana.
That's where her Aunt Louise,
Her Mother's sister, lived, alone.

On the 25th day of October,
One of the nicest girls from Ottumwa, Iowa,
Assisted by Saint James Hospital
Medical personnel, in Butte, Montana,
Gave birth to very healthy and pretty twin girls.
Named them Connie and Cathy.
Connie weighed 6 pounds 7 ounces, with blue eyes.
Cathy weighed 6 pounds 6 ounces,
Also, with blue eyes.

On May 17, a windy day with lots of
Chill still in the Air,
Aunt Louise drove her to the Montana Drivers'
Exam Station, the one over on Wynne Street.
She passed her tests: the written and the driving.
That was her sixteenth birthday present
From Aunt Louise.
She never heard anything
From that Billie Dent boy.

What do they say on this particular Mother's Day,
The second Sunday in the month of May,

When the gravesite of a dead mother is visited?
A day when heavy rain pours and now two larger,
More understanding children start to weep,
As they stand, looking down on a cheap headstone,
Sitting on a mound of dirt, soaked in water,
And inscribed:
Always to be Remembered:
Falasade Foluke Evans,
1979 – 2000.

Two children, a boy and a girl, being told
By their grandmother
The older, more stable,
Surviving family member:
This is where your Momma,
My oldest child, is buried.
Lord bless her soul. She was a good girl.
Don't yaw'll forget it, you hear?
'Cause no matter what other folks say,
Your Momma, Falasade, was a good,
Sweet, and loving child.
She just had too much to carry on her thin shoulders.
She tried her best, though, being so young and all.
So, don't yaw'll ever forget.
When yaw'll get old enough to come here by yourself,
Please, no matter how busy yaw'll be,
Take the time and visit
Where your Momma be resting.
Yaw'll hear what we tellin' yaw'll?

And from a side road, Mister Smith,
The neighboring man
Who drove them to this place,
Blows his car horn – two, then three times.
Walking between the grave sites,

With red mud splashing onto Pepsi Delight's
Bargain-basement, patent-leather sandals
And Escalade's Puma sneakers, they,
The girl and the boy,
And the grandparents weep
And wipe their sadden eyes.

After a short while, the graveyard
Is two miles behind,
With its mounds of wet dirt,
Red mud, puddles of water,
Cheap headstones,
Newly purchased plastic flowers,
And everlasting miseries,
Will be quickly forgotten as Falasade's
Bones continue to rot.
Mister Smith, the neighbor, listens.
He sees the tears. He says nothing.

Suddenly, thunder starts to roar,
Lightning strikes an electric power line,
Knocking out juice to the television news
That tell of diseased people,
Starving people, just-got-out-of-jail people,
Demonstrating-for-freedom people,
Homeless people, rich people,
Wall Street people, terrorist people,
Movie star people, football, basketball people,
All doing whatever they do -
Causing a man to reach for another can
Of Lucky Time Beer and say:
I hate this fuckin' weather.

Pause:

Lucy, her common-law, step-daddy,
Big K, kept on telling her,
Whenever they were by themselves,
And nobody but the two of them could hear;
Would tell Lucy she looked better than her Momma.
Her Momma and Big K were common-law man and wife.
Big K's name real was Kelvin,
But everybody, all over, called him Big K.
Told Lucy, Big K did, every chance he got,
How good looking, how fine she be; especially
For somebody just turned thirteen.
And, Lucy being kind'a slow on the sense side,
Always blushed when Big K told her she was so pretty,
So sweet, so good-looking, and so special.
He was tall, rawboned, and sweaty - Big K was,
Like them giraffes she saw in the animal picture books
She kept under her bed.
He had long legs, too, just like them giraffes
In her animal picture books.
Always when nobody be looking
And her Momma be gone,
Big K would start touching
And tickling and rubbing on Lucy.
Making her laugh. Making her think she be happy.
Telling her she ought'a be in one of them
Television soap opera shows
So the whole world could see how beautiful she be.
How sexy she be.
Lucy, 'bout to turn fourteen,
She started thinking she grown,
'Cause she knowed girls be sometimes cute,
Maybe 'special ones be pretty,
But ain't no girls she knowed 'bout be beautiful

And be sexy at the same time.
Only grownup women, like her Momma,
Be beautiful and sexy.
When Big K wasn't working 'round the house,
He would be down some road
Helping folks fix fences or cleaning trash
Out of back yards, but all the time,
No matter what he be doin,
He always be thinking them sho-nuff
Devilish thoughts 'bout Lucy.
Them Lucy kind'a thoughts all the time
Made him 'bout to explode cause 'a
All the shameful things rumbling all over
And through his mind, and the stirring and
Paining and the growing bigness happen'
Tween his legs that he couldn't stop from
Rising when he all the times was thinking 'bout Lucy.
Things got to bothering him so much, he had to start
Taking heaps of that Standback Powder and
Drinking apple cider vinegar with honey mixed in
Just so he could get his mind straight.
One Monday morning,
When they were all by theyselves,
Just the two of them, Big K and Lucy,
With nobody close to the house but the two of them;
Was not another soul anywhere near to
Hear what he said and what Lucy said.
And what they both did. And how they acted.
Anyway, to be on the safe side,
Big K peeped outta the window and closed the curtains
Before he told his common-law wife's child,
To come with him to his and her Momma's room.
The room where he and her Momma slept and
Did all the other things common-law married people do.
Made her come with 'em.

Told her they be the only ones' in the house
And wasn't nobody outside.
Nobody, in or out, 'cept the two of them.
And, she did. Lucy followed Big K
Into her Momma's bedroom.
Over the months of listening to Big K's words,
She had started expecting she done become all grown,
'Cause she was, 'cordin' to Big K, beautiful and sexy
And sweet-smelling like one of her momma's roses.
Big K told her to wrap her arms 'round him.
And, Lucy did.
She wrapped her arms 'round Big K,
Hugged him tighter than she
Had ever hugged anything in all the
Years since she be born.
Felt him hug her back.
Felt him squeeze her so hard she was 'fraid
He might break her apart.
She started to shiver when he ran his fingers down
The middle of her not-yet-wide back.
Then he started whispering big, sweet,
Confusing words into her thirteen-years-old ear.
Felt him move his lips, Lucy did, to her face.
Her Momma's man then put his tongue right
Upside her neck, and then she felt him lick it,
Her neck with his wet tongue. Up and down he went.
Then, he put the tip of that wet tongue of his
Into her ear and moved it 'round and 'round, in and out.
Lucy felt him kiss, then suck, and slobber on
Her shaking fingers. Then fo she knowed it,
Big K went and took that long, snake-like tongue
Of his and put it right 'tween
Her trembling lips, down her quivering throat.
She almost, but not quite, fainted.
Almost, but not quite, peed on herself.

Wanted to say: "Lord, have mercy," but,
Was too confused to remember the words.
Lucy, almost, but not quite,
Believed she was floating on one of the
Lord's clouds up in Heaven and was 'bout
To say something only Jesus would understand.
Big K's great-big hands — rough, scarred,
Bruised hands, moving like a snake,
Touched her small, almost boy-like chest.
Her almost fourteen-year-old tiny knobs sitting there,
Hard like they be marbles they sell in the
Toy department at the big Kmart store on Sawmill Road.
But, her tiny knobs — her marbles — were aching,
Boiling and 'bout to burst wide-open and explode
And make her sure 'nough lose the rest of her mind.
Lose what sense she still had up in her head.
Big K asked Lucy, kinda soft like;
Like he be one of the actor she see on television;
Asked her to take off her dress.
She was feeling too much to be understanding
Exactly what he meant — slow minded and all —
And stirred-up so much.
So, Big K, with them rough hands,
Reached down, pulled the summer cloth
Up over her head, eased down the moist,
Cotton panties her momma had bought for her
At that Dollar Store out on Sawmill Road,
Not far from the Kmart store.
Too soon, much faster than it should have been,
Lucy didn't have a stitch of clothes on her frail,
Shaking-all-over body.
Not understanding too much and about
To be taken somewhere else, Lucy was naked,
Petrified and still not a bit smarter.
Big K, he, yes, he did,

Laid her almost 14-year-old body down,
Right there on his and her Momma's queen-sized bed,
On the spot where he had placed three old towels
On top of an old, thick blanket
So the bedspread wouldn't get soiled.
He had told himself to take his time,
To go slow and be real gentle.
Told himself how he didn't want to hurt Lucy.
Had kept reminding himself how she was a virgin
And how she might start screaming and yelling his name.
So, for all these reasons, because he had told himself
What might happen, he promised himself
He would take his time, use the Vaseline he
Had hid under the side of the bed,
And go real, real slow and easy no matter
How anxious he became.
He crawled 'tween Lucy's little legs
That had never been splayed open
For anything like what he was gonna do to her.
Before long Big K started grunting and forgetting
All the things he had told himself he would and
Wouldn't do.
Lucy, in some kind'a sho-nuff pain,
Was hurting and feeling real bad.
Then, she, confused Lucy, started to bleed.
Big K, not payin' no 'tention, kept on grunting.
Kept on pushing harder and harder and further and
further than he had ever pushed into her Momma.
Fo long of 'em started to sweat sho'nuff hard.
Blood was coming from Lucy onto the three towels
And the old, thick blanket.
She was feeling pain all through her body.
All at once she started hearing strange things
She hadn't ever heard and seeing things
She had never seen before.

Poor and pitiful Lucy, all of a sudden
Was thinking things she never thought 'bout
Thinking in her whole life on Earth.
Big K, started acting wild-like,
Started licking Lucy, started kissing Lucy,
Squeezing Lucy, breathing hard on Lucy,
Promising Lucy; swearing fo God,
Pleading like he be done gone and lost his mind.
Saying how much he loved her.
How much he needed her.
Lucy sobbing. Lucy hurting from all that pain.
Lucy bleeding. Lucy almost fourteen.
Lucy telling Big K
She loved him more'n he loved her.
Telling him she needed him more'n he needed her.
Then, Big K made Lucy swear on the Bible
Her Grandpa had left for her Momma.
The one they always kept on that
Table next to the bed.
Lucy swore on that Bible that she would
Never tell her Momma or any living soul,
Less she wanted to die and go live in hell with the
Bad, ugly, mean and black-as-midnight,
Devil who would do nasty things to sweet girls, like Lucy.
Lucy, 13-years-old but almost fourteen, hugged Big K
And swore some more on her Momma's Bible.
Then she went to the bathroom
And using wet toilet paper washed and scrubbed the blood
From 'tween her legs and from her thighs.
She looked at the wet toilet paper, covered with blood,
And then she flushed that paper down the toilet
Like Big K had told her to do.
Then, she came back into her Momma's bedroom,
Put on her tiny panties, her simple dress,
Her sandals, and whatever else she needed to put on.

Did all of that 'cause Big K told her to do it.
Lord, 'fo you know it, she, Lucy became fourteen.
'Cause her mind was becoming slower and slower;
Slower than it was before, when she was thirteen,
Her Momma decided Lucy should stay at home,
Away from schoolhouses and all the teasing and
Bullying the other girls and boys would surely do to her.
Without much warning,
Her Momma started making her cook,
Clean the house and do a little washing and some ironing.
"Make yourself useful," her Momma would say.
"You're a big girl, now. You gotta help out."
Every Monday, Wednesday, and Friday
When her Momma be gone to the rich folks' part of town
To take care of things for Mrs. Sheppard and Mrs. Duff,
Big K and Lucy had their way with each other.
For some reason, Lucy, at fourteen,
Was becoming less smarter than the thirteen-year-old Lucy,
While at the same time, becoming Big K's other woman.
He told her so. Made her believe his every word.
Started saying his real woman was her, Lucy,
Not Lucy's Momma, but her.
Lucy, all the time wanted him to tell her that.
Got to where she wanted him more'n he wanted her.
Couldn't wait for the Mondays, Wednesdays, and Fridays
To come 'round so she and Big K
Could do all the things she and Big K done
Figured out how to do to make each other
Feel better'n they ever felt in they lives.
Then one Tuesday,
a day when Lucy's Momma ain't had
To go see 'bout Mrs. Sheppard and Mrs. Duff,
She decided to send Lucy down the road
To the Darby's Grocery Store.
Told Lucy, she should, on the way to the store,

Stop and spend some time with Miss Patterson,
Their longtime neighbor, church member and friend.
Said she would telephone Miss Patterson
And let her know she would be coming down
The road and would be stopping by
To talk for a while.
That way Miss Patterson would be
On the lookout for her in case she, Lucy,
Couldn't remember where she 'spose to stop.
Told her to take her time talking with Miss Patterson,
Stay with her an hour or two, and then go on to
The Darby's Grocery Store.
Tell Mister Darby that everything is alright
And that she praying that his wife is getting better.
Leaving home Lucy was happy as she could be.
But, being slow-minded and all and with so
Much of Big K's happiness all the time
Flowing through her body and her mind,
She forgot her small, red, and green,
Patent-leather, pocketbook
That she took everywhere she went.
The red and green pocketbook was her good
Luck piece that Aunt Strawberry had
Given her on her tenth birthday.
She felt really sad and unlucky 'cause,
Thinking so much 'bout Big K, and thinking
'Bout seeing Miss Patterson,
She had gone and forgot her good
Luck pocketbook and left it,
If she remembered right, on the Kitchen table.
Pocketbook had the note and the money her
Momma done gave her.
Her head hanging, so sad, she being so hot,
Feeling so unlucky, Lucy walked slowly back
To the house to get her little Patent-leather,

Good-luck, pocketbook and the
Darby's Grocery Store note and the money.
Lucy came up the front porch steps 'specting her
Momma to hear the door opening and to meet her
All worried and ask her why she back so soon.
But, her Momma didn't meet her.
So, she went through the front door,
Heading straight for the kitchen,
That's when she heard her Momma moaning
And making noises like the way she,
Lucy had learned to moan and make noises.
Looking through her Momma's slightly
Ajar bedroom door, she saw Big K on his back,
On his and her Momma's bed,
With her Momma straddling him
Like Big K had taught her, Lucy, to straddle him.
Shaking like a mangle dog,
Lucy grabbed her little pocketbook and went
Running and a crying, and saying nasty words,
All the ways down the road.
Head bent, she walked right by Miss Patterson's house
Without saying a single word.
Didn't even look at that old woman and her
Ugly yellow house.
Went into the Darby's Grocery Store.
Mr. Darby gave her everything on her Momma's list.
Lucy spent all the money her Momma
Had put in her little pocketbook.
Spent all but one dollar and 65 cents.
But, she spent that, too.
Bought a small box of "Rat Free Rat Poison,"
She seen on the Darby's Grocery Store's shelf.
Six months later, Lucy and her Momma - both of 'em -
Got all dressed up on a windy Wednesday afternoon.
They were wearing sad-looking black dresses,

Like the ones women folks wear if they be going
To somebody's funeral.
Lucy's stomach was a whole bunch fatter now;
Sticking way out, tight 'ginst her
Going-to-a-funeral black dress.
But, she didn't care, didn't give no never mind.
Had not a single worry 'bout her at all.
She did cry though when the preacher
Talked 'bout Big K and all his goodness;
How he had been one of them big strong men,
Always a provider, a giver, a hard worker,
And a protector of the community.
Preacher told how Big K took care of everybody;
Treated everybody as good as anybody ought
To be treated.
These days, Momma and Lucy,
Both of "em, when they walk 'round the house,
They always be looking funny-like at each other
But they ain't doing too much talking.
Both wondering who done went and done what.
Who gonna do what. Who knows what?
Wondering, Momma is,
Who it was that made Lucy's
Stomach all fat with a soon-to-be-born baby.
Wondering who Lucy got with on them
Mondays, Wednesdays and Fridays
when she was at Mrs. Sheppard's and Mrs. Duff's.

What do they say when the smiling,
Vicious, low-life pimps,
In their purple suits,
Red shirts, black scarves, green shoes,
Cheap gold, and silver-filled mouths,
Stand in the narrow, darken hallways,
Or slouch in their professionally detailed

Pimp-cars on the polluted avenues and in
Trash-filled, rodents' infested, alleyways,
Counting the twenties, the hundreds
They've taken from tall or short, skinny, or fat,
Troubled and drugged-filled young girls
Who sell their bodies up and down the
Contaminated routes and byways?

Who complains about young girls
Jumping into slow-moving,
Expensive cars owned and occupied
By potential customers?
Young girls hoping the drivers
Are sane and not sadistic.
Young girls selling their mouths,
Their cunts, their asses, their hands to
Movie stars and starlets, bankers, lawyers,
Politicians, college boys or just plain,
Hardworking folks for two hours at the most,
Fifteen minutes at the least,
Or for all night if you drive a Bentley,
understand hedge funds, own a mansion,
Deal cocaine, own or play for the Knicks,
The Cowboys, the Heat, the Astros.

All the while the teenage girls keep throwing
Warm, soapy water, mixed with vinegar,
Into their crotches –
Attempting to make their cunts tighter.
Rinsing their mouths with Listerine or
Baking soda, while ensuring their stockings are
Straight and not too torn, then, inhaling
Colombian white powder into their noses.
Hoping it, this Colombian white powder,
Will cause them to be less aware, uncaring

More desensitized, blasé, more shameless
Before placing their high-heeled feet once
Again onto sidewalks crowded with people:
Lonely people, beautiful people, desperate people,
All looking for someone to lay with; young,
For-sale girls, for the fewest of dollars or for free,
Before the men wearing uniforms and badges,
And legally carrying guns, driving slowly in their
Police wagons become more vigilant than they
Were before that teenage girl in the Valley
Was murdered while they paid no-never-mind
And pretended not to care.
Now, because of political pressure,
They chase the teenage girls to homes
Where one, two, sometimes three
Well-fed children, are sound asleep.

As the church bells toll on Sunday morning,
A tired, Twenty-four-year-old mother,
After only a few hours of sleep,
Barely alive, gets out of her bed,
Prepares a breakfast of biscuits, sausages, and eggs,
Then dresses her two precious ones:
Kenneth and Susie.
She kiss their cheeks, and watch
As they walk two blocks,
Holding hands, to the
Mount Eden Baptist Church
To Attend Sunday School, then,
Stay for the eleven o'clock service.

Kenneth and Susie,
Always being respectful
As people say to them:
Kenneth and Susie, yaw'll look so sweet today.

Where yaw'll Momma at? She sick or what?
Hearing Kenneth and Susie say:
She's at home, resting. She's not feeling too well.
While the nosey,
In-everybody's-business church member says:
Sho hope she be restin' good.
By the way, where it is she be working at nowadays?

Soon, everybody is sitting straight
And wrapped in the Holy Ghost
As the most Reverend Silas Pickens
Shouts and explains for
Thirty-two hallelujah minutes,
The gospel according to Ezekiel, Chapter 37.

The Reverend talks and explains
'Bout them *Bones* to one hundred
And seventeen sweating church folks
Who will donate nine hundred dollars
And thirty Cents.

Reverend Pickens tells them 'bout the terrible
Conditions man done placed himself in.
Tells them 'bout prophesying about them *Bones.*
Then, he asks them if they remembered the day
They were saved by the Lord,
Causing Mrs. Annabelle James to shriek:
Lord, Jesus, I sho do!

Look around and you'll notice that the dance halls
Are overflowing with an intolerable stench,
With the slime and the no-counts, the abhorrent.
The human vultures, buzzards, and scavengers are
Peering through banks of smoke and clouds of
Desperation, trickery, and deception.

These buzzards are always leering,
Are always on the prowl, in search
Of weak, vulnerable, and easy-to-conquer,
Nearly dead, female flesh.

These leech-like, women haters,
Always crowd into these defiled spaces;
Spaces reserved and allotted for their blood
Sucking and their soul taking from the pitiful,
Jittery, and shameless women/girls who
Themselves possess little dignity, few scruples,
And even fewer morals.

Women/girls waiting to
Relinquish what tainted probity they still,
Against all odds, have held onto.
The all-seeing vultures are drawn to
The prized female meat that
Waits and wants to be ground
Into an unrecognizable substance
To be devoured, enjoyed, and wrecked.

These scavengers know these women.
They know that these girls greatest desires,
Are, sadly, to be humiliated even more;
To be further and permanently transformed
Into non-returnable, unserviceable,
Condemned, and unrecognizable throwaways.

And, the females,
Mostly single heads-of-households,
Already, most of them, with children too many,
Shake their asses, pout their lips,
Adjust their store-bought, imported hair;

Touch their breasts. Rapidly move their hips
To the beat of pounding drums,
The sound of magic horns,
And repetitive human chants coming
From desperate voices.
Each beat, every note from the horn,
Every relentless chant;
Every sound urges the vulnerable
and the weak, the already and always
sexually driven, to give up the body,
To say bye-bye to self-esteem,
Bye-bye to character.

And, before long there are even greater,
More enticing undulations and movements
Which ask for, beg for the opportunity to be
To be used, to be manipulated,
To be abused, and continually disrespected.

Lust and sweat compete with sordid,
Wretched, and fleeting respectabilities.
Riper, rawer, erotic, explicit lecherous
Desires are on full display
Until they manifest themselves into
A beating, syncopated, hypnotic delirium
That rake the bodies,
Like the Flames in *Dante's Inferno*
Raked its residence.

Then the buzzards, the vultures, pounce.
Always the same question: *Your place or mine?*

The woman/girl timid but consumed
With intense sexual cravings begging
For sexual liberation and satisfaction,

Offers the half-hearted refusal:
I don't even know you.
This causes the buzzard to respond:
Yea, you don't, but I'm navigating a brand new,
Just-left-the-showroom, Porsche Nine-One-One.
The woman/girl,
Already creaming and wet,
Thinks she'll permit a kiss to the neck.
Maybe a rubbing of her tit.
Allow a finger to massage her begging cunt.
Already a little bit afraid, she is, but
The goddamn pounding and the relentless
Cravings keep growing, keep pleading.
The motherfucking itch is multiplied
With each gesture, each sigh..

She is beyond thrilled. She's electrified.
The Porsche speakers emit
Beethoven's *Melody of Love.*
The ride is smoother than
Any ride she's ever had.
Then, her quick appraisal:
He does not look too bad. He smells good.
He's driving this fancy car.
Probably has lots of money.
He speaks well. He likes high-class music.
Has good teeth. Bet he has a big dick.
Probably likes to eat pussy, too.

Folks at the Human Services Offices,
And all the "Help the Poor" outreach places,
Keep believing most of the begging, unwed
Mothers are worthless, shiftless, and lazy.
Believing they, these single mothers,
Are not good examples for their children.

Experience has taught them that begging,
Unwed mothers produce begging children.
That promiscuous behavior generates future
Promiscuous behavior that becomes a lifestyle.
They know, because they hear it all the time,
How people are tired of their taxes going
To support these unwed, welfare mothers
Who are always on the dole,
With their sex-starved
Habits and their addiction to illegal drugs and
Their belief in ridiculous get rich schemes.
Do the mothers, when sensing these attitudes,
Feel ashamed, dismayed, or disheartened?
Do they leave these offices in tears
Or, do they display dignity and self-respect?
Or, do they say, under their breath:
You think I care 'bout what low-salaried,
Government employed, sa-ditty motherfuckers
And the rest of you stuck-up motherfuckers
Think about me? Well, I don't give a fuck!
I don't give a good goddamn, So, fuck off.
Do they silently utter these words and
Behave in a disdainful fashion while all the
Time chewing and smacking their chewing gum
And daring any fucking body to say any
Goddamn-fucking thing
Or look at them in any disrespectful manner?

What thoughts go through the
In-need mother's mind?
What does she think when she stands
Before the Master-Degreed Human Service
Worker who is trying her best to hurry and
Not to appear uppity or better
Than the poor, in need, woman;

The in-need mother, standing before her?
The Human Service worker rushes to see
If the single mother qualifies for an EBT card
Or an increase in the number of her EBT benefits.
What must the single, in-need mother think
While she watches the government worker
Continually input data into her
Government computer.
Watches the government worker's
Insincere smile and her display of
An insincere gesture, maybe a smile,
While believing, the Government worker does,
That the in-need mother,
Just might trade her benefits
For Illegal drugs, more wine,
More *Popeye's* chicken,
A little bit of cocaine or
A bag of dynamite marijuana.
Maybe these young and older mothers
Look into the social service
Workers' eyes and say:
You are right.
I am an unemployed mother.
But, you are wrong when you think
I am not a decent member of this society.
I might not be as productive a person as I ought to be,
But goddamnit, I am a decent human being.
Things will change. I swear to God,
Things will change. I swear. And, I'll be better.
God's gonna look down on me and bless
Me and my children. I know it.

In a nearby waiting area,
A nosey somebody,
With keen ears and probing eyes, mutters:

These girls be too young
To be out here asking for
Any kind of government handout.

Pause:

I always, all the time,
Every day, prays for the "Miracle."
If the Lord sees fit to bless me
Like I keep praying for Him to do,
We be moving outta this goddamn place.
Me and my babies, we be long gone.
Going back down South where folks
Got some sense.
Knows 'bout respecting each other.
First thing I do when
God's "Miracle" happens:
I'm'a get us a brand new car:
One of them big Mercedes,
Maybe one'a them big Lexus or a BMW.
Gonna get me a whole bunch'a new clothes:
Shoes, good stuff from one of them stores that
Ain't in this pitiful neighborhood.
A store like that Macy's or that
Saks Store over in Manhattan or
Some other place where they located.
Buy these po-ass children of mine
Whatever they want.
Throw a party and invite everybody;
Even the bastards I can't stand; the ones I hate.
Might even invite these children's Daddies.
Get me some of the best liquor I can find
And some of Leroy's best blow.
Just a little bit, don't wanna get too fucked up
And then act like a fool.

If the Good Lord sees fit to bless me,
We be on the road to Natchez and fishing
And good barbeque and good Christian people.
To hell with these New York sonofabitches.

What do they say when the
Street corners are without the loathsome
And pathetic bragging men and
There ain't no more of them
Long-legged street walkers wearing
Their tiny skirts and skimpy blouses?
Ain't anybody here and nobody there.
And, ain't nobody anywhere doing
What they ought'a be doing ?

You think the people gonna
Run to the church, the synagogue,
To the mosque and find peace,
Find comfort, find some semblance
Of peace and salvation, or redemption?
Could be, they think they need to
Be touched by the hands of the minister,
The rabbi, the priest, the imam,
By the matted-haired, Abracadabra Lady
Living back in the swamps among the
Wildest and strangest animals
And the poisonous insects
And among those who
Can decipher mumbo-jumbo.

But if the church, temper, synagogue
And mosque have locked their doors
And the pulpits, the rostrums, lecterns,
The platforms and the soapboxes are all gone;
And the preachers, the ministers, the rabbis,

The priests and the imams are all unavailable;
And the stained windows no longer have stains,
And the Abracadabra Lady done left the swamps –
Will those in a hurry for a new kind of salvation
Bow to the falseness of concocted gods, or,
Will they wildly rush onto the avenues, panting,
Breathing too hard; screaming, wanting someone,
Anyone to notice to hear, to offer a guaranteed
Absolution and a cleansing of their soiled souls?

But, without sure-fire absolution and cleansing,
Do they make their way back to
The places of pleasure?
And, should those places: the casinos,
The dance halls be shut and all the
Other haunts of entertainment,
of fun, of music that caters
To the *beautiful* people,
The self-gratification people,
Be silent, will the young mothers,
Alone, destitute, sheathed in invisibility
And eternal grief, having
Nobody but the children;
Will they finally call upon the children's
Lost, damaged, and Most likely,
Eternally ruined and damned fathers?

What will they say when the older folks look
Back on lives filled with misery and little hope;
Remembering old friends who've been moved
To other places: penitentiaries, old-folks-homes.
Who have become too sick to leave
Whatever rooms they've been assigned
And those who were too poor to even get a room,
Or even to enter the worst of homeless shelters;

Who carried themselves to unknown,
Ugly places so they could die unclaimed,
And uncelebrated without ever having been
Visited by a son, daughter, brother, sister,
Mom, dad, a deacon from the church, or a friend?

And, what about those who once were
Strong and full of fiber and
All the right things that turned youngsters
Into good men, good women;
Into quality men, quality women;
Men and women who cared too
Much but were too young and too good
To know any better or to know why,
And who never expected any kind
Of compensation or reward?

Some of the men and women
Have gone to other corners, newer streets;
Taking their romanticized old lies
And confusing dreams in garbage bags;
Talking about grandchildren, great-grandchildren,
And sandlot ballplayers
Who could have turned pro,
Who could have made it in the
Majors if it hadn't been for the
Fuckin' bottle or that goddamn dope,
Or some good-for-nothing heifer
Or some sorry-ass no good, down-and-out,
Who made all the girls,
Good ones and bad ones, pregnant.

And, don't forget the older ladies,
With bosoms that once stood straight,
But now hang and sag.

Who move their jaws up and down,
Round a little bit, adjusting their false teeth;
Who keep asking each other if they watched
That *Oprah* show about them folks who is big
As a house, fat as a cow?
All the time knowing
Somebody is bound to speak
Up and say something, like:
Honey, that Oprah all the time got
Some funny stuff on her show.
That's how come she so rich.

Pause:

Anybody know the name of that senator
Who wrote that evil bill that puts
Poor people in the 'lectric chair;
Or have 'em tied down on a cheap gurney,
Waiting on the executioner's needle;
Or the crying ones waiting for the hangman's
Noose to be put 'round their necks,
Or the trembling ones lined up fo a firing squad?
What was that evil senator's name
Who wrote that evil bill?

What about that all-the-time, out-of-work man,
Who use'ta run fast as a rabbit,
'Cause they both, he and the rabbit,
Both of 'em be hungry;
Runnin' for somethin' to be put in they bellies?
Anybody 'member who that was?

Then, there was the man who washed his
Feet twenty or more times a day
'Cause they always smelled and itched, so he thought.
Washed them nearly raw.

Ended up having to go bare-footed and walk all funny.

There was this one fellow
Who didn't eat nothing but okra.
Fellow ended up with a slimy and slippery mouth
And a real slick disposition.
Always slippin' and slidin', he was.

Somebody over in the west part
Of town is always talking
About that family who never
Turn their house lights off.
Said they be 'fraid of the night and
Suspicious of the natural daytime.

Not long ago, word is,
And most words spoken 'round here
Ought to be mostly honored,
'Specially the good ones,
Ought to at least be heard. Anyways.
Word is, this sho-nuff rich man went
To the courthouse and cussed out this old judge
Who he had went to grade school with,
'Cause the rich man's sweetheart was
Locked-up in the city jail.
Had been caught, she had, messin' 'round,
Selling her womanhood on the side.
So, the judge gave her ten days to be spent
Doing whatever the jail folks told her to do.
Made no difference bout the city jail being
Too crowded and all. Gave her a speech too.
Speech was harder for her to take, so they say,
Than the city jail time.
Judge told his grade school buddy she belonged
Where he had put her, 'cause she had even tried

To get him, an elected judge,
To do the nasty with her.
Wanted to charge him a few
Of his hard-earned dollars for
A few minutes of her time.

Sad, ain't it when the best ladies,
Who ain't never looked too good,
But who possess sharp and unfettered minds;
Who got the best recipes and the best intentions;
And who mostly never escape loneliness,
Rarely find peace and seldom get French-kissed?

When a 45-year-old,
From a single-parent home,
Who never found out who his father be,
Who her father be;
Who had a mother
who is long dead and buried,
Takes the oath for mayor, or coroner,
Or the Supreme Court;
Do the people, who always gossip about
The past and who whisper evil words;
Do these gossipers and evil whisperers
Await some new revelation,
some damaging headline
From the news reporters,
the stabbers-in-the back,
That will bring the 45-year-old,
Dartmouth Law School graduate,
Down to where the dead mother's
Child and children
Like him/ like her, belong?
Or, do they rejoice, not caring too much
About what the child's momma did,

Or about the struggles, and the hardships
The dead mother was forced to endure?

Proudly, with heaps of energy,
Someone just might up and sing,
God Bless America.
Some, thinking 'bout a certain history,
Thinking 'bout what
Was celebrated long time ago,
When things were
Either Black or either White,
Might be heard bellowing:
Lift Every Voice and Sing.
Somebody else might hum,
This Land is Your Land, even,
Dixie, or *Yankee Doddle Dandy.*

All the while, a 68-year-old neighbor,
Wrapped in a new,
Semi-expensive winter coat,
Coughs, wipes her nose and
Remembers the long walks,
Years ago, with the
Dartmouth Law School educated
Child's mother,
Through Baltimore's poverty, violence,
Drug Infestation, and frozen snow.
How they waited in the cold
At a desolate bus stop
For the ride to a street lined
With ladies of the night.
The stroll they always made to
That all-night coffee shop,
Where they imagined,
As they drank their hot tea,

That one day their children would
Never have to do what they be doin'.
That the children would 'mount to
Something worthwhile.
Would never have to live
In some two-room dump.
Would never have to think
'Bout their next *trick.*
Praying they would not be attacked
And robbed of their meager earnings.

Pause:

A good and honorable woman,
A loving and caring mother,
Requested some wings.
Wings that would help her fly to places
She's only read 'bout, done seen only in
Her mind and in the fancy magazines.
Places, maybe she done heard some cousin,
A soldier home on furlough, talk about.
The good and honorable woman,
The loving and caring mother asked humbly
For a ticket to a place away from where she be.
Not a ticket for a bus that would stop
In every tiny town but a ticket that would
Guarantee she keeps riding til she gets to somewhere
Nice and sweet.
A ticket that will take her and her children
To the Rocky Mountain part of Canada, maybe.
Or, Taiwan or even Istanbul. A beach-town near Lisbon.
Maybe, even a place in Switzerland, or Finland,
Or Paraguay, or Bergen, in Norway.
Away from all the mess that be surrounding her.
From the ruined, damaged and the
Never-will-Get-any-better place where

She rises each day.
From all the infested intentions.
And cesspools of defeated intentions.
To a place where sincere words,
That are lined with truths,
Come as easily as sincere words
That are lined with lies.
And, compliments are as common as complaints.
Where peace is admired and cherished,
And violence is never glorified.
A place where women can become ladies
And girls are allowed to become something
Other than whores, outcasts, beggars.
The good and honorable woman,
The loving and caring mother requested a
Ticket that would let her, and her children fly
Away, sail away so they can breathe new kinds of air.
Air that will sooth their lungs and uplift their spirits.
Air that contains no pollution, no fear, no corruption,
No abasement, no thuggery.
A place where the water is purer than
The bottled water rich people buy from their rich stores.

Please, the mother begged, let us receive a ticket.
We want to fly or sail somewhere,
A long ways away from right here;
From this no-good-life we've been living.
Just somewhere where we can all the time
Stop crying and complaining and start
Laughing and rejoicing.
A place where nobody will ever again ask:
What do they say when the babies are born
And the mothers die while the fathers are
Not too far away telling their sweet tales
To other little schoolgirls?

A SMALL ROOM IN PIERRE, SOUTH DAKOTA

In a small room in Pierre, South Dakota,
A lonely, middle-aged man rested his
Overweight and most unattractive body
In a cheap, soiled and smelly, cushioned chair.
His fingers continually punched and pounded
The Dell computer keyboard he had recently
Purchased with an over-charged Visa Card.
He was corresponding with other lonely persons.
Persons, who too, were in desperate need
Of companionship.
Any kind of companionship.

He knew because he had heard
It many times when he
Long ago got his hair cut
How being alone, by yourself,
Is the most atrocious,
The most grievous, the most painful
Punishment anyone will ever endure.

Because of this, he had decided,
Back in January, when snow
Covered Pierre and searches for someone
To talk to, be with, and to escape with,
Were most urgent. And, seldom achieved.
Because of this and his quirkiness,
He establish a personal on-line clinic
For those in dire need of communicating

With someone, anyone, suffering from
The trauma of loneliness; of being alone.

Duron Scopate, had become his fake name.
He liked it: Duron Scopate.
The way it sounded when he said it.
The photos and self-description posted
To his 'Clinic's" webpage
Did not come close to resembling
Him or anything about his character.

After the first two months,
He had become completely absorbed
By his ability to comfort those
Who were seeking an end to
Their loneliness and to help
Dissolve their disengagement.
His eating habits deteriorated and
His personal hygiene became unbearable.
He did not care.

His newly found "Calling"
Was to save those souls who were
Being lost to unfulfilled dreams.
So, being as resolute, determined,
And dedicated as he could possibly be,
He regularly communicated with more
Than five thousand pitiful, grievous,
Tragic, and painful souls.
Mostly women and young girls.
Some were even below the age of twelve.
Some were above the age of eighty.

After several months,
He thought he had mastered his

Universe and he enjoyed
Every second of his mastery.
Some of the lewdest correspondence
Reflected what had happened
To a politician or Hollywood celebrity.
Many of the more lonely and bold
Correspondents wanted to experience
Cunnilingus, fellatio and sodomy they
Imagined the politician or celebrity
Had found pleasure by engaging in.

The most daring of the lonely writers said they
Wanted to be treated and used the same way
Submissives had been treated and used.
They sent him nude pictures
With their lips puckered
Or with a dildo being sucked or licked.
Some of the photos showed
A dildo in the rectum.
He responded with titillating suggestions
That magnified their warped fantasies.

He was amazed by the countless women
Who were bent on being misused and
Abused by men who were in controlling
And powerful positions.
Many said they would beg,
As they supposed submissive women beg,
At the feet of a powerful master.

A BOY AND HIS GRANDPA

The young boy rested his body on his bed
And tried to remember what his Grandpa
Had told him about fishing and hunting
And how peaceful it usually is when you
Are alone on a riverbank or deep in the
Woods sitting silently in a camouflaged
Hunting blind watching and waiting and
Thinking.

His Grandpa had said some things
That a young boy is afraid to remember.
Even though he never meant to frighten
His young Grandson, some of his words,
And the way they were said, would
Even scare older boys.

All the time he ended his stories
By saying something about right and wrong.
Always saying it's better to be poor and right,
Than it is to be rich and wrong.

Resting in his bed,
The young boy had a tough time
Believing this piece of advice.
He always wanted to have enough
Money to buy all the things
He thought he wanted and to buy,
All the things he thought his
Mama wanted and

The things she needed.
Like the things he always heard
Her praying to the Lord for.
And, all the things he knew his
Grandpa deserved.

Other things his Grandpa told him
Had to do with the people in charge
Of the town, the county, the state
And the country they all lived in.
He always said, these things while
He slowly peeled an apple taken
From one of Mister Harrison's
Apple trees, not too far down
The road from their house.

Always said he wanted the Grandson
To grow up and be smart
As he could ever be.
Wanted the boy to be recognized
As the smartest and the
Best-behaved child to ever come
From the family's tree.

Said one other thing, though,
That made the boy wonder:
Said he didn't want the youngster
To end up in politics.
Said politics and the politicians
Had ruined the town they lived in,
The whole state and all of the
United States of America.

Said the worst politician in the
World was the current president.

Told his grandson that the
Current president, who everybody
Called a "Sweet-Talking" man,
Was nothing but a skirt chaser
And a low-down good-for-nothing
Disgrace.

Told his grandson that the
Folks in Washington, D.C.
Were gonna kick the President's
Sorry ass outta office.
Said most people he knew,
Agreed with that notion.

He told the young boy,
About the corrupt people in congress:
People who were rotten and sullied
To their core, but who had
Gotten tired of the president's lies,
His cheating, his wars, and, his making
Women he done made pregnant, have
Abortions.

Grandpa said everybody was tired of
Him having his way with women
In the very office where he
Signed all them bills
That put America into war.

One bill he signed,
Grandpa said, was meant
To stop the government from
Feeding and housing poor people.
Another one he signed,
His Grandpa said,

Was to start putting more
Black people in jail.
But, he didn't sign any bills
Stopping his own whoring-round.

The young boy was kinda confused
But his Grandpa kept right on talking
Till that apple was all bit-to-pieces.

Any youngster would be a little baffled
And puzzled if the Grandpa they loved
And respected told him he wanted the
Youngster to achieve wonderful things,
But didn't want the youngster
To get into politics and maybe
Become president.

He wondered, the boy did,
What the president had done,
Besides cheating on his wife,
Getting into wars,
And putting more poor people in jail,
That was so bad to make
His Grandpa say what he said?

He told himself that he would ask
About the president and all of
What he did wrong on Monday,
When he went to Miss Lawson's
Civics' class.

JUST A PIECE OF METAL

In so many places in this America,
Populate by people who resemble each other,
Events of an indecorous kind were taking place.

It was just a piece of metal.
Weighed less than a pound.
Easier to carry in a pocket than a book.
A piece of metal gripped by fingers
That break pencils and rip
Apart paper that is supposed
To be written on.

Somebody. Anybody. Whosoever.
Does not make any difference.
This is gonna be just another
Occurrence that will appear
On page five of the tomorrow's
Local newspaper. Tonight's news.

His tired ass. His po ass.
His afraid ass. His Black ass.
His ain't-never-knowed-his-daddy ass.
His almost-in-prison ass.
His almost-in-a-grave ass.
His wanting to be a dope dealer, ass.
His not-worth-a-good-goddamn ass.
His ain't-never-been-to-church ass.
His damn near illiterate, Black ass.
His not-worth-a-good-goddamn ass.

His soon gonna cry sorry-ass-tears, ass.

See that boy over yonder,
That boy, 'fo next week,
'Fo next month, sho nuff, 'fo next year,
That boy gonna be dead and gone.
Might be dead 'fo I walk back into
My cousin's run-down, raggedy,
Grease-smelling, too-crowded,
Too fuckin' little shack,
She and the rest of us, call our home.

I ain't no bettin' man but if I was
I would bet that 'fo that boy eats
His next meal, he just might get
A bullet right through his shaved head.
Gonna die the way we know how
To make Black folks die.
Gonna play tough, he is,
Till some other dying-too-soon riffraff
Shows him a Beretta Pico
Piece of iron, he be holdin' stacked
Wit seven of them kill'a-nigga bullets.

Boy ain't gonna run.
No matter, he be lookin'
Death straight in the eyes.
He'll just stand there, like a damn,
Too-proud-to-run fool,
Looking at the barrel of that Beretta Pico,
Then looking down at the spot
His soon-to-be Black ass gonna fall
And start his slow, wrenching,
Hurting-like-hell, death.

A crowd's gonna gather and watch
The blood come outta the
Holes them Beretta Pico bullets
Done put in his once braggin',
Swaggin' and loud-talkin' ass.

Shooter, can't be no more'n sixteen,
Will claim he had to get his rep back.
Boy don't know the whole word, so,
He says "rep."
He even be thinkin' he gonna
Have the young, sweet
Bitches talking 'bout him.
Thinkin' the bitches will be
Sayin' how he be so brave.
How he be the baddest nigga
They done seen since that dead nigga,
Blac-Ink, used to walk these streets.

'Member when Blac-Ink capped them
Four motherfuckin' college niggas?
Said them college niggas was using
Words he didn't understand.
Wasn't that was back in '09,
Around the time Busta got shot?
Blac-Ink should still be free.
He woulda never seen no jail
If it hadn't been for that loud-mouth,
Scared-ass nigga, DayOne.

Blac-Ink, now, tough as he was,
He went and died in prison,
But, he still be these boys' role model.

'Fo he got locked up,

He got more pussy
Than a man who be
Owning a pussy farm.
All these ain't-got-no-daddy
Youngsters wanna be like Blac-Ink.
They be going 'round braggin'
And boastin' how they gonna
Kill some stupid-ass, shufflin';
Some jivin', boot-lickin',
Scared-as-can-be, nigga.

They be walkin' 'round actin'
Like they ain't livin'
In the sho-nuff real world.
Actin' like they ain't got a fear
Nowhere in their bodies.
Folks look at'em like they
Still be children acting mannish,
But they know, and we know,
They be old enough to die;
Old enough to make somebody
Else die, too, 'fo they die.

That boy's old lady
Already done started
Her crying and mourning
'Cause she knows he wasn't bullshittin'
'Bout finding and killing that
Smart-ass motherfucker
He all-the-time been lookin' for.

There he be. See 'em?
That be him in the orange
Colored pants and white t-shirt.
Got that poky-dot rag

Tied 'round his head.
That's the boy who sho-nuff
Gonna die fo the wind starts blowin'.
That's the young motherfucker.
Somebody better hurry up and call
Smith Brothers Funeral Home.
Make an appointment,
Cause at least one nigga gonna
Die in a few minutes.

That boy, the one who
Gonna do the killing,
He be totin' his Beretta Pico.
Loaded with seven rounds.
He probably gonna fire all seven
At this skinny,
Poky-dot-rag-tied-round-his-head,
Nigga's ass.

Here comes the shooter.
What you gonna do, you, Skinny,
"Orange-colored-pants," nigga?
You gonna play like you got courage, nigga?
You, gonna act like you ain't 'fraid?

Don't try and be like you be a man.
Here he comes. You ought'a run.
You ought'a fall on your knees,
Nigga, and start praying.

You showed that boy who toting
That gun and who is sho nuff
Gonna shoot your ass, no respect.
Remember how you grinned in his face?
You called him a name you knowed

He didn't 'preciate.
You messed with his manhood.

You talked 'bout him in front of
Sheleka and Maysue and Ritha.
See what kinda talkin' you gonna
Do now, nigga, when he fires his
Beretta and take you outta this world.

Did you see the look on
Ritha's freckled face?
I betcha she peed on her
Motherfuckin' self.
Sheleka and Maysue just
Stood there with no expressions.

Them young hoes didn't even bend
Over to help the dying motherfucker.
Both of'em looked at the boy holding
That piece of metal, and then they
Sorta smiled.
Smiled the way they probably use'ta
Smile when they was 'round Blac-Ink.
They probably got all hot and bothered, too.
Probably wanted to suck the shooter's cock or
Give him some of their young booty, right
There. Right then. While everybody watched.

But, Ritha, man, she started actin'
Like she ain't never seen a nigga
Kill another nigga, which I know
Ain't true, 'cause 'round here
A nigga kills another nigga every
Goddamn day.
That be our fun. Our recreation,

Our thang to do.
We done become experts at killing
Other Black folks.
Now, he's walkin' – swaggin',
Slow-like, cool-like, hoodlum-like,
Back towards his Mama's place:
Thirty-Two C, over on 25th.
She might be at work,
Downtown mopping floors at
One of them big government buildings.
Doing shit this nigga swears
He ain't ever gonna do.

Here comes the 'bout-to-die
Po boy's, ain't turned thirty-five,
Momma, looking like she fifty
Watch'er, fo she get too close she's gonna
Fall to her knees and start wailing
Them miserable and sorrowful moans
We done learned how to moan
From all the tragedies we done
Had to go through;
Causing everybody in the near
Vicinity to stop doin' what they be doin'
And stare at her sobbing,
Snot-coming-outta-her nose,
And, wonder what's wrong
With her pitiful,
Looking-like-she's-homeless, sad ass.
She sheds her stored-up tears;
The ones she's been reserving for
Another of the misfortunes she's
Been counting on to happen.

The news folks:

One television van.
One newspaper writer. A photographer.
Bunches of cell-phone cameras
Hurriedly taking pictures.
Three reporters with microphones,
Pencils, pads and sly smiles.
They see the 15-year-old Black boy.
A bony child.
See his shaved head and one
Shiny, silver-capped tooth.
His blood done stopped flowing
And his heart no longer
Beats against the white t-shirt
That has turned red.

The Momma, 'bout to turn thirty-one,
Looks like she's 'bout to
Lose her natural mind.
She ain't got no insurance,
She is already worried
'Bout how many dollars
It's gonna take to bury
Her boy if he died fo' she died.
She always told him he was gonna die in
The streets or was gonna rot in a prison.
She even told everybody,
Who already knowed what she knowed,
That her son would be visited by the undertaker
Before he reached eighteen.
Sho nuff before he reached twenty.
But, now, she's wondering if the
Church people at the church,
She used to go to might, out
Of the goodness of their hearts,
donate enough to put her dead

Boy in a decent casket
And let him be buried in a
Respectful graveyard.

She knowed he had nothing
Waiting on him but trouble
And more trouble,
And a violent death.
She knowed 'fo he was
Three-years-old that
He be facing the man below or prison
Before he be old enough
To understand trouble.
She had told him so.
He had grinned in her face.
Told her he would rather die
Than work for folks he hated.
Told her he didn't give a good-goddamn
About any motherfuckin' school.
All he cared 'bout were the bitches
And how much he could screw 'em.
He told her he was gonna be the biggest,
Baddest, blackest and richest coke dealer
In the District, in PG County,
And was gonna buy a great
Big house for her, in Fairfax.

Guess he be wrong.
Now he is just another dead Black child.
Just another pants-hanging-too-low,
No-count nigga; one of them scary things
Decent folks do their best to avoid.

He ended up being just a prediction
That done come true.

Another child trying to
Falsify manhood. He be dead.
He ain't even worth a
Fifteen-minute celebration
Where folks wearing cheap clothes,
Chewing on hog maws,
With messed-up teeth,
Carrying two-hundred pounds
Of overweight girths,
And behind-rent-payment statements,
Will notice. Will remember.
Will talk about. Will shed tears about.

No one from 'round here
Could ever recall hearing anything
About the dead boy's daddy.
No one in the near vicinity could
Recall hearing anything about the
Shooter's daddy, either.
Not a word.

REVEREND EDMORE SAUL

Reverend Edmore Saul,
Originally from that real religious place
That ain't far from them five-curvy roads,
About nine miles outside, Barnsdall,
Which ain't too far from one of them Indian
Places that's always been part of Oklahoma.

Reverend Edmore Saul done learned to preach
From listening to all the preachers in his family:
His Daddy, three uncles, six cousins,
Both Grandpas and one of his Grandmas.
Though, he always was told by folks who knew;
None of'em could preach as good as he preaches.

He knew every word in the Bible:
From the first word of Genesis,
Starting the Old Testament,
To the last word of Revelation,
Ending the New Testament.

Since coming up to this big city,
Where troubles all the time seem
To grow in bunches
And then come pouring down on folks
Like great big buckets of steaming rain,
Causes him to be saying over and over again
That the world done gone crazy.
He be telling how he has to use every word
Of every one of them books in the Bible

To try and explain away and remedy the hate
The fornication, the stealing, and the killings
Be happin' all 'round him and Inez.

Back where he come from,
There be plenty folks living in poverty.
Folks who ain't ever had no more'n a
Cent or two to carry them from one week
Through the next week.

Folks, back yonder,
In the little place he be from,
Never complained.
Nobody hated their neighbors.
They sho-nuff didn't get all riled-up
And crazy and then go out
And shoot somebody.
Some fool, now and then,
Might'a took a switchblade and
Scared whoever they be arguing with.
But, a gun, no, Sir.

Edmore Saul told his wife, Inez,
Who was part-Shawnee and part-Negro,
To make sure she started crying kinda loud
When he got to the part of the sermon
About young folks dying 'fo their time;
'Fo they ever get a chance to see
What is on the other side of them
Dreams they been dreaming 'bout;
What's on top of them hills they
Be anxious to climb.

Told Inez to make sure she
Started crying when he tells the

Congregation how some of
These youngsters gonna soon be gone;
Gone forever before they ever
Smelt anything but over-cooked lard,
Boiled okra, and fried river-perch.

Told Inez to shout like she learned
To shout back home when he
First started preaching 'bout how
Children be too young to be dying
From slaying one 'nother.

She smiled at Edmore and told
Him she knew what to do.
Said she had enough practice
With all these killings that be
Going on in this city;
With all the rich folks on the one side
And most of the fools and po folks
On the other side.
Told Edmore to just pay 'tention to his part,
'Cause she had her part down pat.

Edmore went to the corner
of the little room, behind the kitchen.
He set down and took out his
Fractured funeral-preaching Bible.
He turned that old Bible
To Romans, Chapter 6, Verses 1-7,
And read out loud:
What shall we say then?
Shall we continue in sin, that grace may abound?
God forbid.
How shall we, that are dead to sin, live any longer therein?
Know ye not, that so many of us as were baptized into

Jesus Christ were baptized into his death?
Therefore we are buried with him by baptism into death:
That like as Christ was raised up from the dead
By the glory of the Father,
Even so we also should walk in newness of life.

Edmore had become one of
Them preachers who was in
The business of always burying Black folks.
Most of'em, the Blacks folks he buried,
He figured, didn't have no business even
Being here; hadn't done no good for the
World or for they own self.

Years ago, fo' triflingness took over,
He was all the time marrying
Black men and Black women.
But, Black men stopped marrying
Black women when they found out
They could get what they wanted
From Black women without making
Them their wives.
Found out they could lay wit'em,
Knock they asses up and move on
Without ever paying any mind to
The babies they be leaving behind.
That's how come,
And he knowed it to be the truth,
The marrying side of his preaching
Wasn't bringing in a dime.

At a dead man's funeral,
He knowed if he preached the part
About how the dead would end up
Being free from all the sins they

Have done, the congregation would
Start to moan, groan, and shake;
Throw up and wave their hands,
Saying, "Praise the Lord" and believe
The dead boy who been shot dead
By another soon-to-be-dead boy,
Would somehow be freed from all the
Gang-banging, freed from his no-good-shit,
Freed from the violent acts his
Not-worth-a-bus-token ass did when
He strutted down the streets and ended
Up killing either a good human being
Or a no-count, never-worked-a-day-in-his-life,
Sorry ass, just like his
Laying-in-a-donated-coffin,
Sorry ass.

The Most Reverend Edmore Saul,
Speaking loudly, asked Inez, his half-Indian,
Half-Negro squaw to pour him a little-bit
Of that store-bought bourbon they had
Up in the cabinet, behind the can of
Maxwell House coffee.
Told her he needed more stimulation
Than the stimulation he gets from preaching
About another dead youngster.

Weimar is the German national cultural monument, formerly the city of the German classicists, who through their works gave German emotional and intellectual life its highest expression. Buchenwald (as it was later named; originally it was called Ettersberg) is a natural forest area. It is a monument to the new German sensibilities. Thus, a new set of connections was created: the sentimentally preserved museum culture of Weimar versus the uninhibited brutal desire for power of Buchenwald.

The Buchenwald Report

Translated, edited and with an introduction by
David A. Hackett

Their gaze will temporarily rest on the clumsy noblesse of the Hotel Elephant, for this is the anteroom of Weimar's living Valhalla, where all the great names in art, economics and politics traveling through the town have spent the night.

Weimar -- Text by Bodo Baake

WEIMAR AND THE
HOTEL ELEPHANT

November 9, 2pm.
Frankfurt International Airport, Terminal 2.
SiXT car rental.
I picked-up an Opel Astra.
Driving fast, 160 Km an hour,
I made my way onto Autobahn 5.
Towards Kassel.
Passing exit signs that read:
Bad Homburg, Bad Nauheim, Alsfeld.
I kept moving. 190 Km an hour.
Stopped in Bad Hersfeld.
Got a bottle of water.
Got a rhinwurst. Got a Snicker candy bar.
Autobahn 5 became Autobahn 4.
Heading towards Erfurt.
Germans were driving like they were
Competing at the Nürburgring racetrack.
Their lights flickering, advising slower
Drivers to get in a slower lane.

Another hour I was
Onto Bundesstrasse 85.
B.B. King's CD, "Why I Sing the Blues,"
Was playing and keeping me company.
I was trying not to be distracted

By the lyrics of:
Ghetto Woman and *The Thrill is Gone.*

A lady, at a Farmer's Market,
In Ojai, California,
Had once mentioned Weimar.
She and I decided to sit,
Have a coffee and a sweet roll.
Said it was a rather smallish place.
Said it was a kind of beautiful
Place in the country's Eastern part.

Said, Hitler always booked a room at
Hotel Elephant, whenever he visited Weimar.
Thomas Mann, Norman Mailer,
Tolstoy, Liszt, Goethe, Bach, and
Schiller also stayed at the Hotel Elephant.

Weimarians, she told me, have an
Overwhelming pride, an intrinsic
worldly knowledge,
And a peaceful outlook.
Months later, after many
Conversations about Weimar,
With this middle-aged Ojai lady,
I decided to fly from Los Angeles
To Frankfurt, rent a car and drive
To Weimar.

Soon I would discover a
Quaint and uniquely refined city,
With high sophistication –
Engulfing sensible and exquisite
Qualities, but not a shred of shame.
No reflections. Not an ounce of

Remorsefulness. No looking back.

Driving through the undersized streets,
Onto Weimar's Marktstrasse,
I finally see the Hotel Elephant.
I park the SiXT rental car,
Carry my bags to the front desk.
I go through the check-in procedures.
The receptionist: slim,
Young, smiling, attractive.
A redhead Fraulien, with freckles.
She tells me how much
I will enjoy the hotel and all of Weimar.

She is pleased when I display ignorance.
I tell her I know nothing of anything;
Especially, concerning the culture of Weimar.
A culture, I am sure, that has been
Rearranged so as to forever purge
The current genteel inhabitants of
This town of all sins against others,
They once obediently engaged it.
Those unimaginable sins during
That barbaric and dreadful *Era*.
That *Era* they thought they,
These Weimarians,
Would never have to explain, or sadly,
Have to remember, because as *winners*,
They were made to believe,
They would never need to explain
Whatever behavior, no matter how evil,
That was responsible for their winning.

But, lo and behold,
The winning never arrived.

Meaning, they, with
Their pompous asses, lost.
Still, these Germans, in Weimar,
Will more than likely whisper
Smart and confusing statements,
And to be accurate, behave with
An Eastern German dignifying grace.

I am certain they have made
Themselves believe
They are a more dignified,
A more educated people,
A more morally correct and erect people,
Than the likes of
People resembling me
Who are rarely seen
Strolling their streets.
But, being good Germans,
They are wise enough to know
What Americans fail to know:
That the constant replaying
Of parts of a country's
Most despicably and ugly history
Tends to stymie
Social and cultural progress.
Someone says:
"Let me tell you about Goethe.
Have you read Goethe?
I will take you to his house,
Not far from here;
Today is a very beautiful day.
Let us go."

I immediately think of Mephistopheles'
Statement in Goethe's "Faust:

In the end, you are exactly--what you are.
Put on a wig with a million curls,
Put the highest heeled boots on your feet,
Yet you remain in the end just what you are.

"Weimar," he continues,
"Is such a wonderful place
Of enlightenment, don't you think?
That hotel, the Hotel Elephant,
The place you are staying,
It is the best, most prestigious hotel in
The region, in all of Thuringia."

A few hours later I walk ever so casually
Through the short Fussgangerzone,
Noticing the small cafes, quaint theatres,
Well-lit Thalia Bookstores,
The pastry shops and ice cream parlors.
The people of Weimar nod as I walk
Their peaceful and very clean streets.

They break into beautiful and welcoming
Smiles when I enter their shops;
However, they tense when I approach
The preciously designed porcelain figurines
That are being displayed. I don't blame them.

But, no one, as of yet, has mentioned
Konzentrationslager Buchenwald,
Elie Wiesel or the Jews.

I enter the *Gelateria Giancarlo's Ice Cream Parlor.*
I start eating and enjoying
A strawberry-spaghetti-ice.
I want to remain alone.

I've become pensive.
I attempt writing notes.
And a few rural Alabama aphorisms.

I try remembering the appropriate words,
When someone, from what direction he came,
I don't know, sits at my table,
Across from me, without my invite.
He is an older man. I notice the
Purple veins set in his nose.
His body shakes.
Maybe he suffers with Alzheimer's.
He asks if his presence will
Disturb whatever I'm doing.
He tries to smile but he appears
To ache with each try.
He asks where I'm from.
I tell him I'm from America.

The old man, maybe with Alzheimer's,
Or maybe, something worse,
Says he once worked for
An American law firm.
Did its litigations in the
Firm's Hong Kong office.

His bee-bee eyes are blue,
Bright, and darting.
Four years he lived in Hong Kong.
A single man, easily aroused, sexually,
He explains, by smallish Asian women.

Says the Chinese ladies of Hong Kong
Are the world's best.
Much better than the cold

And dispassionate German
And most European women.
Better, even, than American women.
I agree. He asks how I know.
I tell him I spent
Eighteen wonderful months,
During one of my previous lives,
In Kowloon-Hong Kong.

He tries to drink his coffee;
It spills from the cup.
I steady his hands, assists him.
He tells me I should visit Dusseldorf.
Says it is a much better place than Weimar.
I say I've visited Dusseldorf many times.

Then he tells me a lengthy story
About the city of Aachen.
While he speaks,
I think of *Count Roland*
Fighting so valiantly as he ,
Looked northward out of Spain,
And then dying, so Charlemagne
Or Charles the Great,
Or as the Germans would say,
Karl der Grosse,
Could proudly return to Aachen
From his long war with the Spaniards.

This Alzheimer's - or maybe,
Something worse - elder man,
Is dressed like
An older aristocratic gentleman;
One who is arranged by a housekeeper
To makes sure he, with his peculiar,

Elderly ways, is presentable for his
Daily sojourns through
The city's tiny streets,
Where he tells whoever will listen
About the delicate skins and
Sweet scents of Chinese
Women in Hong Kong.

But, no one, as of yet, has mentioned
Das Konzentrationslager Buchenwald,
Paul-Emile Janson, Caracho Path,
Elie Wiesel or the Jews.

I return to the Hotel Elephant.
I enjoy a superb meal.
The servers are extremely
Professional, prompt,
Pleasant, and polite.

In my room - Room 330 –
I watch CNN International,
Hear about politics in the USA;
Wondering if it matters;
If I'll ever again care.
Voting, I think,
Just might be a worthless endeavor:
Sorta like what Marx said about
Religion:
"Die Religion … ist das Opium des Volkes."
(Religion is the opium of the people.)
One could substitute the
word "religion" for the
Word "voting" and arrive
At the same conclusion.

CNN International commentators
Are trying to explain how the young
Governor from Mississippi had won.
They talked about the vote out west,
The Black vote, and the Hispanic vote.

Someone says the new
President will be different.
Another someone says he will
Be like all the others.

I am tired. With my clothes on,
I fall asleep.
When I wake up, it's only 2am.
Opening the curtains,
I look onto the market square where
I see a few lighted clubs, bars,
Restaurants, a small theater.

Two young women are walking
Across the cobblestones,
Then, as if jerked by a puppeteer's string,
Their heads turn in
The direction of my window.
They see me. I wave.
They don't return my wave.
They continue walking. Start laughing.

Sitting at the room's desk,
I pick up one of
The hotel's magazines,
An English edition.
Weimar, it says,
Is the home of Classicism.
There's a picture of

The Grand Duke Carl August
On his horse on
The Plats der Demokratie.
A picture of Adolf Donndorf's sculptor:
"Mother and Child,"
On Rittergasse and Windischenstrasse.
And, there is
The *Goethe and Schiller monument*,
In front of the
Deutsches National Theater;
The one I saw earlier when
I walked across the plaza.

The next morning, at Goetheplatz,
I'm told:
Take Bus number 6. The one right over there.
It departs 12 minutes after the hour.
Four-euro and 70. Danke.

Drizzling rain. Dreary, cold, dark sky.
A day for sleeping, writing,
Drinking warm tea.
Not a time for doing much else.
The bus travels
Along Schopenhauerstrasse
And then, Karl-Liebknechtstrasse,
Near the train station,
And close to ugly,
Multi-storied, apartment buildings.
Down a nice, tree-lined street, it goes,
On through a suburban neighborhood,
Then turns left onto the road that leads
To the *Camp*.

I'm heading to a place
Where thousands of

European Jews, Gypsies
And *Others* were
Killed, butchered, slaughtered,
Put in ovens because they were
European Jews, Gypsies
And *Others*

This place, I am soon to learn,
Is always desolate and windswept;
Always gloomy, always cheerless
And void of the slightest hints of
Shame, remorse, or regret.
I am the one paying attention to the signs.
I notice the Germans
Who are on their way
Home or someplace other
Than the place I'm going.
This bus route is repetitive
And routine for them,
Nothing new; nothing to be inquisitive
Or curious about,
With the exception of the tall,
Very dark-skinned,
American man on their bus.

I refuse to be too judgmental,
Too condemning. Too accusing.
Don't want to be an *Ugly American.*

Don't know why, but riding this bus,
I feel the same way I felt, back in 1961,
Returning to the Alabama Delta,
Aboard a Greyhound Bus,
After having lived in Amsterdam.
I feel the same detachment and fear of what
I will witness, and what the accompanying

Emotions might cause me to do.
I'm suspended in the middle of *here* and *yonder.*
Here, being a few paces before Hell.
Yonder, being the doors of Hell.

The bus stops.
Silently and tentatively
Four people and I get off.
Most of the riders remain seated,
Not looking to their left towards the *Camp.*
The entrance to this dreadful place,
Appears to be waiting and
Beckoning for another condemning,
Cynical, German-hating tourist.

I walk across the huge parking lot.
A young German,
Exhibiting his best Aryan traits,
Stands outside smoking a cigarette
And watching my approach.
He does nothing in the way of a salutation.
I enter a sterile-smelling,
Sterile-looking room.
No emotions here, either.
There are books, magazines, CDs
And other such items in this place
That one can purchase.
The female worker, with dark hair,
Does not smile.
There is no entrance fee.
There is a sign saying
Donations are appreciated.
I drop a 10 euro note in the container
And walk onto the *Campgrounds.*

The entrance gate,
High and ugly, reads:
Jedem das Seine. (Each to His Own.)
I see the clock
With the time frozen at: 3:15,
Indicating the hour and minute
U.S. troops arrived and
Liberated this hell hole.

Four hours go by.
I am feeling the frigid air
And having weird
And imaginary thoughts.
Thoughts of the grim
And hideous horrors,
And the inhumane activities
Committed by the so-called brilliant,
Always correct and cultured
People of Deutschland who
Would, after their shellacking,
Beg the world to believe, that they,
The majority of them, had no clue as
To what was transpiring a few kilometers
From their doorsteps.
My blood boils.
Yes: *Jedem das Seine.*
(To each his goddamn own!)

As I move through the nasty, dark,
Clouded history of those barbaric acts,
I wonder how a society that produced some
Of the world's greatest composers, philosophers,
Painters, scientists, and inventors could
Engage in and support such abhorrently,
Uncivilized behavior.

Each passing moment,
I become more and more depressed.

Who were those Germans?
How could they embrace the notion
That they were somehow superior?
Did they really believe that –
Because their eyes were blue
And their hair blond and because
They had many guns and a loud
Talking and boisterous leader - they
Were *die Herrenrasse* (*the Master Race*)?

The dampness, the coldness,
The sorrow, the evil deeds of the
Past almost suffocate me.
I go from one spiritually and
Morally depressing building
To another that is equally depressing.

Walking the grounds of
This former concentration camp,
I have an unrealistic fear of being the next
Non-member of *die Herrenrasse* to be
Exterminated, cremated, burned in an oven.
The next to be robbed of everything I possess.

Over the crunched rocks,
I enter into cold spaces
And ghost-filled quarters.
I see the discarded shoes worn by the
Jews, the Gypsies and the *Others*
Before they were put to death.
I see the grotesque ovens where
Bigoted and sadistic Germans
Cremated their former neighbors.

I stand between Blocks 63 and 66.
Tears escape my eyes.

I'd seen and participated in war.
I'd tasted and wallowed in carnage.
I'd seen body bags
And soldiers with no limbs.
Why, then, am I crying?

Then, I know: I realize that humans,
Supposedly, possessors of some of the
World's great scientific and creative minds,
Not too many years ago, diabolically and
Cavalierly exterminated millions of
Innocents children, the very old and
Everyone in between.

Wiped away those
Who were their neighbors,
Their doctors, their musicians,
Their butchers,
Their artists, and
Their most successful
Entrepreneurs, engineers,
And professors.
Erased their schoolmates
And schoolmasters;
Their best-of-friends and
Their everyday playmates
Because they, those eliminated,
Were German Jews,
Gypsies and the *Others*.

I shed tears because
I realize that some of
The exterminators and
Many of their offspring
Continue to live in palatial castles;
Continue to attend exhilarating
Operas written by Wagner, by Strauss;

Still drink their beer and wine
At sidewalk cafes,
Parade about in their designer fashions;
Still find comfort in the beautiful hotels
That line the grand boulevards of Munich,
Berlin and Baden-Baden,
And they still walk
And ride their bicycles along
The banks of the Elbe, Oder, Rhine,
Danube, Moselle, and Main.

I cry because no other emotion,
Other than anger and rage,
fits the moment/
And being here in Weimar, as a tourist,
Rather than exhibit anger and rage,
I choose to walk among these buildings
And shed tears.

After a while, calmer,
I sit in a tour guide's small,
Japanese car. A Nissan, it is.
She had spoken pleasantly
To me during the tour.
Her car radio is tuned to a station where
Soft, delicate, classical music is playing.

The driver says she is very, very happy
To be driving me back to Weimar.
Says to me: *The Hotel Elephant,*
You are staying at the Hotel Elephant, yes?
It is the best hotel in Weimar.

Her words seem befogged.
She is fidgety.
I suppose I make her nervous.
She asks: *And, where are you from in America?*
I say, *Alabama. Selma, Alabama.*
I ask her: *Have you read about Alabama?*
She mentions Martin Luther King, Jr.
Wasn't he murdered there, in your hometown?
I tell her he was shot and killed in Memphis,
In the state of Tennessee.
Her response: *How sad. People of the United States*
Do many tragic things, yes? It is so terrible.
So insane. Such a violent country.
Don't you agree? Why it is so many Americans kill
So many other Americans and foreigners, also?
I sigh but says nothing.
After all, I consider who is making this statement.

She says she takes care
Of her 92-year-old mother.
Her husband died five years ago.
She is very lonely.
Without her work she doesn't know
What she would do.

She touches my thigh, up high.
I feel nothing. No arousal.
No stimulation.
I know I will not attempt to satisfy

Whatever sexual cravings she might have.

I listen intently to the radio's music
While thinking of the
Cooled and sad rooms
Filled with the left behind shoes.

She's such a plain, out-of-date,
Dowdy woman. She is too humdrum,
Stodgy and outmoded for me.
And, every day, she is surrounded
By death and horror.
Her fantasies will have to suffice.

Later, in a dimly lit bistro,
I look over my notes.
For some reason I'm reminded
Of an incident that
Took place, several years prior
In New Zealand.
The two women I love most,
And I, were dining at one of
The best restaurant we had
Visited in Christchurch,
While all the time feeling unsettled as
Other diners, probably, New Zealanders -
Kept staring, making faces,
And whispering.
We wondered if they
Were overly inquisitive,
Or just unashamedly curious.
Maybe they were simply fearful or amused,
We surmised, by the fact
Black Americans were eating at one of
Christchurch's best restaurants.

Same thing, without the similar overtones,
Sitting in the *Zum Zwiebel,* on Teichgasse.
I order six Nuremberg sausages with
Sauerkraut, and a large Milch im Café.

I am surrounded by alluring,
Young, anxious and eager Fräuleins,
And several "out-for-an-evening's wine" Fraus
Who keep casting sly looks and discreet,
Suggestive smiles.
The studious appearing men,
Talking to companions, or in deep thought,
Also keep glancing, nodding, but not smiling.
All are, probably, wondering who I am
And why I am in their city.
Probably thinking:
There must be a jazz concert
Some place nearby.

The crowded restaurant fills with
smells of beer, wet dogs, grease,
And unwashed German bodies.

Ist dieser Sitz frei? (Is this seat free?), she asks.
I notice the green
Scarf hanging from her neck,
Her radiant smile, and her green eyes.
I nod, yes.
She continues to smile and says,
In perfect English, *Thank, you.*
I smile back. I think:
How does she know my language?

She orders a glass of white wine.
We start conversing.

She is impressed when
I say Hotel Elephant
Then, she ask:
Why have you come to Weimar?
Are you a professor? A musician?
Maybe just a tourist?"

I tell her I am just a lonely man,
Traveling, searching, wanting to know
Too much about too many things.
She reply by gently touching
My hand and looking
Directly into my eyes:
Maybe you are a philosopher
Or someone who is what we
Call a romantic, yes?

She is a professor, she tells me,
Of architecture,
At the nearby Bauhaus University.
She orders a small vegetable salad
And more white wine.
The conversation soon turns
To politics, art, music,
Travel, and relationships.
We talk for more than two hours.

She laughs. I laugh.
We flirt with each other.
She continues touching and
Slightly squeezing my hands.
Giving strong indications that
She is interested in something more
Serious than a restaurant conversation.

She tells me she is thirty-five-years-old.

She has recently gone
Through a terrible divorce.
Because of the divorce, she said,
She is thankful
No children were involved.

We meander through the Fussgangerzone,
Passing over quiet side streets
And shop-windows.
I tell her how much I
Admire German architect.
This causes a change in direction.
Soon we are standing in front
Of a small shop with displays of
Architectural drawings in the window.
She points to an intricate sketch,
Says it is one of her designs.
Then she give me a short education
Regarding modernism, classicism,
Angles, and different
Architectural movements.

After we share a bottle of water,
At a small café,
We walk, holding hands,
To the Hotel Elephant.
The young and pretty receptionist looks
At the professor, smiles,
Blinks her eyes, blushes,
Places the room key in my hand and says:
Have a pleasant night.
I'm certain she imagines
What might take place.

We take the elevator to the third floor.
The professor says she wants,
Very much, to continue
Conversing with me.
This, she believes, will make
Her very, very happy.
Because she has no classes
Until Monday afternoon.
She intimates that she can
Stay and talk all night.
She has no place to go other than her
Empty and sad apartment.

Sitting in my room,
We attempt to dissect the
Relationship between German women
And men of the darker hue.
We agree that Black men
From America and German women
Seem to be more sexually compatible
Than any other couplings.
For whatever reasons
They appear in the same
Emotional and sexual troughs.
She reaches, caress my face and

Suggest we stop talking and make love.
I explain that my visit to Weimar does not

Include the notion or desire to have sex.
She ask me if I find her unattractive
Or maybe I am afraid she might have
Some sexually transmittable disease?
I tell her she is beautiful, intelligent,
A pleasure to talk with

And that I do not believe
She has any sexually transmittable disease.
Without warning, she is in tears.
She says all of our talking has made her
An extremely aroused woman.
Says I have no idea how badly she wants
To be with me, to be held by me, to kiss me.
Says, now, she feels embarrassed,
Ashamed and stupid.

I hear water running in the bathroom.
After several minutes and many
Flushes of the toilet, the door opens.
She has washed her face.
Her makeup has been scrubbed away.
She looks not like a professor but
More like a second-year college student.
I tell her that I do not want her to leave.

Soon we are embracing, rubbing,
And kissing each other.
She says she believes I have made
Love to many women;
That I probably have had too many
Experiences. She feels I might be
Disappointed by her performance.

Says she's had many dreams and fantasies.
Even, though she was once married,
She believes she has very little experience;
Therefore, I should be understanding
And patient with her.

Within seconds we are
Both without any clothing.

The few strands of blond hair
Surrounding her Cunt matches
The hair covering her head.

With trembling hands she
Squeezes my hard cock.
She does not stroke it – just holds it.
Squeezes it.

Her face is clean from the scrubbing.
She is so fucking beautiful.
She tells me she wants
Me to do to her the
Things her husband
Had always refused to do.
She wants to be spanked.
Wants me to whip her pink ass
In such a manner she
Will never forget.

Says she wants me in her mouth
And down into her throat,
The way she has always dreamed of
Sucking a Black man's cock.

She will allow me, she says,
To make love to her in all
The manners I have ever imagined
Making love to any woman.
She says she especially wants
Me to savagely sodomize her.

While telling me this,
She is slightly curled, with
Her head resting on my chest.

I rub her ass, pinch it, gently slap it.
She purrs, turns and smiles,
Then bites my nipple.
She laughs and tell me
I am being too timid.
I am being too thoughtful.
Too deliberate. Too respectful.
Too considerate. Too gentle.

I grab her shoulders and roughly
Place her across the side of the bed.
Her breathing quickened.
She places one of her hands on her
Ass cheek and says that is where
She wants my hand to land.
But, she insist that it land
As hard as I can land it.
Soon I am spanking
Her ass with as much
Force as I can muster.
Instead of asking me to stop,
She begs and cries out for
More and harder spanks.

I rise from my crouched position,
Go to the chair where my pants
Are hanging and retrieve my belt.
I look at her German ass.
It is as red as a ripe strawberry.
I am afraid I have spanked her
Too long and too hard,
Yet I am being driven;
Being urged to apply more pain.

She sees my expression and says
Maybe she has had enough.
Says she does not want any more.
Tells me she is afraid of the belt.
Still, her ass remains upright,
An open invitation for more
Pleasure and punishment.
So, I commence to apply the belt.
She cries out.
Places her face into the pillow.
She has several of her fingers
Probing her pussy.
Soon she is screaming,
Saying she is cumming.
Saying she is my slave,
My whore, my woman.

She tells me I am her master.
Her big, Black, strong master.
I am suddenly overcome with
Sexual desires I have
Never before experienced.
I look at the red welts
Covering her ass and I
Become aroused beyond belief.
My throbbing cock is as
Hard as it has ever been.
It seems as if the length has grown
Two additional inches;
While the circumference
Appears more rounded than my wrist.

Using juices from her pussy,
I grease my cock, all eleven inches,
Lifts her beaten ass

From the soaked bed,
And enters her moist behind.
Inch-by-inch, I slowly move
Into her rectum until ever piece
Of my cock is imbedded in her
German ass,
Which I relentlessly pound.
After a short while
I have no choice but to empty
My cum into her well-beaten,
Well-fucked ass.
A few minutes later,
She hungrily sucks my cock
For what seems like an eternity.
I am fully spent and cannot release
One additional drop of cum,
Which frustrates her.
My cock, though, is still hard.

I kiss her.
I lick and suck her huge tits.
My tongue and lips touch,
Caress and linger on her
Smooth and hard stomach.
She is moaning in anticipation.
Slowly I move my head
To the blond hairs
Surrounding her damp cunt.
Playing with individual hairs,
I continue to tease her.
Her begging, twisting,
And moaning increase.
With my lips and tongue,
I make contact with her cunt.
I enjoy her smell, her taste,

Her hunger for pleasure.
I eat her like a starving man eats
A deliciously prepared meal.
With my fingers,
I pry open the tender
Lips of her sweet cunt
So I can go deeper and deeper
With my hard tongue.
Then, she explodes
And keeps exploding.
I keep licking.
She is trembling so intensely I think she
Is going to have a seizure.

I go to the bathroom,
Wet a towel, bring
It back to the bed and put it
Over her face and head.
I repeat this process
Three separate times.
I retrieve two aspirin
From my travel bag.
I ask if she is allergic to them.
She says no. I order her to take them.

After a short nap, we are awake,
Smiling and once again
Touching each other.
Then, she lays face down on the bed.
Again, she places a pillow
Under her stomach,
Pushes her ass upward,
She ask me to please,
Once more, fuck her ass.
I honor her request.

After a longer nap,
We stand before the room's mirror.
We are naked, hugging
And caressing each other.
We see our reflection:
A tall, muscular, Black man
And a beautiful, blond German woman
Who have just experienced
The most erotic and exciting sex
Any two people could possibly experience.

We lay back down and start talking.
She once again plays with my cock.
Finally, we drift into
A long and peaceful slumber.
We stir from our sleep.
We hug each other.
We kiss, very passionately.
Both of us are sore.
We both know my time is running out.
In two days I will be leaving.
Thinking about it makes me shudder.
I crawl on top of her.
Tease her. Suck her tits.
Play with her blond hair.
Touch her face.
We simply cannot get
Enough of one another.
Together, we take a shower.
Afterwards her sensitive mouth
Once again encircles my now
Cleaned cock and sucks me
Better than she has previously.
Then she crawls on top of me.
My eleven inches enters her pussy.

She bends forward. I suck her breasts,
Going from one to the other.
I reach around to her asshole and
Press two of my fingers into her hole.
She moans. She groans. She whimpers.
Spinning her around so I can be on top,
I press deeper into her.
I feel my cock touching her bottom.
I can tell she has entered another world.
Once again, she erupts.
As usual, she shakes all over.
Finally, I feel the rush of an orgasm.
I fill her with my cum.
Some of it overflows onto
The already wet bed.
She raises herself up and once again
Place my Black cock
Between her pink lips,
Sucking and licking
Away the remaining thick fluid.
She smiles as she savors
And digests my white cream.

At 10am she walks out of Room 330.
I relax on my bed and
Think about the topics
We have discussed. How we debated
Politics and economics;
art and history, and romance.
How she has explained her passion for
Architecture and teaching.
I recall Fanon's *Black Skin, White Masks,*
And what he wrote
About the sexual prowls
Of European women and their

Warped mindset
Concerning the animal-like sexual
Capabilities of the black man.

But, no one, as of yet, has mentioned
Konzentrationslager Buchenwald,
the Crematorium, Maria Forescu,
Georges Mandel, Elie Wiesel or the Jews.

Later in the day, tired but happy,
I once again
Stroll through the Markstaette,
Back across Schillerstrasse,
Near the Clever-Fit Gym,
Which is atop a Deutsche Post.
I start wondering if this visit was a waste:
Coming to this small town.
Maybe I should have gone
To Dresden or even Leipzig.
Other than the sorrows felt,
And the history
Taught by Ettersburg-Buchenwald,
Where the great Goethe
Composed "Iphigenia,"
And where between
Fifty and sixty thousand
Innocent Jews Gypsies and *Others*
Were put to death,
What have I been made more aware of?
What else have I learned?
What else have I found in Weimar?

Well, I now know
More about Goethe, Schiller,
The Schillerhaus, the Zum Zwiebel pub.

I know there are still
Many oversexed German women
Lusting after the few Black American
Men who occasional grace their pubs,
Their Fussgangerzones, restaurants,
Hotels, and their beds.

Because of Weimar,
Despite its history,
I feel, somehow, much cleaner,
More pleasant, more at peace, at ease.
The people have certainly
Given me more than I
Deserve to have been given;
More than I've given them.
Maybe there is also something truly
Negative and grotesque about this place,
Other than Buchenwald,
Something negative that
I might later discover –
After reflecting –
While resting in some hotel
Room in Bangkok or on
A park bench in Taipei,
On a beach in Panama City,
or at the Einstein Cafe,
Near the Vienna University, in Vienna;
Maybe while eating enchiladas in an
Out-of-the-way Mexican restaurant
In Santa Cruz or Santa Fe.
Maybe during a tour of Cape Town,
Boulder, Lyon, or Santiago.

One day, in some other place,
I'm certain I'll remember something

About Weimar that
I thought never happened,
That will cause me to laugh,
Smile, frown or utter profanities.
Just maybe I'll think
About the daily breakfasts,
At the Hotel Elephant,
Eating raw salmon,
Or lounging at
the *Zum Schwarzen Baran*,
Not far from the *Schlossmuseum*
And its haughty art presentations,
Or the house where Liszt lived,
On the west side of Ilm Park,
On Marienstrasse,
With his music flowing
Through every plank
And speck of dust in every room.
I just might think about
The bus ride that went by the train station
On the way to that "Camp,"
And the too-plain, but kind tour guide.
But, most probably, I will always remember
Something I never thought worth remembering.

> *But, no one, as of yet, has mentioned*
> *Konzentrationslager Buchenwald,*
> *Ernst Thalmann, Andree Peel,*
> *Elie Wiesel or the Jews.*

Weimar's *Anna Amalia Library*,
All oak-paneled and refurbished,
Is another proud attraction, especially,
For the people of Weimar
And all of Thuringia.

A place to brag about the
Progressive movements
That have taken place in the
Former East German, Soviet-controlled,
Once repressive towns that
Happily, before the Soviets
And Americans came,
Hosted and toasted their
Seemingly omnipotent
And omnipresent Nazi friends.

I'm quickly approached
By a tall, statuesque,
Superbly stunning woman.
She offers a broad smile.
She lightly licks her lips
With her darting tongue.
Her eyes flutter, penetrate and invite.

The library's illuminated
Entrance is spotless.
There is a huge room
With three long tables.
Two young people appear to be deeply
Engrossed in some type of study.
I ask the overly attentive
And superbly attractive
Female worker if the
Library carries English publications.

> *Oh, yes, we have a section of books and*
> *magazines; all in English."*

Once again, I'm asked if I'm a writer,
A professor, a musician?

Why am I in Weimar?
A slight breeze from
Somewhere touches
My bare head. I turn.
The female attendant,
Has placed herself extremely close.
She is almost touching me.
She is breathing rapidly and hard.
She explains that the
Official name of the library is
The Duchess Anna Amalia Library.
Speaking with an ingratiating demeanor,
she says:

> *This is the best and most visited library in the*
> *State of Thüringen. Surpassing even the one in Erfurt.*
> *Parts of the library were ruined, in 2004, by a fire.*
> *So many precious books, from ages, were destroyed*
> *and can never be replaced. How sad, yes?*
> *Are you familiar with the German philosopher,*
> *Friedrich Nietzsche?*
> *Well, this very library houses his archives.*
> *We can go to that area if you like.*

I peruse several rows of
Books and magazines.
The attendant inches even closer.
I can almost taste her perfume;
Still smiling, still inviting.
She asks if I'll be in Weimar for long
And in what hotel I am staying.
When I say Hotel Elephant,
She grabs my hand,
Looks into my eyes, and tells me
I've made a great

Choice by choosing the Hotel Elephant.
I am still sore and tired from what had
Taken place several hours earlier.
Because of this, I don't accept the
Librarian's obvious offer to
Give herself to a Black man.

I leave the library and hire a taxi.
I asks the driver to s
Sow me all of Weimar.
Anxious to practice his English,
He tells me he
Wants to go to New York
And become a New York City taxi driver.
If not New York City, maybe Miami.
He no longer likes Weimar.
The people are too poor.
Weimar people have no money
To pay for good taxi drivers.
Says everything was better before.
Twenty-, thirty-years-ago everything
Was much, much better.
Now, he claims, there are
Too many foreigners with nothing
But their hands sticking out.
All the time these foreigners
Keep coming from Russia, Poland,
Turkey, the Czech Republic,
Places he does not like.
Bad people, from bad places,
With no money.
A two-hour ride,
With two months of conversation.

My last night.
Weimar has sapped my strength.
I fall asleep dreaming
About something remote.
The phone rings, awakens me.
It is Jennie,
The best sex partner I've ever had.
She begs to come to the Hotel Elephant
And see me one last time, to give me a gift.
She says she will come to my hotel room.
Will not stay long, unless I say it is ok.
She arrives. I tell her I am still sore.
This causes her to laugh.
She says she is also sore, very sore.
She rubs her ass and says: *Especially, here.*
She is dressed in a very expensive-looking skirt,
And an equally expensive-looking blouse.
She is not wearing a bra.
We both laugh, embrace,
And kiss passionately.
We fall onto the bed,
And despite our soreness,
We are once again engaged
In energetic and beautiful sex.
My cock, and for sure her cunt and ass ache,
Yet, we cannot restrain ourselves.
I bite into her cunt, licking and
Slurping like I am crazed.
She keeps saying how much she loves me.
She get on her knees, look up at me,
And sucks my nearly raw cock until my cum
Over-flows from her mouth
And down her throat.

Holding each other, we do not move.
We remain stationary, still, and thoughtful.
Finally, she tells me that she would
Do anything to keep me in Weimar.
To prevent me from going back to America
Says she makes enough money
To support the both of us.
I tell her I have to travel to Bogota
For a very important reason.
Tells her I will stay in contact.

For breakfast we have boiled eggs,
Sliced tomatoes, cold pieces of salmon,
Bread with jam, and strong, black coffee.
Like before, she starts to cry.
Other hotel guest attempting to enjoy
Their breads, salmon and coffee, look at us,
Probably wondering what cruel things the
Black man might have done to make the
Beautiful German woman shed tears.
We carry my bags to the rental car.
She gives me two gifts:
An architectural drawing
Of a house overlooking
A body of water and a
Small book about Weimar.
I give her a hug,
A compliment and a short,
Framed poem I'd written;
Not about her,
But nevertheless, a poem.

The day before, after leaving
The Anna Amalia Library,
I had stopped at a bookstore

And purchased the inexpensive frame.
I tell her she is the most
Magnificent woman
I have ever known.
Ensuring I can depart Weimar
Without difficulty,
She gives me directions
To the autobahn.
We kiss. Hang on to each other.
Tell each other how much
We are in love with each other.
She takes my cell phone and programs
In her telephone number and
Other vital information.

Lastly, she tells me that last night,
Though she does
Not believe in God,
She had prayed that
I would impregnate her.
That she had taken no
Birth control measures.
She prayed I have given her
A beautiful Black child.

I look at the Market Platz
Where farmers are busy
Selling their products.
Someone waves and says:
> *Come back, again.*
> *You are always welcomed in Weimar.*

> *But, no one, as of yet, has mentioned*
> *Das Konzentrationslager Buchenwald,*
> *the Corpse Wagon, Black 50;*

the sign that says: Jedem das Seine;
Fritz Czuczka, Herbert Sandberg,
the Little Camp, Marian Filar,
the 56,000 who were murdered;
Baron Otto of Schmidburg,
Almeric Lombard de Buffiers de Rambuteau,
Armand de Dampierre; the mad, sadistic doctors:
Gerhard Rose, Waldemar Hoven, and Hans Reiter;
the Hanging Post, Children's Block 66
Caracho Path; the dog kennels,
SS Hauptscharfuhrer Sommer,
the Disinfection Chambers, the Goethe Oak,
the Hygiene Institute – Block 50,
the Pathological Facilities,
the Execution Cellar, the Crematorium,
the Sinti and Roma victims,
the Watchtower,
or the famous survivor: Elie Wiesel.

BACK WHEN

No longer do I daydream while
uttering indistinguishable sounds,
while facing strong winds with my head bowed
as I hoof onto Hawaiian beaches, Copenhagen
pathways and Barcelona's Gran Via;
smelling dirty waters
and looking for miles outward
to the East, to the West
seeing lands and peoples
that would one day teach me so much.

There were those days when
I thought I could actually see the wind
touching the wings of birds,
causing them, those birds, in flight,
to adjust their courses.
I believe it was the same wind I now feel,
chillingly, blanketing my thin, in need of food, body.

Back when,
before I said goodbye to everything alcoholic,
I tasted the cheapest vodka, cognac, and warm wine
in hundreds of small European towns.
I was, most times, with other starving poets
and foolish, misinformed sages who always
claimed we were alike.

All of us stole
fruits and vegetables from farmers' markets,

bedded whores we could never satisfy,
while talking endlessly about Marx or Kant or
nothing worthy of remembering,
in those quaint dives,
in the alleyways of Trier's Porta Nigra.

Even then,
I, as well as my friends, to be sure,
lost more poems, more thoughts,
more innocence and more love
than we could ever hold onto.

Sometimes I gave mine away:
my poems, my thoughts,
my innocence, and my love -
mostly to sophisticated,
well-educated ladies
with cigarette stained teeth
who were usually married,
or were being kept by some wealthy sponsor.
Ladies who provided me
places to sleep, foods to eat
and, other equally pleasing comforts.

Later on, during the somewhat better years,
I deluded myself into thinking
I was somehow more
informed, more insightful and more suave;
a better lover
because I was able to dine,
in the Australian city of Melbourne,
on glorious meals,
sleep in huge and expensive suites at
the Grand Hyatt, on Collins Street;
the Langham, on Southgate;
the Stamford, on Little Collins;

the Windsor, on Spring Street;
and, the Park Hyatt, on Parliament.
Sometimes, to try and relax,
to think about home,
I would stroll along the banks of the Yarra,
smiling to myself and
taking for granted the many
conquests that occurred on Lygon,
Victoria and Little Collins,
or somewhere along Saint Kilda
or Toorak Road, and Flinders Lane.
Or, Brighton, or further out, in Mentone.

I was always smiling and thankful for the
lavish meals eaten at Silks, Station Pier,
Jacques Reymond, Nobu and other similar
restaurants; all paid for,
Down-Under, by curious,
Australian women who spent
parts of their lives fantasizing
and dreaming about Black men.

Now, getting older,
yet, still moving, searching;
almost on the verge of giving in,
I wonder what parts of this life could have
been prevented, or made better?
Or, was it all meant to be as it has been?

Those serious, all-night repartees dissecting
Camus, Fanon, Mao, Santayana, Nietzsche,
Descartes, Spinoza, Ovid, Kierkegaard;
I will always wonder if any
of it was significant, with meaning;
had any worthwhile value.

The heat, smog-everywhere
days in Los Angeles;
casually strutting down Crenshaw,
holding a bag of Leo's Barbeque ribs,
collard greens, and cornbread.
Thinking about that club
I went to in 1960,
maybe, 1961, maybe '62;
hearing Sam Cooke sing and
tease the lonely women with:
Darling, You Send Me.

And, there were the long,
mystifying and anxious nights
in Hamburg, Rotterdam, London,
Geneva, Prague, and Nice,
when I danced like I was crazy
to really fast Jimi Hendrix's
music before Jimi died.
And, in San Rafael, Oakland,
Marin City, and Sausalito where
I gazed at reefer-filled blonds
and redheads, before going to
that corner store and buying a
small can of Vienna Sausage,
a bag of potato chips and a Pepsi.

Doggone shame, Sam dying so young.
That jealous woman, messed up on
some kinda drugs or just messed-up,
when she fired that cheap pistol
and sent Sam, straight from that
Figueroa Street motel, right
through the flaming gates of hell.

Remember that time in Tokyo hearing
Japanese singers trying to sound like
their favorite Black, soul singer.
Sitting in some dark,
too-much-smoke, room,
on Minami Aoyama, in the Roppongi District,
trying to understand some
drugged-filled Japanese,
while holding a cup of steaming,
green tea in my right hand
and some unknown Shoji's
breast in my left.
Wanting to explain why Gakushi,
all 98 pounds of'em, was not a good
imitator of his hero, James Brown.
Gakushi screaming:
"Please, Please, Please".

But these are memories not worth one euro,
one yen, one peso, or one dime.
Just thoughts anyone might have.
Memories, from years ago.
That's all.

Remembering times when there
was no air conditioning keeping
us from sweating, and no television
telling us 'bout the news we already knew.
Times when discipline was
dispensed by neighbors
sitting on their front porches:
watching, correcting,
helping to raise young boys, young girls.
Porch-counselors, seeing children
going to and from school,

or playing hop-scotch, street ball,
maybe, just strutting;
wanting to gain attention.

There we were, back when,
dancing, late into Saturday nights,
acting like a fool,
in a cement-block, tin-roof, blues' shack,
that had been built in the middle
of one of Black farmer's vacant fields,
somewhere in the very rural part
of Dallas County, Alabama,
where the women, jet-black or high-yellow,
fought better'n the men.
Women willing to end your life if you
acted too cheap or showed no respect.
But, who would make love to you all night,
if you acted right, bought a few bottles of
Falstaff, a fish sandwich,
and added a few sincere compliments.

Those were the times when
the strongest, best, most wrongful
things we put inside ourselves
were too much corn-liquor,
too many pig feet,
and too many chitlins

Back then the people looked at me;
always shaking their heads
because they knew, they said,
I was kind'a special.
Telling me, at least once a week,
I didn't belong in anybody's cotton field.

Remembering the evenings
on the way home from working
at Carter's Drug Store, on Broad Street,
a few blocks from
the Edmund Pettus Bridge;
that ugly bridge stained by horse hooves,
human blood, screams, fears, beatings,
and the desire to slaughter freedom.

And, those real hot days in the Delta;
where we moved without
the least bit of hurry.
Stayed cool by fanning ourselves
with them Miller Funeral Home
hand-held fans.
Watching-out for the flies,
 mosquitoes, the red ants, the gnats
that were all the times crawling,
flying 'round us, on to us, biting, stinging -
knowing they, the flies, mosquitoes,
red ants, the gnats were
the real rulers of Alabama.

We would sit in our front yards,
or on porches surrounded by screen wire,
sometimes no wire,
but, all the time surrounded by
sho'nuff Alabama heat.
Everybody looking at everybody else:
at the people walking,
in no hurry, waving, like they tired.
Asking, "How Yaw'll doin'?"
Hearing, every-now-n-then,
a car coming down the road,
everybody getting ready to look -

see who be driving, who the passengers be.

Remember back when the insurance man,
no matter how hot it be,
always wore a suit, wore a necktie.
Collected fifty cents from Momma.
>		*Be back next week, Miss Alma.*
He, all the time said,
>		*Unless you want to pay now*
>		*for the whole month.*
>		*Ain't but one dollars and fifty cents,*
>		*like I said, Miss Alma for the whole month.*

I always knew, years ago,
times could always get a whole
lot harder, a heap more tougher;
but might, if I prayed hard enough,
get somewhat better than the times that day,
that hour, that right-now moment.

Another continent, here I come.
I'm on my way to somewhere else unless
I've already there and don't even know it.
Some other city. Some other country.
Different mountains.
Another stretch of a long river
winding through lots of countryside,
towns, and villages.
Hearing more strange
and confusing languages.

Been thinking how similar
all these places are.
Almost the same, these countries,
these cities, but, they all

have their differences.

Learning, these people –
in these different places,
are always learning why Black men,
especially the ones from Selma,
Dallas County, Alabama,
be the most intriguing men
in the entire world.

Vienna: A seven-hour train ride from Mainz.
I looked at the countryside:
the farms, the cathedrals, the castles.
I was on one of those fast trains, speeding
through Germany on into Austria, to violins,
operas, and the best Wiener Schnitzels in the world.
I rode through Wurzburg, Regensburg,
through Lenz.

Two ladies from Budapest shared
the same compartment with me.
The three of us.
We smiled at each other and
engaged in several hours of small,
inconsequential conversation.
They flirted. The ladies wore no bras.
They showed lots of cleavage
and lots of thigh. Neither wore panties.

Playfully, they hugged and kissed each other.
Looking at me,
they squeezed each other's breast.
One was twenty-one.
The other, twenty-three.
They wanted to know what I thought

of Hungarian women.
They told me Hungary had the
best looking and most
desirable women in the world.
They said men from all over
the world came to Hungary to be with
Hungarian women because
the women of Hungary
loved having sex. Any kind of sex.

The train entered the Vienna West station.
It was close to mid-night.
It was a warm night.
I said goodbye to my
two Hungarian train mates.
Giving me a telephone number
and an address, they invited me
to Budapest and a good time.
I took a taxi to my hotel.
A BMW, quiet, smooth.
The desk clerk was of Asian origin.
I wondered what circumstances
had brought him to Vienna.
Maybe he was born in Vienna.
I presented my American passport,
and my credit card. Thank you.
I took the elevator to my room.
A small room. An apple and a bottle
of water were on the bedside table.

I smelled really bad. I took a long,
soapy and hot shower.
I searched for but could not
find a Chinese restaurant.
After a while I went into a small,

quiet Italian café, and ordered three slices
of pizza, a large Ginger Ale.
The waitress and I talked about the weather
and, of all things, dogs.

Funny where you might end up.
I was born on September15, 1937.
I'm a Virgo.
Eighteen months before my birth,
My brother, Sonny, was born.
Sonny became
the focal point of everybody's life:
He was born with hydrocephalus:
water on the brain.
Then, he lost all his sight.
At age five, Sonny was totally blind.
In Selma, Alabama,
back in the 1930s, if you were Black,
no doctors were available to treat you,
water on the brain or not.

I didn't know much
about anything, or anywhere, or anybody.
Not even 'bout my own self.
When I was growing up
two things I did know, though:
I knew I would one day leave that place,
Selma, Alabama,
and I knew I was never gonna live
in that place, Selma, Alabama, again.

Picking cotton,
working in a cotton field,
that's tough, hard,
back-breaking, hellacious work.

Getting up before the sun rises,
riding in the back of a rattling cotton truck;
stooping, bending, dragging that cotton sack,
while the boiling sun beats down on you
in a white man's cotton field,
from the time the sun comes up,
till the sun goes down;
and then the steam, from all
that day's heat, starts to come out of you,
making it so you can't get a good night's sleep.

We went to them cotton fields
and picked that
cotton just so we could make one dollar,
maybe two, maybe three dollars a day.

Long time ago,
right there in one of them
Dallas County cotton fields,
some smart fellow,
who had lived up North,
said, like he had learned a heap
of stuff up in New York;
said, while sitting on his long,
dusty sack, filled with cotton:

> *These little white balls,*
> *they done ruined the lives of many a' folks.*
> *Cotton and everything 'bout cotton*
> *caused slavery,*
> *caused the Civil War,*
> *caused us to be in this here field today.*
> *Cotton's been responsible for the killing*
> *of damn-near a million folks;*
> *some from up North, some from down South;*

some black, mostly though, they be white.
Destroyed homes; some big and fancy,
some little bitty, run-down, po folks' shacks.
Broke 'part whole families, entire towns.
Broke 'part the whole damn country.
That's what this goddamn thing,
we call cotton, done always done.

Back in 1947,
my daddy looked at me
like he was 'bout to cry.
Daddy said, with his voice in a mournful,
sorrowful tone:

Boy, your daddy done been through hell.
These White folks done
put your daddy through fire.
I sho hope you don't have to go through
what your daddy done had to go through.

I remember back when
the bill collectors
came to our house,
1500 Weaver Street.
It was in the early morning.
November was just starting,
and it was still hot
'cause it takes a while before it
gets cool in that part of Alabama.
My Mama was gonna be
up no later than 4:30,
but this must'a been a few minutes
before she got up.
She was always the first to get outta bed
so she could make the fire in

our wood-burning stove.

All of a sudden we heard loud knocking
on our front door,
then, not just on the front door
but all 'round the house.
Then, the screaming:

> *Jay Bird, we know you in there.*
> *Get your black ass out here*
> *or we'll burn down*
> *this motherfucking rat trap.*

My daddy's nickname was *Jay Bird*.
Daddy grabbed his single-shot shotgun
and started crawling
on the floor over to a little crack in the wall,
wanting to peek-out
and see who be doing all that knocking.

We could tell he was scared
'cause he was trembling,
not too much, but still he was trembling.
Daddy moved his hand, signaling for everybody
to get off the two beds and get under them.
Odessa helped me lift-up Sonny Boy
and placed him on a pallet.
Sonny Boy and Odessa got under one bed.
The rest of the family
crawled under the other bed.

After 'while the bill collectors
starting hammering onto the house.
Seemed like that hammering
sound kept going on forever.

Even today I can hear that
hammering on our house.
That loud pounding, just a' pounding -
over and over and over – pounding.

All six of us,
still laying on the floor,
under them two beds.
Then the nailing stopped.
It got kind'a quiet.
Quiet enough for us to
hear nothing but our fright.
Daddy, after a while, told
everybody everything was alright.
Said they were gone, and he didn't reckon
they'd be coming back.

Later, when the sun started to come up,
all of us, 'cept Sonny Boy, went outside to see
what all that hammering was about.
Them bill collectors,
them no good, evil white folks,
had nailed, all over our house,
pre-printed leaflets that said:
These Niggers Owe Jameson Loan Company Money.

Them bill collectors probably had a car full of
signs like that that they
went around nailing
on to black people houses.
There must have been fifty
of them yellow and black
signs tacked to our house.
Daddy tore 'em off the house
and burned them in the backyard.

Mama shaking her head
went into the kitchen
and made some biscuits.
That morning we had biscuits
and syrup for breakfast.
But, nobody cried.

My Daddy lived to be eighty-two.
Mama lived to be ninety-two.
Neither one of them ever talked about,
not with us, the children,
what them White folks did that morning
around four o'clock,
when November was just starting.
Everybody pretended it hadn't happened;
went about our lives skinnin' and grinnin',
huffin' and suffin', prayin' and sinnin'.
But, all these years later
I can still hear that pounding
and the hate-filled voice of that
White man calling us niggers.

I wonder, just wonder,
how we be able to carry
such pain, such hurt,
so deep, for so many years;
all the time smiling and forgiving,
and trying to forget.
How can anybody do this?

Years kept on going by.
Before I knew it,
I was in a place called Korea.
The things I remembers about Korea:
more than anything,

are the smells and the women.
The smells I eventually got used to.
The women I became addicted to.

The Koreans and that damn Kimchi
and other smelly, stinky things,
at first, bothered me,
then before long, I didn't even notice.
Even the buses, city streets,
the stores - all had that Kimchi smell.

I first went to Korea in January 1957,
that's when I got to meet,
and have fun with Korean women.
I learned that they are the cleanest,
smoothest-skin women in the world.
After a few visits with girls
managed by Mama-San,
I came to believe that the
Korean woman had perfected the
best and most satisfying ways to use
their sex to please a man, to make
a man stay full of happiness;
to make a man lose his mind,
and to make a man want
more of what she had.

I thought God must have blessed
Korean women with superior talents.
I spent lots of nights
in the bars of Yongdonpo,
watching American men
exchange their money for
an hour or two with some Yobo.

Back then
I constantly listened to the blues.
I always done loved the blues.
I like the way the blues creeps
through the soul, play hide and seek
with the man who carries
the pitchfork and has a tail and horns.
I remember on Friday
and Saturday nights
in the sho-nuff hot Alabama summers,
them blues singers,
with their harmonicas and guitars,
would stand cater-corner
to my parent's house,
next to Mrs. Mary's big corn field.
They would groan, play, moan, and sing
them nasty, dirty-delta, really lonely blues.

Making up songs, they would,
about all the miseries right then taking place,
and the ones happened last week, last year;
and the ones coming in a hurry – 'bout
five miles and forty heartaches down the road.
All the many pains, wretchedness, worries and
troubles that were waiting to be had,
would be coming outta them bluesmen.
Coming outta their voices,
guitars, and harmonicas.
Coming outta their aching bones,
through their snaggleteeth,
and covered with their everlasting miseries.
All the time these blues men were
Thinking 'bout another man's woman
and why a half-pint of
moonshine cost more'n a dollar.

They entertained. Made everyone smile.
Sometimes folks even laughed out loud
and clapped their hands like they were
in church listening to a good sermon.
They always made Sonny Boy
and the rest of us happy.
More often than not, they would yell:
Sonny Boy, how you doin'?
Sonny Boy, with his blind eyes shiny and clear,
would respond by uttering:
Ar-ight.
Then, the blues-men, hardworking men,
not too educated men,
scared-of-White-folks folks, men;
who hadn't bathed in two or three days,
 maybe a week, would head on up the road,
towards Range Street,
to Lannie's Bar-B-Q Spot,
the one on Minter Avenue.
Now-n-then they would spit, in the dirt,
just ahead of their next footprint,
as they went towards that place right
cross the street from where that house
burnt down back in 1954.

At Lannie's they would talk about
next week like it was last year;
eat barbeque pork, fried catfish,
boiled link sausage sandwiches,
some collards, and sweet potato pies,
while drinking moonshine,
Miller High Life and Pabst Blue Ribbon;
all the while getting ready to start playing them
gut-wrenching, baby-making blues.

Sitting on front porches,
neighbors, a half-mile away,
could hear songs of sorrow, of wishing,
of sweet dreams gone awry.
Songs – music, bitter songs, sad music,
'bout too much trouble that was
waiting to intervene and destroy
what little hope still remaining in their
broken down bodies and beat-up minds.
Music silhouetting off the dark,
wishful, longing, desolate, and
deep southern sky.
A southern sky that carried,
what most skies of the
South always carried:
a history of hangings, beatings,
rapes, disrespect; man-owning-man,
miscegenation, and segregation.
Singing really loud, then softly;
singing them pitiful, low-down,
sweet and dirty blues.
Late into the night, they sang.
More pitiful and low-down
by the half-hour, on into the
early parts of the coming morning.

Most of 'em had been on the way home
from the Selma Sawmill Factory, maybe,
the Brick Yard, or Zeigler's Slaughterhouse,
but for some reason, the same reason:
every Friday evening,
they could not make themselves
get further than Lannie's Bar-B-Q Spot.

There are things that can ruin

all the decent memories you
have about the past.
There was this time when
Two of my friends and I were
walking home from the picture show.
We had been to the Roxy Theater,
in the Black section of Broad Street.
The Roxy was an all-Black picture show.
It was owned by a White man,
but only for Blacks.

At the Roxy
we didn't have to sit in the "crows' nest;"
a little balcony section,
a long ways from the screen,
like they had to do at Selma's other theaters:
the Walton and the Wilby.

The sun was almost down,
lightening bugs were 'bout to
get ready to do their flying.
It was summertime.
There was no school anybody had to go to.
The three of us were joyful.
We had just seen three movies for a
single dime: Tom Mix, Roy Rogers,
and the Lone Ranger.
As we crossed the ball field,
at Payne Elementary School,
we saw a police car drive by;
dust trailing behind that police car.

If you were Black, in Alabama,
you had better know, always,
where the police be.

There were no Black police,
in Selma, back then.

All of a sudden
that police car made a quick turn
and started speeding towards the three of us:
Bootney, Carrie Mae, and me.
We stopped in our tracks;
petrified, trembling, scared-to-death.
All three of us were thirteen-years-old.
The policemen, both of them,
kinda young-looking,
got out of their car, guns pulled, they asked:

>*Where you niggers going?*
>*Where you headed to?*

We were well into the Black,
segregated part of town.
Payne Elementary School was
a hundred percent Black school.
This was 1951.
We thought we were gonna go to jail,
be beat-up, or
maybe even, shot dead.
Such was the fear felt by Black youth
being questioned by white policemen
in Selma, Alabama, in 1951.

One policeman said:

> *You niggers*
> *been out fucking, ain't you?*

Having just left the Roxy,
our minds had been on Tom Mix,
Roy Rogers, the Lone Ranger and all
the bad guys they had
killed or beat up, and not on fucking.

Then one policeman
told the other policeman:

> *Make sure these nigger boys ain't*
> *been somewhere fucking this nigger gal.*

Told that other policeman
to examine Carrie Mae,
to see what Bootney and I had done to her.

The one policeman then said
if we had fucked Carrie Mae;
he was going to shoot us dead,
right there at Payne Elementary School,
He said he would kill all three of us
because it was against the law
for niggers to fuck
before the nighttime comes.

Then this policeman
grabbed Carrie Mae, spun her 'round;
held her so her back was up against his front.
He reached around Carrie Mae,
pulled up her dress, tore it a little bit,
ripped her panties, pushed them to the side,

then put his fingers up into
her private parts.
Then he moved his fingers
back-and-forth in her private parts.

Carrie Mae was 'bout to faint;
she was shaking, trembling, crying,
but was afraid to scream.
Her silent tears were flowing
like any young girl's
tears would flow if she were being
handled in such an inhumane fashion.

The policeman, grinning,
finally took his fingers out of Carrie Mae
and said Carrie Mae was not wet.
Said that proved we had not fucked her.

The gun this one policeman
was holding, was put to my head.
He said he didn't like the way I was acting.
Said I wasn't scared enough for him.
Told me he was gonna shoot me.
Kill me right where I stood.
Then the gun made a "click" sound,
but no bullet hit my head.
The policemen, both of them,
laughing, got back into their
police car and drove away.

The three of us started walking,
then we started running,
all three of us were sobbing and filled
with the greatest fear we had ever had.
This happened more'n 70-years ago.
I still 'members it;

'members it like it happened an hour ago.
Bet Bootney and Carrie Mae 'member it, too.

But sometimes there are things
you 'member that always make you smile.
There I was heading south, from Virginia,
through South Carolina,
driving this old Honda Civic,
when it decided to stop
right on I-85, on a Sunday afternoon,
in the middle of nowhere.

I tried restarting the car.
The engine remained quiet.
I took off walking towards an exit road
I had seen a mile or so back.
Got to the exit road
and started walking down this narrow road.
All of a sudden I heard a car coming.
I stopped and started frantically waving my arms.
A Black man was coming.
He was driving a very fancy and shiny Mercedes.
I looked at the Black man in that fancy
and shiny Mercedes, and he looked at me,
then he increased his speed.

I kept on walking on this road
until I came to one
of them run-down-looking, country stores.
Sitting out in front of the store
were four or five White men,
all looking like they didn't want to be bothered.
I went into the store, told my story.
The store owner, he said, he was,
said, *Come with me.*

We stepped outside.
The store owner talked to
this fellow named Ted.
Told Ted what my situation was.
Next thing I know we are in Ted's truck.
He takes me to my broken Honda Civic,
still on the side of I-85 South.

Ted looked like he had
spent most of the day in
a Sunday church service.
He was wearing black pants,
with a short sleeve, white shirt.

Ted messed with some wires
under the car's hood.
The car still refused to start.
Then, Ted got down and just slid
right under that Honda;
black pants, white shirt and all.
After a while, Ted got from
under the broke Civic,
did some more messing
around under the hood,
went to his truck, opened a big toolbox,
brought back some kind of wire,
crawled back under that Honda Civic,
holding onto that wire.
Ted, spent maybe an hour working
on the broken-down Honda Civic.

I watched Ted work and started
thinking about the Black man in the
 fancy Mercedes car who
made his Mercedes go

faster when he saw me, a Black man,
waving my arms, and Ted,
this White southerner,
was doing all this work while wearing his
Sunday-go-to-meeting clothes.

The car finally started.
Ted gave me instructions
On what to do if it stopped again.
I offered Ted seventy dollars.
He refused to take my money.
He just shook his head,
and said, with his very Southern accent:

> *Glad I could help.*
> *Wherever you goin', be careful.*

Sometimes time seems to fly, doesn't it?
But, sometimes time has a way
of not moving at all.
I've been talking 'bout and remembering
 lots of things but I have not mentioned
a certain thing I remember from 1959.
It was during the late summer.
I, this Black boy from Selma, Alabama,
was stretched-out on a big, soft bed,
in the wonderful city
of Cologne, Germany,
with the most gorgeous woman
I had ever seen,
ever talked to, ever been with.
A German woman who could'a,
in my mind, been a movie star.

She had her blond hair
draped over my naked body
She said she was gonna do
everything I ever dreamed a
woman could do to and with a man.
Told me she wanted to know
about all the sexual things
I ever dreamed of, 'cause she
was gonna make all of'em come true.

Her head was resting on my chest.
She was breathing with
a smile across her face.
When we woke up.
She kissed me real hard.
Then, she was sighing and rubbing my
head, entwining her fingers
in my nappy hair.
She kept telling me what wonderful
skin and hair I had;
how she loved my very black skin and
the feel of my kinky hair.

I thought I had been placed
in paradise, in Heaven.
Both of us believed we
were in a different world
being consumed and
driven crazy by each other.

Told me she had never been happy
with any German man.
The German man, she said,
could not satisfy the German woman;
almost all German women, she told me,

when thinking about sex,
always think about Black
men from America.

She looked up at me.
Told me once again
how much she loved me.

I kept thinking 'bout
the folks back in Selma
and what their reactions would be
were they to witness this
German woman being pleased by
A Black man from Dallas County.
The white folks would probably hang me.
The Black women would probably call me a
no good, white-bitch-loving, nigger.
The Black men would probably
want to save enough money for
a flight to Germany.

Just thinking those thoughts,
made me laugh aloud.
She asked why I was laughing.
I said he was laughing because
I was so happy and so thrilled.
Finally, when we were both spent,
we slept.

I had met her at a record store,
on Hohenzollern Ring,
where I had stopped to
browse the latest jazz albums.
I knew I did not have
enough German marks to

spend on anything but
browsing was free.
All I was gonna do was look,
sit in a listening booth
and listen, then leave.

She approached me, smiling.
God, she was so pretty.
She suggested I purchase
the new Sonny Rollins'
album that had just arrived.
I said I did not have enough money
but I would be back in a few weeks.
Told her I was living in
the Rhein-Hunsrück Region,
about 90 minutes away.
She asked me to promise. I promised.

Two weeks later
I returned, wearing a coat and tie.
She was not there.
One of the workers said
she was the owner and was on holiday,
visiting Italy with her parents and her siblings.

I returned a week later,
wearing a different coat,
white shirt, and a tie.
She saw me walk in and she started smiling.
Her smile made me feel good and special.
I purchased the Sonny Rollins' album,
Aix-En-Provence.
She asked if I would be kind enough
to take her to dinner, that is,
if I was not seeing someone else.
Said she would gladly pay.

I had never been in a place
like the *Le Merou Restaurant*,
at the *Dom Hotel.*
She ordered for both of us.
Today, as hard as I try,
he cannot recall the foods we ate.

She told me, in perfect English,
that she had never
been with a black man.
She loved jazz.
Loved seeing black men perform.
Had dreams about being with a black man
but, despite her age, she had never kissed
or even touched a black man.
She wanted so much, she said, to hold me;
maybe I would allow her to kiss me,
to caress me.

She was thirty-three. I was 22.
She was so refined, with lots of money,
Spoke several languages.
I was a former Alabama cotton picker,
sawmill and brickyard worker,
who didn't even speak proper English.
She talked very elegantly
about art, music, writers,
other countries and other peoples.
I was silent, not knowing how
to respond or what to say.
She excused herself, went to the bathroom,
I once again noticed her walk, noticed
her beautifully shaped legs,
nice hips and round behind.

Later, after leaving the *Dom*,
stomachs filled,
we walked over to this big, tall church:
she called it the *Cologne Cathedral*.
The biggest and finest church in Alabama
wasn't as big or as grand as this church.
She paid a taxi to take us to
the place where she lived.
It was in a very rich-looking area.
Her apartment building was high-class.
There was a doorman who opened the door.
He looked at me like I
was some kind of vagrant.

On the stairs to her second-floor apartment,
she moved close to me.
Her breathing was hard, fast.
In her apartment, she kissed me,
gently touched me, bit my ears
and sucked on my fingers.

She kept kissing, moving
her fingers against me.
Then she started removing my clothing,
asking me to do likewise and remove
her clothes, which I did.
We stood, holding each other, naked.

Somewhere along the way, with
the passing of so much time and events,
I lost the Sonny Rollins' album,
Aix-En-Provence.
But, I've never lost the memory
of the talented and lovely, Elsa.

I left Alabama in May,1956.
Tommie, who lived across
the street from me,
talked me into signing up
with the United States Air Force.
That was the single best
thing to happen in my life.
That was how I got out of Selma
with dream, after dream, after dream,
of never returning.

I was raised in a very religious family;
Christian-to-the-bone.
We were Southern Baptist.
I sang in the Mount Ararat
Baptist Church choir.
Folks, throughout the church
used to shout because of my hard,
dedicated and soulful singing.
Everyone told me I was surely
going to be a preacher.

Years, hundreds of books,
and events later,
I would ask questions about Christianity,
about the other religions, too, like:
how come all these religions keep
keeping people apart and
keep causing people to keep hating,
and keep killing one-another?
I would ask why so many believers in God
start wars, build prisons, own guns, tell lies,
deceive their brothers, sisters, neighbors,
even their mothers and fathers?
Nobody ever gave me a satisfactory answer.

Still, despite not being given the answer I asked for,
I still believe strongly in God.

In 1960 I moved to Amsterdam, Netherlands.
A place like no other place I'd lived.
Amsterdam taught me so many
essential things about life:
Where I wanted to end up,
where I didn't want to end up,
what I should expect from others,
how I should approach love and how
to rebuild after suffering great pain.

In Amsterdam,
I learned the importance of
politics, people, art, good food,
and truthful women.
Amsterdam, where
my favorite woman, Alfie,
wore no clothing inside the house;
doing all her chores and whatever else,
buck-naked.
Always walking around with her bare ass,
breasts, and bald pussy on display,
even in the cold, winter months.

Because of Alfie, I learned to tolerate,
even appreciate two women
making love to each other.
I would watch as two exceedingly
beautiful women brought each other
to orgasm after orgasm,
and who would then reach out for me
to join them in a magnificent and glorious
smorgasbord of raw sex.

Our friend, Neshi,
who had migrated from Suriname,
with her parents when she
was five-years-old,
had grown into possibly the most
beautiful woman in all the Netherlands.
She was a top Dutch fashion model;
one of the most photographed
females in all of Europe.
Her chocolate body,
bearing not a single blemish,
was often sandwiched between
Alfie's paleness and my blackness.

We would enjoy each other until
there was nothing more for us to enjoy.
Then, dressed, we would walk near
the *Royal Theater Carre*,
with both Alfie and Neshi
acknowledging and smiling at envious
men and jealous women.
Late in the evening,
in the *Amstel Lounge*,
at the *Intercontinental Amstel*,
we would order our usual:
heated, red wine for the ladies.
I usually ordered hot tea, with honey.

Alfie would always study the people
and their mannerisms.
She was an accomplished artist and
never stopped studying potential subjects.
Sometimes she and Neshi would engage in
passionate kisses,
then they would kiss and play

with me – squeezing my cock –
to ensure our soon-to-be ménage à trois
would take place with a new ferocity.
It was in Amsterdam where Rabbi Chayim
taught me the importance of not
succumbing to peer-pressure.
There were so many drugs:
hash, marijuana, coke.
All kinds of drugs.
Most of my friends, associates,
people I admired
had constant cravings for
whatever drug was available.
Yet, I never touched not even a cigarette.
Never got high.
I was always afraid of
developing an addiction,
of becoming and looking unhealthy;
of having rotted teeth, smelly breath.
Of returning to Selma looking badly.
I was also wary of letting Rabbi Chayim
words go unheeded

I will always be thankful to the Dutch.
The finest people I've known.

I later moved to Japan,
Then, later to Australia.
then back to Europe;
spending very few years in America.
I was always moving in an attempt
to avoid nasty American policemen
and overt, in-your-face, American racism.
Never forgetting what happened,
that summer of 1951,

at Payne Elementary School's playground,
and other incidents that demonstrated
White-Americans' hatred
for anyone not white.

Looking, I was,
all the time, for some place
with just a little bit more of this,
a little bit more of that.
Always being surprised, I was,
By the many folks who,
without being solicited,
rendered a helping hand,
offered a gracious and accepting smile.
Usually, these were folks
of a different culture,
a different country,
who spoke a different language,
but who were always anxious
to talk, to embrace, to share,
as if I had been their friend forever.

I've set, laughed and swapped stories with old
ladies and long-pipe-smoking men in Vietnam.
I've heard the voices of those wearing burqas,
Hijabs in Kuwait City, Muscat, and Doha.
I've spoken with so many Filipinos, away from
the Philippines; realizing that they,
Filipinos, are the real worldly people;
always delightful and gracious;
living everywhere, speaking all languages,
and working harder than most.

Sometimes I have looked so hard
for the best possible place,

the most beautiful person,
the most desirable qualities,
that I have ended up
missing out on the right placed,
the right people and the right qualities.

Australia,
where I attended university
and made the strangest
of love to too many unsatisfying
Australian women,
is another place, like Selma,
I do not want to ever return.
Not just because of its blatant
and unsophisticated type racism,
but, also because of the goddamn flies,
the rats and the weird shapes of the
people's faces and bodies.
I don't ever want to hear
another Australian accent
or place my cock in another
Australian woman's cunt,
ass or mouth.

Years ago, around 1972,
my cousin, Richard,
died in a Texas prison.

Richard was sent to prison more than once.
He had moved to Texas with Aunt Hattie.
Not long after getting to Houston's Fifth Ward,
he stole a gun and then robbed
and beat up another man.
Uneducated, and poor, Richard got 15-years
in a Texas penitentiary for robbing

and beating up that Houston man.
While uneducated,
poor Richard was in prison
he beat another prisoner really bad.

Later on,
according to what we heard,
somebody in that Texas prison
used a hammer to bash-in Richard's skull.
Nobody from Selma went to uneducated,
poor Richard's funeral.
The State of Texas
was good enough to send the
kin folks in Selma a letter.
The letter said, Convict Richard M- - - - -
was buried right there at that Texas prison.

There is this small café, *Café' Jehanne d' Arch*,
on *Place Jeanne d'arc*, in Metz, France.
I used to sit at *Café' Jehanne d' Arch*, drinking
coffee, eating warmed croissants
and watching my life slowly get away from me.
Then I would walk, ever so slowly,
to the *Cathedral Saint-Étienne de Metz*,
on *Place Jean-Paul II*,
go to a nearby ice cream parlor,
and get a cone of vanilla ice cream.

I usually rested in front of the Cathedral,
on a bench, ate my dripping ice cream,
while asking myself questions:

why was I in this little-big city,
allowing my life to gradually get away from me
and where might I be ten years down the road?

Remember the times
sitting 'round the stove
after Daddy had killed,
cleaned and slaughtered a hog,
after he had thrown the hog's
liver into the red-hot ashes.
Kept that hog's liver in them red-hot ashes
'till it got all crusty and sweet tasting.

The time when we went hunting
out in the woods, beyond East Selma.
I had an old, single-shot 22-rifle.
I didn't want to kill no rabbit or anything else,
but was afraid to tell Daddy;
'fraid he would get mad.
All of a sudden this little rabbit hopped
out of the bushes and plopped
down right in front of me.
Daddy was farther along the trail.

I looked at the little rabbit that seemed to be
welcoming me to his neighborhood.
We stared at each other.
Finally I drew back the rifle and threw it
towards the rabbit,
who ran a few feet away,
looked back at me and took off.
I turned and saw my Daddy.
He was shaking his head
not understanding how I
could not kill that rabbit,
take it home, skin it and have it for dinner.

And, there was that time Daddy
got drunk and peed in his pants.
Mamma got really mad;
so mad she started laughing.
Told him he would have to wash his
own piss-filled clothes.

There were days, long time ago,
when I was looking around
for decent places
to lay my tired body down.
A place of rest and peace.
Begging others for a dime,
a twenty-five-cent coin, a dollar;
watching them watch me,
hearing them thinking,
seeing them get disgusted.

Sometimes right ain't exactly right,
and wrong ain't necessarily wrong;
just have to do what you think feels alright,
what you think ain't gonna hurt anybody.
Otherwise, you end up getting all confused,
all frustrated, wondering 'bout codes,
the Ten Commandments,
and them Seven Deadly Sins.
Then, you start doubting who you be;
become unsettled;
want to, then, strike-out at somebody,
even at the ones you most love,
most respect, most care about.

Back when
my head was often resting on some table
in a thousand smoky, stinky, cheap cafes;
in all the nasty places,

all the wretched hell-holes
I set in, alone, wishful and dreaming.

Places I wallowed in, told lies in.
Places where I searched for elusive truths,
concrete meaning, some sort of redemption.
My head laying on them no-table-cloth tables,
somebody putting a bowl of steamy
onion, noodle or potato soup in front of me,
telling me I had better eat 'cause
I didn't look too well.
Saying I was becoming too sick-looking.
They were afraid, they claimed,
something tragic would happen to me.

Back then
there were the long hours and short days
that never ended.
But, sometimes there were
the days that never wanted to get started.
Some days I was high in a mountain retreat,
other days found me shooting crap
in somebody's damp basement.
Yet, I knew through all them days,
with all them times, that,
we, all of us, including myself,
none of us, is too good, too solid
not to be broken down
into little, bitty, non-functioning pieces.

Ain't anybody solid enough,
strong, powerful, resilient,
and talented enough to
withstand the ever-wrenching might
of the bigger-than-man, all-seeing and
all-knowing: *Puller.*

The *Puller* that keeps on
pulling till it pulls
you one which-a-way
then another which-a-way,
'till you ain't nothing
but a broken thread here
and a torn thread there;
a lot of little, easy-to-break threads
looking all the time for your
other blood-related pieces of thread,
'cause they be looking, too, for you.

Back when
seems like nobody cared 'bout
nothing but telling tales,
deciphering what old folks said,
and listening to Gabriel Heater,
The Shadow, Amos and Andy,
Red Skelton, and Arthur Godfrey;
waiting for the Gillette Cavalcade of Sports
to broadcast the Brown Bomber's fights,
where we prayed he would knock-out
another man who looked like the
folks we hated and the folks who hated us.

Or, I would be sitting under Mr. Clanton's
big shade tree, eating peanuts,
while worrying 'bout Jackie Robinson
and them Brooklyn Dodgers and how they
kept on trying to beat the New York Giants
so they could get into the world series
and lose again to them New York Yankees.

Didn't care 'bout nobody, 'bout nothing
but the ones, the things not worth caring 'bout.
Gabriel Heater, The Shadow, Red Skelton,
Arthur Godfrey, Amos and Andy, Joe Louis,
and Jackie Robinson; they took care of
everybody, everything you cared 'bout.
Made all of us take a break from our
daydreaming and wondering what it
would be like to be in a place where
there was lots of snow and never a
southern accent coming
outta anybody's mouth.

Thinking way back,
I saw people going off to war.
Mostly, all, but a few, were going
to a foreign land to fight for their country,
the United States of America.
Everybody on our dirt roads and streets
watched their kin, their neighbors,
and folks they didn't know too much about,
come back from Boot Camp wearing them
pretty and proud-fitting uniforms of one
of the branches of the U.S, Military.
Everybody shook their hands,
Patted them on their backs, and asked questions
they thought were serious and meaningful.

Then in a week or two,
the new military men caught
the Greyhound Bus,
got comfortable in their seats in the back,
and went to places,
nobody in Selma had ever heard of,
to fight and kill people or be killed
by people they had no anger towards.

Few of'em, later on, came back.
Some were limping.
Some were in flag-covered coffins.
Some were still standing straight
and smiling.
All were still Negroes, Colored,
or Niggers and second-class citizens,
coming home to racially segregated,
Selma, Dallas County, Alabama.

Back then there were blackouts;
when the city turned off all the lights
to protect people from possible enemy,
nighttime raids.

To keep people from starving too much,
the folks in power gave out ration cards
and ration coupons just so
poor folks could get some sugar,
some butter, some flour, some lard.

Times were strange, tough and rough;
and punishment was quick,
harsh, and, often, final.

I always paid strict attention to them
steel balls that were chained to the legs of
Black men working on them chain gangs.
The White folks held them shotguns, rode
them big, sweaty horses, and kept their eyes
glued on them Black chain-gangers
who in addition to that ball and
chain tied to their leg, were made to wear
black & white striped prison uniforms.

More'n anything I prayed about,
I prayed the hardest and sincerest that
the Lord would never
let me to do anything that would
cause me to wear one of them
black & white-striped prison uniforms
with a steel ball chained to my leg.

There was a whole bunch of
po folks with no heat.
They were all the time goin' to
the railroad tracks looking
for stray pieces of coal.
Lots of people,
the ones further out in the country,
used kerosene lamps for light.
Folks with nothing to live for,
would fight and die over
a nickel or a bar of lye soap.

Saw two men, way back when,
both lived out in Smokey City,
the toughest part of Black-folks' Selma.
These two men been
best friends for a long time.
But this particular night
they got in an argument,
a real serious, heated and mean argument
'bout something they had read in the
Book of Nehemiah, in the Christian Bible.

They went, like they didn't really want to,
behind this run-down, old house,
these two longtime, Christian friends.
It was a Saturday night,
'close to eleven o'clock.

Nobody followed 'em
behind this run-down, old house.
Just them two men;
best friends and Christians,
from the time they were little children;
wanting to come to a settlement about
what they thought they
may have read in *Nehemiah,*
went behind this run-down, old house.

Everybody standing out
in front of the run-down,
old house, heard the two men struggling,
moving fast saying this
and saying that and whatever;
slowing down, then speeding up,
putting suspense all 'round
and through the small crowd,
sending mystery into the crowd's mind and
causing everybody's imaginations to wander
in the direction of pain, agony, death,
undertaker and graveyard.

Could hear two switchblade
knives slicing through
the hot Alabama air.
An Alabama air filled with:

Alabama-Saturday-night:
must be time for one Black man
to kill another Black man.

Soon there was no more yelling,
no hollowing, no more screaming,
just a few quiet,

After-a-while-I'll-soon-be-dead, grunts
and one or two silent groans and tiny,

Jesus, here-I-come, wails.
A few minutes went by.
Everybody was all hushed,
starting to get further back,
wanting to know the outcome but
not wanting to be a witness.
Then we saw one switchblade
being raised by one bloody hand
wearing a yellow shirt that
done turn nearly blood-red.

He staggered into the bright light
that was coming from a big, orange,
and low-hanging "*Swing low, sweet chariot,
comin' for to carry me home*", moon.

Holding his Hawkbill, pearl-handled knife,
murmuring like he was talking
to nobody but himself, Tad Jones said:

*Yaw'll, I done kilt that motherfucker.
Everybody, I just kilt Little Pete.
Bastard, was my best goddamn friend
and I done gone and kilt 'em.
Please yaw'll, pray for me.*

Remembering the times
walking through Lautzenhausen,
outside Hahn Air Base –
approaching the *Pacific Bar*,
where White American
miliary members went.
Not stopping 'cause I didn't want no trouble.

I was heading for *Charlie's*,
where the black American military members went.
Wanted to drink a Coke, swap lies.
But, that one night, for whatever the reason,
I decided I would go into the *Pacific.*
That's where that ugly Fraulien
threw a mug of beer in my face,
telling me the *Pacific Bar* didn't serve niggers.

Before the first drop of that beer touched me,
I was across the bar with my hands around that
Fraulein's throat.
Next thing I knew I was
beating the hell outta an
American soldier who had
come to the Fraulein's defense
'cause he must not have liked niggers, either.

I beat that White soldier so bad –
broke his face, blood was everywhere.
Bunch of White military folks had
to pull me off of him.

Got word later, the military police
was looking for me.
I never was apprehended.
I was lucky that time.

The trips from Selma,
riding them Greyhound buses
that took me, so many times,
to wherever I had enough money
for them to take me.
Places where I would experience too much,
and too many things;

meet too many folks,
walk too many avenues,
boulevards and streets to remember.

But, everywhere, everything and everybody –
they are still buried in my head.
All of it, deep in the wrinkles of my soul.
But, after so many years, could be
the wrinkles have become
too crooked, too deep,
and the things to be remembered
are becoming too buried.

Without the slightest modification,
I think they better stay where they be.
Right now, ain't no use waking 'em up,
getting 'em all riled and bothered.

'Cause, sometimes
remembering how it was, back when,
ain't what it's all dressed up to be.

DANGER AND SISSY

Yesterday, after work, just fo
I started to crawl under Miss Lawson's car
Guess who came moping by?
Danger and that woman of his, Sissy.
Both of 'em looked like haunts who
done been sleepin' in a graveyard.
They had cigarettes hanging from their lips.
Both skinny as a rail.
They sit they asses on the bench
That Presley built for me last year.
Right a' way, I could tell they be fucked up
off'a that liquor and that dope they aways doin'.
Danger said:

> *How you doin', Apple? You alright?*
> *Hope you ain't been sick.*
> *You still workin' on cars for them*
> *colored folks over in Prichard?*
> *What's some of they names be?*
> *Me and Sissy might know some of 'em.*

I was tired.
Had to finish work on Miss Lawson's
broke-down Oldsmobile 88
That she had been bringin' to the shop
for more than twenty-five years.
All the while I be workin',
she used to sit on a chair
and watch everything I did
like she been doin' for as
long as I can remember.
Never sayin' a word.

But, after having trouble with her health,
she stopped coming.
Stopped sitting and watching.
I asked Danger what it was that caused
him and Sissy to stop by.
Danger told one of his lies –
he had ten million in his head.
Said him and Sissy wanted to stop by
and see how I be doin'.
Said he was one of my kin folks,
Had always liked me and respected me
More'n he liked anybody else that is
related to his side of the family.
He told Sissy that they owed me a
visit and a few kind words.
Sissy, with her crossed-eyes,
Said she had to pee.
Had to go really bad
I pointed to a door and said, *go in there.*
Danger watched her step over a
few rags and tools, I had on the floor.
I got down on one knee and pulled
my Creeper close to where I kneeled.
But, I thought I had better
wait 'til Danger and Sissy
left fo I crawled under Miss Lawson's car.
Sissy came back and told Danger she
was ready to leave if he was.
They looked at each other real hard
and then Sissy laughed kinda funny like.
That's when Danger told me
That they didn't give a fuck
'bout how I be doin'.
They stopped by to see if I still was the
kinda cousin he knowed from years ago

He kicked an oil rag, o
n the garage's floor,
next to the Creeper.
I told'em to get their asses outta my
garage and off my property.
Danger knowed I could and
would kick his sorry ass
if he acted too much of a fool.
So, with Sissy urging him to leave,
They staggered outta the garage
Last I heard, both Danger and Sissy,
Died from the same kind'a cancer.

THE MOON
REPLACES THE SUN

Sitting in your rocking chair and watching
the moon replace the sun
Have you thinking about when you never
had a chair of any kind to sit in
When you had to sit on the ground
in a house with a dirt floor
Where you got your knees and legs
dusty when you prayed
The prayer you had learned years before
while listening to praying old folks
whose prayers sounded more earnest
than any of the prayers you prayed
For things and times to become perfect,
which is better than good
Like sitting in your rocking chair
and watching the moon
Replace the sun

SOUTHERN WOMAN

She was a Southerner
Not a Black Belt type
Southern woman was she,
But a McClean, Fairfax, Alexandria –
Northern Virginia type Southerner:
Immersed in sophistication
Who often attended operas and ballets
At the John F Kennedy Center so she
Could be seen and discussed by other
Northern Virginia Southern Women
Who like her lived by noble articles of
Pretentious and privileged faith
Which had been commandeered from
Eudora Welty, Flannery O'Connor and
Oher Southern female writers but not
From Harriet Ann Jacobs or Anne Moody

CRAZY JOHN

Some sly, slick,
Shrewd and roguish fellow,
He was, this man, John
Swallowed, he did, too much
Of that Beetlejuice stuff
That turn good men into hornswoggles

Those who knew him from years back
Said John came from a decent family
And was a good boy and was
Raised to be a better man
But, once he reached a certain age,
He started using
Too much of that Beetlejuice
Started to hang 'round
Bewildering, older folks

Late one night,
They mentioned, hushed-like,
That God had come to John
And explained a bunch of stuff
Had laid it all out and made it crystal clear
What was gonna happen to those who did
Or did not do this-or-do that;
Who did not obey His words

And, John being the truest of
Believers in every one of God's words
And the best preacher of His words
And the craziest preacher ever to preach

What God had whispered
To him that late night

John, was always in states of bewilderment
'Cause all of the opium
And the methamphetamines were
Taking control of what mind he still had
Which made, with his partial mind,
Him preach louder and more
Rambunctious and more crazy-like

Some of the things he
Said scared most of those
Wanting to be thrilled and
Entertained as they watched
The spit start come out of
John's turned-up mouth
Making some in the hillside crowd laugh,
Especially, when John started
Whooping and hollering
About the Seven Churches of Asia:
Ephesus, Smyrna, Pergamos, Thyatira,
Sardis, Philadelphia, and Laodicea

You see, the crowds were mostly believers
In whatever John said but none
Of them had ever attended a geography class,
Not even in high school,
Therefore, they had no idea where
These seven churches were located
To be truthful, they didn't know
Where Asia was
Even though they were in it all the time

Soon, John started being called,
 "Saint John the Devine,"
A special name for his peculiar

And rare form of talking
And scaring everybody who listened to him

Saint John the Devine,
Knowing he was a better and more
Spirited orator than other spirited orators
Said he would use his words,
As a sword to fight
And destroy all things bad

One time he talked about this woman
Who had had her clothing made by the
Great sun and who walked around
Wearing a twelve-star crown
While she stomped on the moon

Even the ones who were also using opium
Beetlejuice and methamphetamine
Started to become concerned, asking,
 "What the fuck is happening to John?"

BROWN LEAVES

Uninterrupted melancholy,
Little doubt, not a jot of faltering,
A browning covers you like it
Covers the once green leaves
That no longer holds the dampness
Of its fall season

Winter approaches and so much
Of the green starts to ebb
But a leaf, before turning brown,
Does not, always retreat and
Suffer melancholy, doubt, and faltering,
Uninterrupted or not
Like you so often do.
Like I so often do.
Like we so often do.

THEIR TIME

Rachael told Henry that Renee
Was in love with Juan,
But that Juan was smitten with
That old school-teacher lady
Who used to teach him science
When he was in the tenth grade
Rachael looked at Henry and felt
Some sorrow, some regret
She shouldn't have told him
About Renee's love for Juan
She should have told
Him about the sermon
Reverend Jones preached
Easter Sunday or about
The new store she was
Hoping to find employment
Better, yet, she should have
Kept her mouth shut,
Not said a word but that's
The way she was,
Always has been, will always be
Henry shook his head, move his feet
Through the dirt, a little bit
Then he thought about Juan being one
Of his longest friends
And he thought about
Renee and how she always smiled at
Everything Juan said
He thought about the time they had

Gone together to the movie theater
How Renee took the seat 'tween
The two of them and ate her popcorn
How she placed the straw, sticking out
Of her medium-sized coke
Between her lips and sucked like
She wanted Juan and him to notice
When she thought he was paying
Hard attention to the screen
He saw her move her hand to Juan's
Lap and squeeze him and rub him
That should have made him aware,
Told him something
Peculiar was taking place
But, love, everybody says,
Makes you not see things,
Hear things, ignore things

YOUR LAST POEM

Why did you write your last poem
What thoughts rested
Or rushed upon you
Who and what occupied your fantasies,
Your lurid dreams
Were you fearful of being
Overcome by desires too strong
To ever be abated, to be weakened
And, should such thoughts,
Fantasies, lurid dreams
Ever return, and again overwhelm
You with pungent desires
Will you then write, once more,
Your last poem

A WRITER IN MALMO

I sit in the Malmo City Library,
Located on King Oscar vag.
      I am lounging
      In one of the library's secluded
And rarely used corners.
      A place students, housewives
      And avid perusals of books
      Shy away from.
This library, modern and nicely adorned,
With not a speck of dust,
Is a place that is kept alive
By generous public funding, with the belief
That there is goodness in literacy and knowing.
      I look at shelves lined with titles of
      Books, manuscripts
      That give claim to the notion
      That words on parchment
      Are to be greatly honored and prized
      More so, even, than unclaimed gold
      Found in an alleyway by orphaned children
      Who have escaped all but
      The meanest despair.

I will later, after leaving this library,
Walk to Sodra Forstadsgatan.
      Where I'll will spend a few hours, maybe,
      In that coffee shop, the one with five tables
      Pushed scatteringly across
      A wooden floor that is

Chilled even during the warmest of months.
I will probably consume
A few cups of Turkish coffee
While looking through the windows
At casual-strolling women, alone,
Who could be thirty, forty, fifty,
Or twenty or younger,
But surely in some man's heart,
The age does not matter.
Strolling women who seem to be sightseeing and
Watching what the marketers want them to watch.
But they will never notice my large
Hands gripping a cup of Turkish coffee.

Before I was discharged
From the American military,
I would often sit on a toilet commode
At a Forward Operating Base
And write words on toilet paper
That I thought were
Brilliant, truthful
And somehow consecrated.
That was when I had an income, free food,
Free housing and the protection income,
Free food and free housing bring.
When I was discharged I had memories
Of places,
I had traveled to engage the enemy.
Places where I never spoke
The language of the natives
And places where I never understood
The natives' culture.
But, I had tried to learn.
However, laziness always got in the way.
And the truths I thought I had written

On toilet paper, before long,
Turned-out to be tainted and untrue.
>> Then, I started to see
>> My consecrated words
>> As having become
>> Polluted and diseased.

There are moments, now, when I know
It is best that I isolate myself.
>> Move away from all distractions.
>> Cocoon myself for a few weeks in the
>> Small room I am renting from the widow
>> Who lost her husband to heart trouble
>> And whose children, she once claimed,
>> Never come to visit.
>> Never, she claimed, telephone.

I sit in the room
Where I hibernate, and meditate upon notions
That are abstruse, transcendent
And often, excruciating; even
Sacramental, and spiritual.
>> I sit in this room, where I am comfortable,
>> Because I know in this room the widow
>> Will not ever disturb me
>> Not even on
>> The first day of the month,
>> To ask for the monthly
>> Rent money of 2500 SEK.

At times, feeling somewhat depressed, I think
I should give up the idea of writing in Malmo and
Go back to the small Kansas town of Coffeyville;
>> Eat huge steaks at Sirloin Stockade,
>> Root for the Red Ravens'

Football, basketball, and baseball teams,
Meet some Midwestern,
Well-bred woman
Who wants something she's
Too afraid to ask for
Or even imagine thinking about.

Instead, I am in the south of Sweden,
Not speaking the language.
Rarely do I travel to Stockholm.
Rather, on occasions, I go to Copenhagen
Where I usually spend two days
With the same red-haired prostitute who tells me
I am handsome, smart, kind, strong, and funny.

The landlord, widow lady that she is,
I believes she believes she knows
Where I go and why I go,
But she never says.
Could be the widow could offer the same
Things the prostitute offers and with much
More sincerity, efficiency, and passion.
After all, she, the widow,
My landlord, is no more than fifty.
She has beautiful teeth
And a nice Swedish body.
Makes me wonder how long she has been
Without a male or female companion.
I have these thoughts each time I take
The short train ride to and from Copenhagen

The widow asked, several weeks ago,
When I gave her the 2500 Swedish Krona
For the monthly rent,
What did I write about and where

Might she purchase copies of my writings.
>   I told her I wrote books
>   That no one ever reads
>   And that my subjects and topics
>   Are not fit for any decent
>   And honorable lady.
Shaking her head, and smiling,
She took the rent money
And slowly walked away.
>   That day I wrote for twenty-two
>   Consecutive hours.
>   My words, so well-arranged
>   And connected, flowed easily.
Then I slept for a few
Hours before writing more words.
>   In three days
>   My writing consumed
>   More than fifty hours.
During that time, I drank tea,
Ate previously purchased rolls,
With thick slices of sausage
And sweet cheeses.

>   I wrote about the widow
>   And her uncaring children.
>   I wrote how she must long
>   For *someone to* embrace.
>   I wrote how remorseful
>   She has to be when
>   That *someone* is always
>   Absent and never embraceable.

I wrote about the blond hair
That she always ties in a bun
And the heavy breasts she carries upright

And many times, I am certain, without a bra.

Then, after so many hours of writing,
Words pouring forth,
I took a slow walk through Stortorget,
Coming to rest at one of my favorite cafés:
Mello Yello.
>I drank tea, ate a seafood salad,
>And thought about
>Sergeant Major Darrel Hill
>Strolling through Bagram Air Base
>In Afghanistan
>In search of some soldier doing
>Something wrong.
The thought made me smile,
Shake my head and
Thank the Lord for allowing me to survive

>Later, still sitting in Mello Yello,
>I wrote words, rapidly, that were different
>Than the words I had previously written.
They were more serious, reflective, with searching
Language and punctuation marks of every sort.
>It was as if
>I was in too much or a hurry
>To say something
>About something that had
>Long agitated deep inside of me.
So, ordering more tea,
I wrote about the tears
I had long ago cried upon leaving home.
>I wrote how difficult
>It had been to see Andy, my dog,
>Chasing the bus
>And what heartbreak

I felt as the bus passed
The Coffeyville Cemetery
And headed onward to Kansas City
Where the Army was waiting
To take me away to
Places and events and pains
I'd never imagined.

The sun had not gone away.
It was not dark. It did not matter.
I was tired.
The waitress, a well-built brunette,
Told me she had, a few days prior,
Spotted me at the library.
      Looking at the waitress,
      As she walked,
      I noticed that other customers
      Were also looking at her swaying behind.

I started to write about a young recruit,
A female, I often saw
When we were having our evening meals,
In the post's chow hall.
      How we would, across tables,
      And other recruits,
      Smile at each other.
            We were never introduced.
            I created a name for her:
            Mildred Redcliff.
            That is the name I gave her.
            She had red hair and a tiny
            Mole on her neck.

I wrote about things much more
Engraved than Mildred Redcliff

And Coffeyville, Kansas.
        I wrote about
        The first time I fired a weapon
        At another human being.
Of seeing the body falling onto the sand,
As that human was surely dying.
        I wrote about the times
        Ralph and Tommy and Herb
        Had played a game on me,
        Making me think the Afghan girl
        Who worked at a stall,
        Inside our compound,
        Had wanted to make me her secret man,
        Her special person.
Ralph and Tommy and Herb
Had told me it was true,
But like the redhead girl in the chow hall,
Much about this Afghan girl had also faded away.

        When I stopped writing I rose
        And walked onto the street.
I watched the lights and
People, in love or wanting to be,
Holding hands.
Humming a song,
I had always heard at Bagram,
I headed home.
        Rather than entering my apartment
        I knocked on the widow's door.
Neither of us spoke. She stood aside.
I walked in. She watched me.
        She told me where to sit.
        I set.
        She stood over me and smiled.
I smiled up at her.

She went into another room
And returned with a bottle.
        We drank red wine.
We did not speak.
We, just slowly and silently,
Drank the red wine.
        When we had emptied the bottle,
        She rose and without looking at me,
        Took the empty wine bottle
        Into the kitchen.
Then, she returned, walked pass me
And into her bedroom.
        I, the American writer, living in Malmo,
        Followed.

WINTER IS COMING

Surely as you are born,
winter is coming.
Before long these grounds will be covered with snow.
>Cured meats will be removed from
>their places of storage,
>while canned fruits will be taken
>from shelves and eaten in the solitude
>of two-bedroom homes.

Miles from Duluth, Hibbing, and Bemidji;
up around, Baudette, Roseau, and International Falls,
married men will be hard at work
on jobs that are miles from where they rest at night.
>Their lonely women with nothing
>but their iPhones, iPads
>radios and televisions to keep them company,
>will wish for their men to hurry back to them.

Lonely housewives, with their men away, listen
to Superior and Duluth and International Falls
talk-radio stations and watch reality-television shows
as they try and remember the few times
when they really had so much fun that they
would fall down laughing.

>This past summer was especially
>warm and humid.
>Very few thought of heading south
>or to the Caribbean in order to leave behind
>oncoming cool days and cooler nights.

But, now, winter is coming.
Just around the corner.
And piles of snow will be pushed high
against other higher piles.
Lakes, rivers, streams, like always, will freeze-over.
      Older, crazier men, filled with tradition,
      will cut holes and drop fish lines
      through the frozen ice, with hopes of
      catching something besides a cold
      or whatever it was they failed
      to catch in June and July.

Winter, when it does arrive, up in these parts,
usually takes a breather before
becoming catastrophic.
Before becoming debilitating
and downright miserable,
with tree limbs breaking from the heavy icicles
and well pampered dogs starting
begging to get close to stoves
or next to the unoccupied rocking
chair that seldom rocks anymore.

      Years ago when gas was cheaper
      and crime lower, the Mason family
      who used to live down the road,
      would always pack-up in in late September,
      and head out to Arizona,
      New Mexico, or Florida –
      driving the same old Volkswagen bus,
      they bought
      back in 1983, while visiting kin folks
      down in the Twin Cities.

They would head out to
any place that was warm and
could give them a really good tan while they laid
in the sun and talked about the Vikings and Twins.

        Speaking loudly about whether or not there
        will be a winter colder than the last winter
        is a tricky business.
        Some folks count on *Punxsutawney Phil,*
        that Pennsylvania groundhog.
        Other folks count on certain bones aching.
Then there are the folks who count on nothing,
they just make sure they
have enough wood, enough coal.
        Make sure the propane gas contract
        is up to-date.
        Thank God, they had enough sense
        to cured the meats they killed,
        and canned the fruits and vegetables they grew.

KIERAN PADRAIG

A pensive walk, she makes,
Across the floor and onto the Belfast stage
Where words, as if written by a young
And drunk Shakespeare, will be nervously and
Hurriedly read by a frightened Irish colleen
Who prays she will not stumble over the
Clumsily constructed words
Which attempt to describe how foolish it is
To contemplate, to seek love –
No, not love, but simply, to seek being
Tolerated as someone intriguingly mysterious;
Something this Irish colleen has never weighed,
Imagined, nor dreamt of.
Standing before the microphone,
Feeling more terrified than she ought to be
She raises her head, wipes away a strand of
Her brown hair, squeezes the papers
That the clumsily constructed words
Are type-written on in big, black letters.
The nervousness of her father, of her mother,
Of her two aunts envelope her.
Kieran Padraig, the man who wrote these
Badly conceived and ill-manufactured words,
Has been a drunk since the day he was
Accused of molesting a nearly blind coed
Which he adamantly denied and was let go by
The pompous folks at Belfast Metro
Where he often boasted about his
Relationship with the great poet, Seamus Heaney

Over at Queen's University, who had won the
Nobel Prize for Literature back in 1995
The plain Irish, colleen starts to read,
What she had rehearsed too many times,
Kieran Padraig words about redemption,
Forgiveness, and recompense that may
Enthuse his never sober soul and make
Him think he is as good as Seamus Heaney.
But, she, just seventeen,
Has studied Seamus Heaney,
And knows the daily drunk and coed molester,
Kieran Padraig, cannot be spoken of
In the same breath as Mr. Heaney.
She hopes the audience is paying attention
And will regurgitate the foulness she reads
As soon as she reads it; thereby, rejecting
Every word and utterance she makes.
Knowing she is a simple girl who has been
Tasked to perform this scurrilous recitation
Because, she had been chosen by the most
Revered English teacher, Madam Sarah Deeds.
She wishes there were better lighting and
A cooler setting. Nonetheless, she reads:

> *The forever coward bombmakers and*
> *The chicken-hearted assassins*
> *Encased in their never understood hatred*
> *And their never mitigated anger,*
> *Have I seen, listened to, and have*
> *I attempted to reverse that which is wrong.*
>> *One side of us have worshiped the Holy See,*
>> *Residing in Vatican City*
>> *The other side has pronounced obedience*
>> *To the Empire of Great Britain.*
> *The lads, the lass, the old, the young, man, and*
> *Woman, under this mostly brisk sky,*

Have, for reasons, even the learned does
Not utterly understand and grasp,
Contributed to the massacring of Irish boys,
Irish girls – all ages and beliefs;
By demanding their be obedient to distorted
Beliefs coming from those in Rome
Or decreed by the United Kingdom of Britain
And Northern Ireland Parliament.
Like all of you, I've seen the
Gatherings in Mid- and East-Antrim cemeteries;
The City of Belfast Cemetery,
And the Clifton Street one, and Dundonald's
> *Small and sparse gatherings many*
> *Of these burials, with few true tears.*
I've stood to the side, almost drunk,
Near the very back, close to the gravediggers,
Watching steam flow from the boiling
Hate and the simmering need for revenge of
Young lasses and young lads soon to be
Led to Roselawn or Drumbo where
They, being dead and buried,
Will not notice this boozed and disgraceful man
Who choose to attend as many of these ceremonies
As he possible can so he may retire to an
Unkempt bed with a bottle of Bushmills and
His dreams of where he might now be had he not
Been born in Coleraine near the River Bann,
Of parents who – both of them – were caretakers
And boastful drunks with no education,
But possessors of good sense and a willingness to
Obey the law and love their child, me,
This drunk poet but well-versed man who
Is a Northern Ireland disgrace.
> *Whose shameful behavior has spared*
> *Not a meter of this great land that*

For reasons, has been fervently
Nourished by many and
Discouraged by an equal number.

Seek freedom from England, seek self-rule,
Seek something called "Nationhood."
And with passion, those who oppose, who
Refuse to abandon the tit of Mother
England, the two sides, some from the
Same kin, have filled our ancient and new,
Our beautiful and out put-out-to-pasture
Graveyards and cemeteries.

Through the bottom
Of Northern Ireland whisky and gin and wine bottles,
I've witnessed what hate and pride, gassed by ignorance
And recompense has wrought:
Enough tears and sorrow to fill the entire Lough Neagh.

The seventeen-year-old colleen, nearly exhausted.
Steps away from the podium.
Kieran Padraig's words has brought fear,
Not only to her, but the attentive audience
Who throughout her reading of this molester's
Words, have remained anxiously calm,
Apprehensive and ready to pounce in condemnation
Of what they, upon arriving, knew would be foul.
But, to their surprise Kieran had not written anything,
So far, that was too untoward.
After a quick trip to the restroom
And a glance at her parents,
The seventeen-year-old colleen starts to again read:

There have been pain and suffering and
Trouble and tribulation and vexation.
Wives have worried about husbands;

Husbands have worried about wives.
Brothers about sisters; sisters about
Brothers, neighbors about neighbors.
In the midst of their worries about mayhem,
Groceries had to be purchased,
Appointments had to be kept.
Birthdays and celebrations had to be attended
Where drunks like me were never invited,
Or if stopping by, were shooed-away,
Reminded that we, drunks like me,
Are never welcomed around decent folks,
Even if those folks are like the misguided
And crazed, assassinated Maire Drumm,
The Sinn Fein leader, whose hatred was
multiplied by the mistreatment of family.
Yes, cowards wanting to prove their
Loyalty to the Queen, shot poor Marie Drumm dead
As she lay in a hospital bed in an attempt to recover
From eye injury and pain of heart.
I, this drunkard fool who on occasion muster
Enough energy and intelligence to write,
Wrote about her murder and how she must
Have trembled as the assassins approached.
She must have known she
Would never again see her five children,
Her husband, Jimmy, or any of her friends
So, on a rather misty and very cool Fall day,
Smelling of bourbon and unwashed skin,
I stood far away, half-hidden behind the never
Visited tomb of some long-dead gent,
And watched as the children: Seamus, Sean,
Catherine, Marie, and Margaret wept,
While Jimmy, still resembling the prisoner
He had been for so many years, wept not.
I wondered who of the attendees were

Sad and who were joyful and why and why.
Which of them had revealed what ward,
Room and what bed Marie Drumm lay
So they could be praised and boasted by
Those in cahoots with Ulster Loyalists
Who saw such murder as a way of
Expressing, "God save our gracious Queen!"
Reigning from the guarded acres of rarified
London land at Buckingham Palace,
Where she silently and with a nondetectable
Smile, surely welcomed Marie Dunn's death.
No wonder then that I prefer the bottle,
Whether it contains wine, gin, or bourbon
To wash away the perpetual evils that awash
This place called Northern Ireland
One tear, then several started to cover the
Seventeen-year-old colleen's smooth cheeks that
Had been duly scrubbed earlier that morning
As she prepared to come to this venue and read
The words of the molester, Kieran Padraig;
A very foul man whose living in Belfast tainted
All that was beautiful and precious
About Northern Ireland and what
Northern Ireland nourished

She stepped to the side of the podium.
Finally, someone applauded.
Then, everyone applauded.
Then the audience, as one, stood and sang:
"Long live Kieran Padraig
And his righteous words."

A MOTHER PONDERS

Five years she has set in this place
Feels like she has taken a million tiny steps
From one side of the cell to the other.
In the beginning, when it first started,
During those earlier times, she counted them.
Now, they let her walk down the hall
And on occasion into the yard.
No one asks anymore why she is in this prison
Or for so long she has been locked away.
They've all heard through prison's rumors
And gossip and the guards' whispers.
She is good at braiding hair, saying nice things,
And making others feel pretty about themselves.

The man who all the time beat her daughter
And raped her ten-year-old granddaughter
Is long dead, done rotted away into nothing.
It was one rainy Sunday night, when the
House was creaking, and before her prayers.
He begged her to let him come inside
Out from the weather, wanting to get dry.
Then, he beat her with his calloused fists
And an ironing iron she had on the stove,
Before and after he raped her grandchild.

He was somebody who deserved to die slower
Than the hurry up manner she made him die.
She kept on sticking-in and pulling-out the ice pick
From his rounded and soft belly and his hairy chest

His hollowing and screaming and cussing
Almost made her regain her Christian mind.
He stumbled out the back door before he fell
A few steps onto the rained-on crabgrass.
Foam and blood was coming out of his belly
Out of his chest, nose, and out of his mouth.
His eyes were leaned way back
In the back of his shiny, rained-on face.
When her daughter
Came home from where she'd been,
She explained what she'd done then
Showed her where his dead body lay.
In the wet grass

Her granddaughter, God bless her soul
Was still screaming and shouting
Then she went into the yard and spat on him.

Her daughter, the child's mother,
Just stood looking
Through the drops of rain at his dead body

They took her to jail and gave her
Eight years with the chance for parole
For what she did, but she didn't care
Never regretted one thing 'bout what she did
Never lost a bit of sleep 'bout what she did
Told the judge and the jury she would do it again
If he had done what he had done again.

She still reads her Bible, like she used to
Before she got here.
She talks all the time to her God.
But, she ain't asked, not one time,
For no forgiveness or redemption
For no absolution

AN OLDER WOMAN,
A YOUNG MAN

Yvonne Drezler.
She's had had four husbands.
Seventy-one years-old, is Yvonne Drezler.
She is now single.
She has amassed a miniature fortune,
Mainly from her last two marriages;
Particularly, her last marriage to a very corrupt
But wealthy hedge fund director.
She owns several real estate properties –
None exceptionally large, but pricy.

He is a twenty-six.
He claims to be a poet.
His name is Remus Testament.
Remus Testament, by chance, encounters,
The seventy-one years-old, Yvonne Drezler
During a first time visit to Tybee Island.
Remus thinks of himself as
A superbly-brilliant, young poet.
His genius mind far exceeds his youth.
He is a cautious person,
Possessing a sparkling truthfulness;
Always displaying a respectful demeanor
And an unblemished character.

In a Tybee Island bar, not far from
Where the Atlantic Ocean swells,
Leaning across one of the tavern's table,

Her bosom sagging, her teeth gleaming,
Yvonne Drezler speaks to Remus Testament.
She speaks her English
With a strange accent.
Her eyes have red flickerings
Buried in their corners,
Which reminds everyone of a weirdness
They never want to encounter.
She orders another cup of the strong
Black coffee with a pinch of lemon.
>   **And, you, young man, what do you do?**
> *Most of the time I'm a poet. Yes, ma'am, I'm a poet.*
>   **A poet, you say? Is that another way of**
>   **saying you are a goddamn liar?**
> *No, Ma'am, I don't lie. Ever. Never*
>   **Stalin, the man who once ruled the**
>   **Soviet Union, was also a poet and a fucking liar.**
>   **You know that? He was also a murderer,**
>   **and a psychopath. You, know that?**
> *Yes, Ma'am, I've read about Stalin and what he was and*
> *what he wasn't.*
>   **Do you wake up at 4 o'clock in the morning**
>   **with ideas that will never touch paper?**
> *Sometimes that kind of thing happens to me but not*
> *at 4 O'clock in the morning.*
>   **I once loved a poet. A goddamned mad man.**
>   **And the world's greatest liar but he could**
>   **fuck up a storm. Could eat pussy better than**
>   **any man or woman I've ever known.**
>   **He was one of the ones I never married.**
>   **Never wanted to marry the bastard.**
>   **But, Lordy, he could fuck. Could eat pussy, too.**
>   **You were not aware of that, were you?**
>   **Of course not. I never told you or**
>   **anyone about that pussy eating man.**

Never told a soul.
Why do you always talk the way you are talking?
Are you Trying to shock me, upset me?
Fenton Johnson. Now, that was a poet.
Are you that good? What about Langston Hughes?
I'm as good as I want to be. As good as God wants me
To be. I don't compare myself.
What a stupid answer. No, you are not.
Not as good as either Fenton or Langston.
You don't even know me. Have never read anything
I've written. How can you tell whether I'm good or bad?
You are nothing but a goddamn hustler.
A fucking counterfeiter. A fast-talking rip-off artist.
A hanger-on vagabond.
A bogus-traveler with nothing to offer but your lies
and your bullshit.
When I was in Paris with my fourth
husband, before coming to this miserable place,
I went to a club filled with poets, writers,
painters, pimps, and whores.
It was a joy to hear the poets recite their poems,
which I didn't understand.
I was enthralled by the writers and artists
and the whores strutting and rotating their asses.
The luring and lust-filled eyes of the pimps
almost made me climax.
Do you understand French?
What about Italian, Spanish, or German?
Have you ever been to Paris?
What about Rome and Berlin;
not to mention Istanbul or Oslo?
I'll bet you cannot speak proper English.
So, how can you be a poet?
What a dumb-ass you are.
Why do you call me a dumb-ass? You are right, I do not speak Italian or German,

but I do speak English, Chinese, French, Spanish, Russian, and Arabic.
    Would you write a poem for me if I
paid you with my flesh,
with my practiced mouth?
If I allowed you to do all the
things my fourth husband,
God rest his soul, was unable to do?
Would you write me a hang-low, windy,
smelly, burning-up and blistering kind
of poem if I crawled on my knees and
sucked you dry and let you release
in my mouth, down my throat;
and, then before you got soft, let you
go into my about-to-go-sour pussy?
And if you are still hard,
I would let you get behind me and
fuck my long-time-ago virgin ass.
I'll pay you with my body, my sweat,
my moans, but not with my money,
because I will never give a poet one dime.
Not one goddamn penny.
Only sex will I give.

But, based on what my previous husbands
and lovers told me, my flesh is better than money.
So, stay at this table while
I fetch you pen and some paper and
another glass of wine.

When we get to my apartment,
I'll wager you will be inspired
when I remove my clothing:
my bra and my panties. And, whatever
else needs removing; like, my dentures.

Maybe then you will
write me a love poem;
something rather short
and tender but foul, too.

Something like Pushkin's short
and tender poem, "O love You,"
that he wrote for that poor and lonely,
but pretty, Russian girl living
in a run-down Moscow
apartment building.
My, God, you do know who
Alexander Pushkin was, don't you?
How stupid can you be?

By the way, how old are you?
You seem too young to be a goddamn poet.
Any kind of poet.
But, as you probably know,
with poets, age really does not matter.
Does my age matter to you?
Hell, Paul Lawrence Dunbar
died when he was just thirty-four
and Villion when he was thirty-three.
And, then there were Shelly,
Sylvia Plath, and John Keats –
All were dead before turning thirty-one.
And, people have been copying
their stuff ever since they
went into the ground.

Do you think your poems will be worth
copying, worth plagiarizing, worth stealing?
That woman, Edna St. Vincent Millay, wrote
"To a Poet That Died Young," about poets

dying in their early years, she said:
"Growing old is dying young."

Do you like my apartment?
That painting over there,
the small one next to the large one.
I did that ten years ago when
I thought I liked painting.
Can you see what I
was trying to capture?
Of course you cannot.
You don't have that God-given ability.
Afterall, you are stupid. So fucking stupid.

*I'm twenty-six. A few minutes ago you asked my age, but you never paused
for my answer.*

I'm sorry, baby.
Sometimes I ask a question and
becomes too distracted to wait
on an answer. I apologize. Come over here,
let me give you a big, strong hug and a
long and hard kiss. I want to stir you
with intense and widespread passion,
wickedness, desire and lust. I want you to do
things to me that will have you ashamed
or proud for the rest of your life.
I'm talking about sexual things.
Things a boy your age, poet or not,
have never dreamed of.
I want you to quake, tremble,
be on fire and be swallowed up in flames –
while writing my poem.
As you read it to me,
I want you to be buck-naked with
a big hard-on that only
young liars can muster.

And, with your hard-on, will you stand next
to my painting and recite it in your youthful
voice, with your cock still hard?

Ok, gaze, look at me. I'm naked.
What do you think of my body?
I know it has been used, but not depleted.

My first husband was music man.
He didn't play any instrument.
He would whistle the music.
He could whistle Beethoven, Mozart,
Charlie Parker, anybody, and everybody.
We broke up over some silly shit
that didn't make any sense at all.
We were too young and dumb.

Then, I met a man who owned
a clothing store. He was a damn good man.
Too good for me.
So, with him on his knees crying and begging
for me to change my mind, offering me all kinds
of designer clothes and special seats at restaurants
and tickets to plays where I could show
off my designer outfits and flaunt my curvaceous,
sexy and boiling-over-hot body, I walked away.

Number three was a college professor
who could tell you anything you wanted to know
about the human body and what makes the body function.
Trouble was, he was impotent.
Poor rascal could not get his cock to rise no
matter what medicines I made him take.

My last marriage was to a very well-off man.
One of the richest people I've ever known.
That man spent too much money on me and
on the things he thought would make me happy.
I left him after I caught him sucking-off his male secretary.
That's how I ended up so damn rich.

Then, I stopped being with men and started
having sex with young, inexperienced women
who could use their tongues and hands and
all kinds of sex toys to bring me total delight.
Those young girls knew how to please a woman better
than any man I had ever been with.

Are you stirred? Are you quivering and fantasizing
and wondering and picturing us together?
By the way, what is your name?
I don't think we ever got around to that, did we?
But, as you probably know, names are not important
unless they belong to poets. Right?

My name is Remus Testament. Remus Testament, the Second.

Wow, what kinda fucked up name is that?
Who in the hell named you Remus?
And, where did the last name, Testament, come from?
Is your daddy a preacher?

Late one night when we are both drunk from
my expensive liquor, when we are tangled up
with each other, I will ask you what you've written for me.
You will say you've written about people. All kinds of people.
People from everywhere, and by saying that, you will
prove me right: that you are a conniving piece of shit.
Will prove what a flimflammer you are.
What a hood-winker and bamboozler you are.
I will rise and stand over you and tell you what that fellow,

Carl Sandburg, a real poet, said about people.
I'll explain Sandburg's meaning when he wrote,
 "The people is a myth, an abstraction. "
Then he – Carl Sandburg – a real poet, asked:
"And what myth would you put in place of the people?
And what abstraction would you exchange for this one?
And when has creative man not toiled deep in myth."

That is what a real, gen-u-wine poet wrote.
What a real poet, said. And, since you and I,
most of the time, will share the same bed,
why don't you, one evening,
write a poem about me like that poem,
"Toast," that Frank Horne wrote
about that woman he slept with?
Frank Horne, wrote:
"Here's to your eyes for the things I
see drowned in them. Here's to your lips,
two livid streaks of flame …
Here's to your heart, may it be ever full
of the love of living. Here's to your
body a lithesome hill-top tree
swaying to a spring's morning breath …
Here's to your soul, as yet unborn."

Why can't you write something
like that for me? How come?
Is it because I'm old enough to
Be your mother, even your grandmother;
too old for you or any poet to write about?
Is it because you, deep down inside,
consider me a washed-up , shallow, and profane bitch?
If I had an ass and lips like that skinny, blonde,
pornographic-looking heifer,
living in Apartment 409,

I bet you would write all day
and all night long about how beautiful and delightful I am.
But, we are in Apartment 501,
which I own, eating food I paid for.
And, because I'm a seventy-one-year-old
shallow bitch and you are
a twenty-two-year-old poet,
you can't muster up the courage
and creativity to write a few lies about me.
About us.
All I want from you are a few of the lies all
poets, who are masterful liars, write.
Tell me I am adorable. That I am thin.
That I am somewhat holy and somehow pure.

Write a poem about how I inspire you.
How I am the most beautiful woman on Earth.
With your poem, make me believe
that my cunt has not been stretched
to its physical limit.

Write wonderful lies that make
me believe you love me. That you want me.
That you need me. Write that you will
never leave me for a girl like the sex-filled
girl in Apartment 409.

Just give me a bundle of your poems that are
filled with your best vision and best lies.
Let your poem, filled with lies, I beg, capture
my otherworldliness and ethereal exquisiteness.

Tell me, and all who will read your words,
that my skin is flawless,
having not one blemish.

Using the magnificent way poets put things
together, let everyone see how I became
obsessed with your young body, and your
young mind, and with your much
younger spirit and infant soul.

Wrap a verse or two in the flowery garments
of my debauchery, self-indulgence, and decadence.
After drinking a glass of wine,
sit back down and write how I was the catalyst,
the enzyme that generated your gifted writings
of the most probing invasion of my inner secret-self,
so I, alone, with my depleted body and fleeing hopes,
can at least read and shutter as I remember what it was
like to be held and kissed by young, inexperienced lips
and mauled by a cock that never tired,
that kept pounding every hole in my body.

Now, I will be silent and allow you to
concentrate, to fathom thoughts that
I'll later, no doubt, cherish.

You have spoken without saying anything significant.
Your tongue is covered in foulness that would make repugnant
whores sashaying through Delhi's infamous G.B. Road blush.
Maybe because of my youth and my sexual impoverishment
and my lack of discovery, you think I am not worthy of anything
but your vulgar language and your fractious and antiquated behavior.

To be sure, I find your obscenity and coarseness sad,
worthy of a cheap clergy's sympathy.
Yes, there it is: you are nothing more than
a sad, obscene, and coarse woman; a nasty woman;
a woman in search of ladyship; some degree of dignity.
That is, if you have ever searched for such a thing.

You ask me to write a poem populated with untruths
because you claim all poets are untruthful;
therefore, any poem I write, particularly one about you,
will reflect nothing but lies.

Maybe your assessment is correct;
for me to say you are beautiful, would be a lie.
To say, even using obscure words,
that you are sensuous or physically desirable, would be a lie;
not to mention my saying you are intelligent,
worldly, well-read, or imaginative would be nothing
but falsehoods, untruths, fabrications, magnificent lies.
With your disgusting, contrived and well displayed ignorance
and your horrid manners, you dishonor the
mother that brought you into this world,
the father that gave his seed while rewarding
whatever child you never gave birth.
Your presence on Earth pollutes every
centimeter of ground you see and step upon.
Without insight or knowledge, you assume
you shall lure me into your bedroom and do
as you please with my body;
thereby, torturing my mind and blemishing my morals.
Morals inculcated in me by a long history of
honorable and highly renowned forebearers.
I know very well the foul languages: Arabic, Russian and Chinese.
I am fluent in each. I am also fluent in my native language,
English, as well as French.
These, as you surely must know,
are the five official languages of the United Nations.
I know these languages almost as well as
I know their governments' penchant for inflicting
the most diabolical, barbarous, and magniloquent
inhumanity ever thought of, ever dreamed of.
According to native speakers of these six languages,

I speak each of them without a flaw.
Yet, you, without any evidence, accused me of ignorance.
You called me a dumbass. Why?
Have you, not, in the many years of having men ejaculate
into your constantly used cunt,
become pregnant with any of those men's child?
If so what happened to that child?
Were it crudely aborted in the same fashion
your senses have been forever erased?
But, were you a mother, I doubt if you would approve
a wretched and damaged old hag saying harsh, vile,
and reprehensible things to your child or to anyone you love.
Being true to my feelings and my need to know
and my desire to render a degree of pain
I would very much like to penetrate each of your
outmoded and aching-for-penetration holes;
ripping you in such a way you will beg
and scream for a mercy God has yet designed.
You are silently hoping and praying that my youthful
and elongated prick will treat your cunt in the same
manner your cunt, when it was in its youth prime,
treated the many pricks it once engulfed.
Yes you hope that I will flood your cunt
with twenty-six-year-old cum that will overflow
onto your stout thighs and mingle in that hairy bush
I now look at and onto your rounded and swelled belly,
I now must turn from.

Yes, I will fuck you — not as a young poet —
but as a demon released from years of rehearsal in hell's
university obtaining a PhD in how to best
fuck older and decadent cunts.
I will fuck you until there is nothing left of you
to be fucked, to be used, to be destroyed.
Then, with nothing more to gain from your tired

and musty, stale, and widen cunt, I will attack
your rounded, wrinkled, and fat ass by first
plunging one, two, three fingers —
my entire hand into your behind and watch
as you turn and wither. And, I will listen as you
whimper, bellow, and beg for more.

Beg, you will, that I turn your ass
into a welcoming sexual retreat.
Yes, I will go deeper into your rectum
than any person has ever gone;
ripping your bowels and making you
lose all sense of being alive,
of who you are, of where you are.
This — all of what I've mention, and more,
if I'm able to conjure much more,
I will do with joy and conquest crusting my soul
and with happiness rippling throughout my young blood.
I will reawake and provoked urges and sensualities
that have been dormant for years, not in me, but in you.
You will relearn how it feels to emit your sticky,
and ill-smelling cum and to reach a level of bliss that has,
for your entire life, eluded your sad soul.
You will gladly lick my youthful balls
and run your abominable and foul tongue into my ass.
And, like a crazed woman, you will,
as if interlocked with rampant spirits,
emit joy at the heights I have brought you to;
hence, you will wallow like a captured fish.
Then, suddenly, you will become silent
and totally submissive and quiescent.

Hesitatingly, Yvonne Drezler
rose from the cushioned chair.
Her bloated belly, resembling an oinker's;

something no one would ever want to see,
touch, lay next to, and surely, never embrace.
No semblance of a man, especially a
young poet, would want to embrace
Yvonne Drezler.

Trying to forget how she had allowed
herself to come to this,
she contemplated gathering the clothes
she had haphazardly and hurriedly thrown
from her depleted body and onto the floor
and the chair that the maid had
yesterday cleaned.
She thought about placing her bra
around her sagged and bruised breasts.
She knew she should retrieve her tiny
red panties, soiled with her cum;
that covered the slit that was
barely noticeable because of her
folded, bunched-up, obese flesh.
The slit that, at one time,
had been penetrated by large
and small human organs and
man-made toys; all of which she
had pretended to be apprehensive about,
But had in the end, enjoyed.
Only to reach this point in her life
where she could not even convince a lying
poet who is young enough to remain
stiff for hours, to enter her antiquated
and shriveled hole.

Not wanting to utter a word,
she did not touch
her designer pants and blouse.

Nor did she pick up the tiny panties
or the stockings or her pride
or her debasement.
She simply set there with her
long-time-ago seductive body
that had pleased four husbands
and forty or fifty or sixty
other men and wondered what
had made the young poet so brave.
Much too brave for even a wise
and well-travel woman of shameful
and distant fame and sorrow,
mixed with a type bemusement only
the most despicable experiences.

She may weep which may cause
wrinkles to form which may be a
masquerade to gain a degree of mercy;
maybe an ounce of sympathy,
that will seep into
the young man's mind,
and juggled his youthful senses,
thus, mollifying his courage and
make him want to say he is sorry
for the lewd words he has spoken to her.
Still naked, she leans back in her chair,
wipes her cheeks, pucker her lips,
spread her legs.
After a while, she smiles.
She places her hands on her lap.
She again licks her lips.

**Being brilliant, so you claim, does not,
for sure, amputate an unkind and
braggadocious nature. Rather than**

admonishing, you choose to eviscerate,
not only my swelled sense of delight,
but also my very desire to imagine beyond
the realms of the greatest of all imaginers.
You choose to cauterize, to singe my fantasies
for one final sexual spasm.

You, with your fluency in the five
United Nation languages, reversed the table,
making me the ignorant one;
the one with tainted money and
even more tainted scruples.

I stripped every piece of clothing
from my body and stood naked before you.
I pleaded in a non-subtle,
non-sophisticated manner,
for you to ravish and use me
in any fashion you saw
fit but my nakedness and my
shameless groveling for your cock
did not stir you, did not cause you
to be aroused, not even for a second – I noticed.

Now, humiliated and reminded that there is
no place for old, worn-out hags, I must ask
you to please leave me alone so I can drink
myself into oblivion.

Maybe later into this night or tomorrow
morning I will masturbate with my
old fingers and think of you and the poem
you will one day write about an older
woman, like me.

ON THIS DECEMBER DAY

On this December day,
Not far away from where
We might eventually arrive,
We watch an older man's
Left arm wrap around a
Matured lady's waist
We watch how they guide each
Other along the wide sidewalk,
Grass on both sides
They stop as if to catch their
Breath and to look at
And smile at each other
Then, slowly he bends his head
While she raises her's,
Their lips meet
We are certain their souls
Are joined into one;
Their joy is singular
After their embrace, after their kiss –
They continue their gradual walk
His left arm wrapped around her waist,
Slightly breathing, smiling
Going where we need to
Go but are afraid to try,
On this December day

ANGRY POETRY
OF THE BLACK POETS

As hard as I try I cannot locate the word Negro
Or the words Black, or African American,
or Colored, or White
Or Mexican, or Chinese, or Englishman,
or German, or Japanese
There are no profane words like motherfucker,
Bitch, sonofabitch, goddamn;
No phrases like "Kiss my ass," or "Fuck you,"
Or "Suck my dick,"
In Langston Hughes' poem, "Harlem,"
Which asked the question:
What happens to a dream deferred?
    Using a magnifying glass
    I searched for some type ethnicity, race,
    Religion, or cultural disparity
    In the poem "Sympathy"
    Surely, there must be something
    Bespeaking bigotry, race, religion,
    Or cultural variation embedded
    Among Paul Laurence Dunbar's
    Well put together words.
    This Dayton, Ohio boy,
    Insightful beyond his years, saying:
    I know what the caged bird feels, alas!
    And, later, saying:
    I know why the caged bird sing, ah me,
    When his wing is bruised and his bosom sore.
        Try as I might,

> Analyzing throughout the night,
> Having read and re-read Jean Toomer's
> "The Blue Meridian,"
>> I cannot tell you –
>> Not from the poem –
> Mr. Toomer's race or religion.
Let me in my attempt to transcend
What can be rarely transcended: Race.
Let me, like Hughes, Dunbar, and Toomer,
Write at least one poem or some type prose,
That goes beyond race, religion, culture,
Ethnicity, sex, or politics.
>> Let one day go by without
>> Me having thoughts of
>> Revenge or speaking about
>> Reaping what has been sown.
> Rather, allow me to compose sentences
> Impregnated with love and beauty and
> Winsome dreams.
Should I not construct such sentences,
Will it be because I have never known love,
Have never seen beauty,
And cannot have winsome dreams?
Then, please allow me to find a place,
Anywhere, where I can at least
Enjoy the loveliness of silent disappointment
But never remorseful revenge

PAINT ROCK

Eleven people in that one box car –
Hobos, riffraff, drifters
The year was 1931,
In the midst of the
Post-Antebellum South.
A South still in the throes of remembering
It's defeat to the hated and reviled,
Yankee-North

March 25 - eleven young people riding
In heighten fear,
Through Alabama darkness
Heading into a most damning misery
And a deformed story to be later told.
They never could have guessed
That was waiting for them.
A damning misery and deformed story
That would canonize,
And bastardize these eleven souls.

Even Melampus could they have
Predicted The troubles and pains
These tracks would bring.

Two girls, both poor.
Both as filthy, and as vulgar
As the Alabama dirt that
Produced them.

Some eighty-or-so miles west
Of Chattanooga, Tennessee,
At a Alabama place
Named Paint Rock,
Seventeen miles west
Of where that train's engine was stilled.
Where its boxcars were stopped.

Alabama mosquitoes,
Gnats, lighting bugs
And cottonmouths all of a
Sudden ceased moving
So they could get better looks.

A fat man, with tobacco
Juice escaping his lips;
A man with a sheriff's star pinned
To his heavy coat.
Had a pistol on his side
And a shotgun cradled in his arms.
Slowly, he strode to that boxcar
Breathing and sweating
Harder than he ever remembered
Breathing and sweating.

Other men, some skinny,
Some stout, most with no
More than a grade-school education,
Stood behind the fat sheriff.
Each, also, had a star pinned to a coat.
They were the fat sheriff's posse.

Every last one of them,
Carried rifles, shotguns pistols and
Every bit of hate, animus, revulsion

Viciousness and fear,
Jackson County, Alabama
Had, since the day they were born,
Taught them and boasted about it.

Two women: one 17-years-old
One 21-years-old;
Matted filthy, blond hair
Both wore too-big, oversized, coveralls.
Both slick about the ways Southern
White women use to get out of trouble.
Two Huntsville girls –
Cotton mill working girls
Leg-spreading, seldom bathing, girls.

The nine men, well boys, really;
Twelve to twenty-years-old.
All nine stinking, hungry, full of dread.
This was March 25, 1931 –
Ten days after the soothsayers
Ides of March predictions take place.

Victoria, 21 years of evil,
Incased in a devilish soul,
With a body filled with
Loathsome and damning diseases,
Along with 17-year-old
But far from innocent, Ruby,
Slithered against the boxcar's back walls
Making themselves as invisible as possible.
Hiding, they thought, in the dark.
Not wanting the fat man or his
Posse with their pistols, rifles
And shotguns to notice.

But, the nine boys had nowhere to hide.
Had nowhere to run.
They were too scared to even move.
They said prayers to their always deaf, Jesus.
Snot and tears were running into their mouths.
Still, they prayed the different prayers
They had heard others, much older, pray.
Too afraid, they were,
To reach up and wipe away
The flowing snot and the cascading tears.

The two girls, when discovered and
Realizing they were in trouble,
Employed their "set-me-free" code
That all such females, North or South
Were made to believe,
When properly applied,
Would indeed set them free.
So, they commenced screaming
Their all-encompassing
Guaranteed, set-me-free screams.

Victoria, her breath foul from onions,
Cheap whisky, and rotting teeth, said:
They raped us.
Dem niggers made us do the nasty wit'em
Made us fornicate wit'em. Put they big thangs
In our tiny holes. Made us scream.

On and on she bellowed
She broke down and cried like
Rhett Butler's lady did in that movie.
She trembled like she was crazy.
She fell into the stained dust that trains emit.
She puked, squeezed her head.

The fat man with the pistol and the shotgun
And his posse, kept right on pointing their
Weapons into the faces of the nine boys.
At the nine boys stomachs and private parts.
Daring the nine boys to belch.
To scratch. To look cross-eyed.
To wipe away the snot or tears.

> Looking at the
> Seventeen-year-old girl,
> The fat, out-of-breath sheriff,
> With the biggest star
> Asked the skinny girl,
> Wearing the over-sized britches
> What had happened to her.
> She simply said, in a hushed tone
> Because she was crying too hard
> For a girl her size: *Me, Too.*

Seventeen miles from Paint Rock
Set another Alabama town:
Scottsboro, seat of Jackson County
Not counting red ants, coons, and possums
In 1931, Jackson County,
The entire county had 37,000 people.

Back then, between 2,300 and 2,400
Of Jackson County's folks lived in
The county seat, rundown and
Poverty-ridden, Scottsboro.

And, yes, it would be unsightly Scottsboro,
Not ignorant and more pathetic Paint Rock,
That would ring in infamy for the
Dastard and deformed decisions –

They called Alabama Justice -
That emanated from the
Jackson County's courtroom
And generate decades of American shame.

A courtroom with an Alabama flag
Flying next to an American flag,
With Bibles being held by most attendees.

Fifteen days from that March 25, 1931, day
To that other day, April 9, 1931 –
Just fifteen day; not a whole month
After their Paint Rock arrests,
All nine of the males were found guilty.
Eight of these were sentenced to
Fry in Alabama's electric chair:
Big Yellow Mama
>   Haywood Patterson, 18-years-old
>   Clarence Norris, 19-years-old
>   Charlie Weaver, 19-years-old
>   Andy Wright, 19-years-old
>   Olin Montgomery, 17-years-old
>   Ozie Powell, 16-years-old
>   William Roberson, 16-yers-old
>   Eugene Williams, 13-years-old

Roy Wright, Andy Wright's brother,
Was only 12-years-old, therefore,
He was spared *Big Yellow Mama.*
Instead he was sentenced to life in prison.

Law schools of the South
And of the North, with their steeped
In jurisprudence courses
And their pontificating professors –
Will enunciate –

With a sophisticated drawl –
How law, justice, truth, and legitimacy
Are the pillars of a *just* society –
And how America
Is the most *just* of all societies.
      They will spend less than
      Two minutes on the infamous
      Scottsboro Boys' lack of justice.
      When they speak about "due process"
      They, all of them, fail to mention
      Paint Rock and the Scottsboro Boys.
Still, prestigious law schools
From Harvard and Stanford
To less than prestigious ones,
Like, John Marshall and Thomas M. Cooley,
With pride, constantly instruct on the
Rules of law and the
U.S. Constitution, while being
Oblivious of Paint Rock,
Scottsboro, and nine Blacks
Who were treated as if no law,
Not even one prescribed by any
Of Jesus' Holy Disciples or
By Jesus, Himself, existed as
A protective shield.

THE KILLINGS

EIGHTY-SIX YEARS, 1882 to 1968.
EIGHTY-SIX YEARS of lynchings,
Of hand wringing
Of hiding and running deeper into
Snake-filled swamps

EIGHTY-SIX YEARS, 1882 to 1968.
Right around 4,742 lynchings;
That is four thousand,
Seven hundred, forty-two
Americans who were alive
And going about their way;
Citizens of the United States of America,
Who were lynched, were hanged,
Were burned at stakes;
Beaten till they no longer sighed.

And the black funeral homes,
When finally made aware,
Sent their death wagons
To carefully roll across the grass, the dirt,
Across a farmers' pastures,
Down near the river,
Where the death wagons gently
And quietly rolled
Through the cotton fields
And beyond crumbling shacks.

The needed-to-be-greased wagon wheels,
Of the Douglas Funeral Service, creaked
As the perspiring horse, *Good Sam,*
Knowing he was carrying the results
Of an ungodly deed,
Sank into Southern dust turned to mud,
As he slowly carried to a safer place,
A mutilated, rearranged, breathless
And dead body that almost everybody,
Because of downright fear,
Persuaded their eyes not to see.
And their ears not to hear.
And their minds not to fathom.
To forget and never to remember.
To leave it to God.

    Eighty-six years,
    And way before that,
    Starting in earlier years –
    To the finish of 1968,
    Four thousand,
    Seven hundred forty-two
    Black Americans lynched
    And ain't no telling how
    Many thousands more killed
    For no reason.

    According to the folks who arrange
    Mysteries but who cannot read nor
    Write words or count to high numbers
    But who can explain to those who listen,
    Who sit still without stirring;
    A heap more were made died because
    They had smiled when they
    Ought to have looked away or cried.

And a heap more, that ain't been counted,
Got kilt from the tar and the rope and the
Beatings 'cause they acted brave.
Brave in a way that evil and ugliness
Could not tolerate:
Looking straight into a man's eyes
When he shoulda looked down.
Shoulda knowed he had no business
Looking into that man's eyes.
For that, for that look,
For that bravery,
Someone was to be kilt.
Was to be dead by sunrise.
And, they, the ones made dead,
Were the docile and the brave
Black boys.

Some, they say, were even defiant.
Some described them as arrogant.
Some chose to be intelligent.
For that they had their private
Parts separated;
Sawed-off with butchers' knives
Or the hunting squirrels'
Skinning knives.

    Some had a heart removed while
    It was beating and in search of the
    Tiniest bit of some type salvation.
The good Christian folks in attendance
Looked on and marveled, pointed,
Made jokes and laughed at the removed
Private parts.

A few shuddered when a hatchet
Was used to open the chest and
Wring away the heart.

Children stood amidst
The crowds so they
Could make themselves
Strong for the future
Times when other Black boys
And no-good Black bastards,
Resembling the ones
They now saw dangling
And dead will, too,
Hang from a not-too-tall
Oak tree near that creek in the back of
Mister Crenshaw's plantation.

Wanting a precious souvenir,
A poor farmer,
With his wife
And six-year-old son
In tow, steps forward,
Reaches in his pocket for two bits
And a dime or even four bits,
Wanting to purchase a prize:
The long black penis and testicles;
Or the Black bastard's heart that's
Gonna cost more, much more;
Even more if it still beats before
Becoming silent, before the dead
Black bastard stops moving.

But, those,
Four Thousand,
Seven Hundred and Forty-Two,

Lynchings, of which 3,445 were Black.
Those numbers – covering more than
Eighty-six years, is horrendous, shameful,
Barbaric, and uncivilized.

Horrific as they may be,
Those numbers are
Small when compared
To the numbers for
The years, 2015-2018.
In those years, 2015-2018,
In the United States of America,
Black men, the descendants
Of Blacks brought across the
Atlantic from West African lands,
Decided they would imitate and magnify
European Americans' ugliness,
Evilness, and barbarism, by creating an
Epidemic that could not be contained.
Someone is referring to this epidemic as
The: *Black Fratricide Syndrome*

Over that four-year period 30,176
African Americans were victims
Of the *Black Fratricide Syndrome.*
Of this horrifying number, 25,890
Were African American men:
The traditional "bread-winners"
Of the nuclear family.
It did not take long before
The *Black Fratricide Syndrome,*
A most shameful man-made disease,
Started to ravish most
African American communities,
Afflicting the young, the old;

Every professional and income level.

>Data, from many sources,
>Show the ridiculous and sad
>Dilemma Blacks regard each
>Other's life and existence.
>Tablets filled with numbers,
>Note the colossal numbers of
>Black male Homicide victims.
>Between the years 2001 and 2019,
>More than 100,000 Black men were
>Murdered; mostly, by other Black men.

>That's nearly 6,000 per year.
>Add the numbers. Do the math.
>Do the research. Weep and moan.
>Wail long and pitifully. Deflect.
>Cast blame. And, then ask:
>"Who has the power to
>Rid the world of this
>Dreadful *Black Fratricide Syndrome?*
>Who can find a fix for this ailment?

>For some reason, these monumental
>Number of homicide Black deaths
>Has not generated the protestations,
>Anger, denouncements, examinations,
>Nor demonstrations deserved, but
>Lo-n-be-hold, ain't never been expected.

>Cries for remedies and agitations for
>Punishment for those who spread the
>*Black Fratricide Syndrome*, are never heard,
>Never seen, never talked about on any
>Radio station or television.

There are no discussion
About finding a cure.
An astute observer told a close friend
That if he would ever get more'n a few
Thousand dollars he was gonna invest in
Funeral homes, hearses, embalming fluids,
And casket making.

Told his friend that that
is where big money can be made,
'Cause, as sure as the sun rises,
There's always gonna be lots of killings as
Long as the *Black Fratricide Syndrome* exist.

Get mad at each other over things
Like cheating at dominoes,
Stepping on someone's foot,
Or looking too hard
At another man's woman,
At another woman's man,
Playing the dozen or saying the
Wrong things about the wrong things.

Yes, investing in funeral homes
Like the ones on the South Side,
Near the juke joints and the churches,
Is the way to go.

But, the *Black Fratricide* Syndrome
Extends beyond homicide,
Or murder, or the killings
Of walking-around folks.
It reaches into the bellies of bunches of
Black women who find joy, it seems, in
Getting rid of the babies their lovers and

Haters have impregnated them with
By going the *Abortion Route,*
Which is always the winner of the
*"Black Fratricide Syndrome Most
Killed in a Single Year Award."*

The *Abortion Route* wins because it
Is the most ballyhooed and promoted
Method to rid the world of Black children
Before those children can ever see the light
Of day or feel a raindrop fall on their heads.

From start of the year 2001 until the end
Of the year 2017, according to some folks,
Black women, unbelievably, killed
Between six million and seven million
Black children while those children
Rested in their Black mothers' wombs,
Unaware that these mothers were making
Plans to destroy them.

How can such self-imposed tragedy beset
One people – a people who have always
Been overrun with mischance and every
Conceivable hardship and misfortune any
God would place upon any group of people?

But, here,
In the land of churches by the
Thousands, where Black people constantly
Offer prayers, it seems as if their prayers are
Never heard, or if heard, they are ignored by
The good Savior and then transferred to Satan
Who smilingly arranges for greater casualties
Of the *Black Fratricide Syndrome.*

SPARROWS

So good at shooting birds with his bb gun,
This man was,
He could shoot a sparrow right out of the sky.
One time he shot his bb gun ten times
And killed eight,
Flying through the sky, sparrows.
Tied them, 'round his waist with
A brown-colored rope.
Came strutting down the road with
Them dead sparrows hanging.
Stopped, he did,
Across from an old house
That had one window in it.
Asked Miss Slaney,
Who was sitting close
To her front door,
If she wanted two
Of them little birds,
To mix with her mustard greens.
Miss Slaney,
Without saying a word,
Rose and went back in the house
So she could peep through
Her one window.

JUST MISSING EACH OTHER

He turned North onto First Street
She must have turned South onto Third
He went into a café that specializes in seafood
She took a seat in that Mexican restaurant
He prefer reading French authors
She, mostly, reads American writers
One day, God willing,
They will sit in the same café
Drinking the same kind of wine,
While eating at the same table
They will smile and wonder
Why it took so long

THE PIANO

His parents, to be sure,
With the scantiest income
And no such thing as
Social Security or Medicare
Bought him a piano
Put it in the front room
Sent him a mile down the road
To a piano teacher's house
So he could learn how to play that piano
After several months and
Spending their income
His parents discovered
He was missing more
Lessons than he took
He preferred playing baseball
Twenty-years later, with a scotch
Whisky on his table
Sitting in the Jazz Workshop
In San Francisco's North Beach
He watched a man play the piano.
He heard the applause,
Saw the happy faces
He watched the man take a bow
He saw him wipe his face
He noticed how the women
Looked at the man with adoration
He thought about the piano
Back home still sitting in the front room
That his parents, thinking about his future

Had purchased with so much
Of their hard-earned money
He, too, clapped his hands
Smiled a sad smile,
And walked onto Broadway Street

JUNE BUG

June-Bug, Natty's youngest.
Smartest, too
Made better grades, ran faster,
Sang better than anybody.
June-Bug, waited on the
Steps for his Momma to get home
A whole block away
She could see June-Bug
He was sitting,
Kinda hunched over
Like he was feeling some kinda pain
Natty, naturally, felt a worry streak
Hurry from her knees to her spine.
Didn't know exactly what it was but
Something had to be wrong.
Long time ago, growing up in
The place she grew up,
She had learned to smell the aroma
Of things gone wrong,
So, even with a bruised heel
She hurried her steps,
Arms quickly swinging
June-Bug looked up, straightened up
Then he stood up,
Then he smiled
Then, he walked,
With his arms spread wide
Grinning real big
Threw his thin arms round his tired,
Worried, and bruised-heel, Momma,
Said, very sincerely, a tear falling:
"Momma, I love you. Happy Birthday"

HISTORY

Point to me a history that says
I must be fearful and forever
incapable of solving differential equations
and biological magnification.

Is there a history that explains why,
in my design of verses,
I must call women whores,
bitches, skanks, hussies?

What history dictates that I should never
marry the woman I impregnate?

What about a history glorifying the
number of women I mistreat,
I leave crying and in ruin?

Is there a history smiling at me
because I do not take care of my
little girl, my little boy?

Years ago I went to a faraway place
looking for something
Called "My History"

Looking for something to explain
why I am fearful of differential equations
and why I could never understand
biological magnification

Every way I turned I saw people
resembling my physical makeup
I saw wide hips, broad lips,
long and short legs
I saw straight and nappy hair

Going inside a small coffee café
I spoke American English
I smiled my American smile
And I smiled it with pure truthfulness.

A dark-bronzed woman placed a
steaming cup of coffee on my table
She looked at me. Hard
She smiled. She had dimples
You are not from Lagos;
you are a foreigner?
Asked me where I was from,
From what region I came from
I am from here, from this place
Is what I told her, still smiling

Told her I was carried away from
From where we were talking
Many, many, many years ago
Now I'm back looking for my history
Wanting to gather with my people.

She sat across from me
If you are from here why do
you speak so strange?
Maybe, she said, you are from Kano.
Are you from up north
Is Kano that your home?
What about Sokoto, you from there?

When year did you leave your home?
Maybe I know some of your people.

I told the dark-bronzed woman that
the last time I was in Nigeria was 1737.
Laughing, she backed away from the table.
No longer was she smiling.
Once back behind the counter
She pointed her finger at me and
Yelled so everyone could hear:
For sure that man, that man there,
Is a child of Ekwensu.

MODERN ALABAMA

Outside the "Summit" in Vestavia, Alabama/
She held his arm/ he squeezed her behind.
He recited nasty, disrespectful words
Only a nasty and disrespectful person
Would appreciate and praise.

With his messed-up, profane words/
So badly, but loudly, pronounced/
He referred to his mother as a rung-out bitch/
His sister, he said, was just another Black whore/
His Daddy became a no-good-motherfucker/
His brother, he bellowed, was a nothing but
A locked-up nigga, faggot.

With her blond hair, in braids,
She leaned into him and
Licked his left ear/
Ran a hand over his crotch
Told him in her somewhat-refined
Southern voice/
So those staring could hear/
"You be my nigga/

Surely, somewhere in the annals of time,
there is someone/
Some gifted and righteous smart person/
Some soothsayer
Who knows how to untangle
The pamphlets of history/
And read to us about the beginning of time/

Someone who may examine closely
The things that can be examined/
After spending years in Princeton's
Reference Center
And asking the esteemed professors
At Harvard/ Oxford/Yale

Asking the purveyors of ancient histories
To point to the times when men and
Women so brazenly belittled each other

Asking the esteemed professors/
Asking the purveyors of ancient histories
To point to the periods in time when
Brothers rejoiced in the killing of brothers/

Asking them to be reveal the history of
Those who refused to establish proper shelter
For their children and their children's mates
And who with blasphemous words,
Dishonored their mothers and their fathers/

Ask them to show us who prescribed this
Type behavior for future generations

A STRANGE OCCURRENCE

I move my fingers, ever so lightly,
from the side of your left rib,
Just beneath the beating
Of your palpitating heart/
Your eyes/ like mine/ are closed

I can feel the tightening of
Your stomach muscles

     My tongue brush your parted lips
     I inhale the aroma of your smallish,
     Unbathed, yet, scented, breasts

With your eyes tight/
Your breathing, as does mine, increase/

     My lips trove your lower parts/
     Hoping to find your fleeting thoughts/
     So I might ingest them

You whimper an unrecognizable sound/
Though not spiritual,
You utter something spiritual/

     Then, you speak the words
     Oh, shit and goddamn/

     You beg me not to stop/
     You call out a name/ Not mine
I pretend I do not hear/

I pretend you meant to call mine/
    So, I continue/

    I lick tiny beads of perspiration
    From your skin/

    You place your hands/
    Both of them, on my head/
    Then, gently, you push downward/
    I know where you are pushing me/
    Where you want me to go

Again, you speak your
Favorite curse words/

    With eagerness,
    I go where you are pushing me/

    My tongue anticipates your taste/

You say that name again/ not mine,
Someone else's/ I don't care/

    I hear a female voice/ A calming voice/
    "Sir," she says,
    "Can you hear me?
    Is everything alright?"
    I say: "Everything is perfect."

    The voice says:
    "You should be able to go home
    by tomorrow afternoon."

HEALING

An act of kindness/
A healing process/ a lifting up
Only a second/ never more than a few/
A smile/ a nodding of the head/ a helping hand/
So far away/ so remote/ lost/ at a distance/
The offering of a praise/salutation/best wishes/
An acknowledgement/
All, thrown into a polluted ocean/
Into a raging fire/ into a swamp of reptiles/
Onto an erupting volcano/

Healing:
A smile/ an embrace/ a praise/
So easy/ yet, so hard/ too difficult to do/
To say/

TRAVEL COMPANION

Was a young woman I met in 2002
On my way to from Stuttgart to Brussels
She was standing outside
A petrol station near Koblenz

Rain, mixed with snow
Had made the day miserable
      I got a large coffee mixed with lots of cream

Walking back to my car
I could see her moving her feet
Her arms tightly folded
As she tried to stay warm
      I was about to leave the parking area
      I paused and reversed the car

Smiling, she placed her duffer-bag in the trunk
I turned up the heat. Her hair was wet
She looked nearly frozen

      I removed a dry towel from the back seat.
      I told her to dry herself

I was on my way to Brussels
She smiled and said she was also going to Brussels
      After a few kilometers, she fell asleep

Outside of Maastricht
I stopped for another coffee
      She came into the café with me.

Each of us ate a bockwurst with fries

She said her name was Millie
A student at the American University, Brussels
Her Italian boyfriend had become angry
His anger caused him to
Leave her at the Koblentz petrol station

    She was a third-year student,
    Majoring in International Studies
    She told me she was from Riga,
    The capital and largest city in Latvia

She gave precise directions
To her Brussels' apartment
I asked if she had enough money
For a meal and other necessities
    She smiled and said she would be alright,
    Telling me I had done enough
I gave her two hundred euros.
    She hugged me

I drove away looking for
The Husa President Park Hotel

    I felt better than I'd felt in several months

HEAVY LOADS

Heavy loads been carried down
And up mighty steeped hills
On broad but tired backs
Set atop spindly legs

From some place not yet noticed
Always comes a whispering hymn
Created by a voice hungry
For relief and salving

Heavy loads with uninterrupted
Burdens and worries
Weighing on shoulders with
Hardly anything but bone

Somebody's child starts to cry
It is in dire need, for sure,
Of a mother's breast or a
Quick rocking till it sleeps

Heavy loads robbing the tiny
Thoughts that used to be
Before the loads became too
Heavy and the hills too steep

THE BOOK

People start dropped to their knees
Like Oymyakon snow in January
Reason being:
Everybody guessing but nobody knowing
It was time for the reading of the *Book of Life*
Too late, they all knew,
If you are not listed among
The blessed and chosen ones.

Listen carefully.
Stop your chattering. Pay attention.
Maybe, just maybe, you'll hear your name.

The *Book of Life* just might reflect names
Like Cao, LiWei, and Umar.
Does the *Book* mostly contain
The names of the French and Irish
With an occasional Basira, Jawahir,
Mawuli, Bengt, and Rufus?

From what city will the *Book of Life*
Be read, what time of day?
Will the reading take place
In Brno at noon time,
Redi Doti at sunset,
Or Nepalgunj at sunrise?

The gathered masses crowding
The streets of Seoul, Pretoria, Ub
And every place – big or small –

Regardless, its religious beliefs,
Will be consumed with hope,
Faith, expectation, and fright.

Police patrolling each gathering,
Will try to ensure quiet and calm
So everyone can hear and understand
What names are being called.

Those who have committed crimes
Where there is no vindication
Or absolution, will beg that they be

Considered or granted a reprieve.
Therefore, with mammoth wishes and
Hopes, they pray that their names,
Before they or anyone was created,
Was mercifully, written in the *Book*.

Goat herders in Arbay Heere, Mongolia
And in China's Changthang plateau
Became stilled; even the goats,
All listening for the recitation of
Names from the *Book*.

The fashion designers in Milan
Salmon fishermen in Alaska
Beach goers at Thailand's Rai Leh Beach,
Pause their activities and await the sound
Of a voice that might
Be feminine or masculine,
Soft or booming;
Speaking in tongues only
The saved will be able to weep
Happily and understand.

Others – those whose names
Are not in the *Book* – will not
Understand a word that will be read
From the nearly eight thousand languages
Of the most precious *Book.*

The pious inhabitants of the small
Village of Busbanza, Tundama Province,
Are confident that their church going,
And their lives of poverty and their
Constant prayers have placed
Them amidst those whose names
Have been written by the *Creator*
Onto the pages of His *Book of Life*
That rang throughout the Blessed Scriptures.

Now, all of them:
Boys and girls, moms and dads,
Sisters and brothers, and neighbors
Stand in towns' squares, massaging
Their Holy beads and rosaries as they,
The weak and righteous ones,
Believe they are destined to have a
Place on God's right side.

A gambling man who is proficient
At all kinds of poker and an
Expert with the dice,
Has never heard of anything as silly as a
Guaranteed victory or a never losing game.
So, he laughs and jokes and makes fun of
Those who say they will stand out front
Of Casino Baden-Baden and the Grand Lisboa,
Putting their gambling aside while beseeching
The Divine Saints and Glorified Angels, they knew

When they were children praying true prayers,
That their names are written in the *Book..*

What sins could one engage where there
Will be no forgiveness and no exculpation;
Preventing those sinners' names from being
inscribed in this most precious *Book of Life?*
Only the Creator knows why names were
And were not placed in His *Book of Life.*

Should the tyrants, murderers, rapists,
Or those who hate God and deny God's
Existence, feel anxious about hearing their
Names not called or do they already
Know they are Hell-bound because of
Their many unforgivable actions against
Their fellowmen and fellow-women
In the many places where even their
Most heinous behavior has
Become blasé and permissible
And where hooligans are anointed
Because of their butchery and the
Amounts of blood they cause others
To shed, and where not one missionary
Or any pious and honest believer of what
Is written in any Holy Bible,
will approach the hooligans
And speak about the *Book of Life*;
About salvation and the *Ever-Life.*
Such a missionary or pious and honest
Believer will be run-off, beat upon,
And even worse by the scums of
Whatever place they prowl and pretend
That they are mightier than God.

So, to these fools the *Book of Life*
Holds negligible significance and
Unimportant meaning.

To the ever praying
Sisters of the Order of Saint Benedictine,
Some acts are beyond atonement.
There can be no placement in The *Book of Life*
Of those who commit the most dastardly repulsive
Sins and with loud boastfulness celebrate their
Disassociation with any and all manners of Holiness.

They are the ones who dance, curse, fart
And belch too loudly whenever
The holy folks mention God.
They are too ignorant or too learned
Or too busy or too rich or too healthy
Or too involved;
To ever tarry with too far away thoughts
Of mystical fairytales and far away, unseen places.

Someone with a short pole made for leaning
And for assisting those who are lame and old,
Asked, "What have you heard?
Do you think our names are
Still written in the *Book*?
She leaned forward on her short pole and heard:
"I do believe they are, 'cause we been good."

CRICKETS

1

I'm in another place.
A place separated from the rest.
But, I'm in the same county, same state,
Populated by people who look like me,
Who attend similar churches,
And walk down somewhat similar streets,
Visited somewhat similar cafes
And grocery stores and places that cut hair,
But not too similar never-manicured parks,
And, surely, not too similar good schools,
And not too similar places of employment.

In this other place, away from
Where I once was but where I
Am at this very time,
I am that one nearly forgotten soul
Who cares not a goddamn thing
About the latest occurrences taking place
Anywhere else on planet Earth,
No matter how catastrophic, how cataclysmic.

2

Nor do I concern myself over Black boys
Being killed by other Black boys
Or some goddamn White boy and
His White, pregnant, and uneducated wife,

Or whether they have pork-n-beans on the shelf,
And a hundred secrets they keep from each other,
Or whether they detest each other,
Or don't detest each other,
Or tell lies for and about each other.
'Cause, they, like the stupid Black boys that kill
The other stupid Black boys, do not realize
That sometimes close to the
Almost same hour of the supposed
To be silent night, in this place, tucked far
Away behind heavily leafed bushes
And tall oaks and big pines
And other kinds of trees,
I forever listens to the chirping sounds of a
Thousand or more crickets,
Probably, all male,
Searching about and trying
Their best to attract mates.
But, for me, their search is too disturbing,
And, too goddamned frustrating.

3

I am already a sadden soul
Who silently awaits some
Ghastly-type, final damnation.
However, should I be lucky
Enough to keep surviving,
Though, I know it, my survival,
Will never happen, not for real.
But, should I be rewarded a
Surprise, and survive longer than expected,
I will then tormentingly linger in wonderment
As to when my newly scheduled ending
Will finally occur. What year? Spring? Winter?

4

These chirpings turn each of my nights
Into constant poundings inside my head.
These poundings, are similar to the pounding drums
Played by amateur street-musicians
So they can entertain visitors coming to a
Southwest Ghanaian Christian's baptizing.
Visitors who usually appear during the later hours
After the sin-cleansed bodies have been removed
From the chilled waters of the Ankobra River.
I imagine on special occasions the baptizer,
Or to be more precise, the *administrator of baptizing,*
With the professional attendees,
Applies his duties seriously,
With dignity and with the blessing of his
Christian God, before a more clamorous
Audience of undignified, obscene and
Non-Christians, booze-filled stragglers,
Who after hearing the beating drums,
Come covered with sweat,
Though the Axim dust,
Wanting to witness another ne'er-do-well,
Asking, before going into the river's water,
That his wrong-doings be washed away.
Another ne'er-do-well who could not
Afford a decent church, or a real preacher,
Or a true, honest, and holy congregation,
But can sway to the sounds of beating drums.

5

On the upper floor or some floor near the
Top, is where I sit. Where I rest on my cot.
Where I take nine steps to the right,

Eleven to the left and where I gaze
At a ceiling that is getting lower and lower.

Here, some stories above the ground,
There are still crickets.
How do they fly this high?
Most of them stop their flight –
I have watched them -
Maybe, around the second, third or fourth tier.
But, determined ones fly outside
My seventh-story window and,
To be sure, peep into my small room..

Still, way up here
Away from the prowling,
Mean-spirited crowds,
Even though, at this moment,
I hear no more chirps,
I know this quietness is just
A twist of my imagination.
Just a mental fancy.
A delusion that is sending me a rapid,
Twisting signal that I must decode,
Otherwise these crickets will keep returning
With their bothersome sounds.

6

Maybe I am madder than they say I am.
More crazed than I ever wanted to be.
Could there are no real sounds, no real crickets,
Not a single one of these critters, anywhere?
Maybe I concocted the word "Cricket."
Maybe the chirping sound is something
My craziness invented.

Could be I desire to have a constant distraction.
Something, no matter how bothersome,
Pestering, and disturbing – to keep me alive.

Sometimes, though, I scratch and pull at my skin
And constantly rub my saliva
Onto the stinging, the crawling and the irritation
I feel creeping over my body,
Even into the folds of my crotch,
In the pits of my arms and deep into my rectum.
This must mean I am not hallucinating.
That I am not imagining.
That all of this is real.

I've mentioned this to no one because they
Will claim I am losing my remaining sanity
Faster than they predicted I would.

There are nights when I see them, this high up,
Surrounding the outside of my room's window
That is covered by three steel bars.
Bars, they say, that are needed
For my protection.

7

LouSill, my best friend,
Oftentimes plays the whist card game with me.
She is the only person, I can ever remember,
Who smiles and laughs with me.
Tells me jokes, teases and tickles me.

She always say things that
Excite and inform me.
Tells me stories, LouSill does,

About the ways of many things
That I can never learn about while living
In this place I'm living and where LouSill works.

Still,
I've learned to solve complex calculus problems
And I know lots of biology and chemistry, too.
I can also talk about faraway places and
Where those places are located.

Most everybody says
I'm smarter than the
Smartest people they know
Or have read about or have
Seen on the television or at picture shows.

8

On Thursdays, Saturdays, and Tuesdays
We walk outside the side door.
Then we go around
Behind the main building,
The one where some of
The people in-charge live.

Sometimes we sing make-up-songs
About the way we understand what we see
And what we feel and what we
Wish we could see and
What we wish we could feel,
Who we wish we could be,
And, who we wish we could love,
And, who we don't ever want to love.

Other times we just walk and kick at little

Popsicle sticks and chewing gum wrappers
People, rather than putting them in their pockets
Or into the trash cans,
Have left behind on the ground.
LouSill says they, the people
who leave the little Popsicle sticks
And the chewing gum wrappers
On the ground, are lazy people who don't care
About keeping the grounds surrounding
The buildings nice and tidy.

9

In the winter when there is snow
Or just cold without any snow,
We look at our breathing
Floating from our mouths;
Then, before too long, we go back inside,
Through the side door,
That LouSill unlocks with her special key.

Then, we get into the green elevator.
In the green elevator I always want to cry
But I don't because I'm a big, grown man.

In my room I lay down on my stomach and rest
While LouSill gently rubs and pats my back.
And, she always tells me how lucky I am to be
In such a wonderful place.

10

In my thirty-two years of living in this place,
I've read book after book after book.
I've read newspapers, magazines,

And anything with words written on it.

I understand what the great writers,
Even the confusing, but great, poets,
Are talking about, complaining about,
Rejoicing about and attempting to describe.
I never forget the writers' and the poets' words;
Always reciting them to myself.

If ever I'm asked to, I can with ease
Talk about Honoré de Balzac.

I can explain to some smart professor
All there is to know about the Russian poet,
Alexander Pushkin.
And, I could, if requested,
Recite his poem *The Gypsies*.
Feeling what I feel when I read *The Gypsies*
Makes my heart go too fast,
And causes me to become irritated and
That makes me turn my
Mouth up in a peculiar way.

And, I can also talk about *The Wish*,
Another one of Pushkin's great,
But short poems.

I dare some smart Mississippian
To quiz me about that Oxford
Mississippi man, William Faulkner.

I would sit and recite for that inquisitor
Every word of *A Rose for Emily*,
The Sound and the Fury,
And *As I Lay Dying*,

And of course,
I could tell that inquisitor where
Mr. Faulkner placed all of his
Commas and exclamation points
In that not-long story of his,
That Evening Sun.

Question me about either
One of the James
And I will tell you that
Henry's greatest piece,
For me, was *The Turn of the Screw,*
Or maybe it was *Portrait of a Lady,*
Or, maybe, *The American,*
Or one of his shorter stories.
I don't like to explain what he wrote.
Makes me more uncomfortable
Than even these damn crickets.

His brother, William:
I could tell whoever wants me to,
How William came up with that clever
Philosophical, maybe it was psychological,
Question, that he believed he was the only
One who knew the proper answer:
Why do you run from a bear?

But, while I discuss this subject,
Let me inject, before I forget,
The name Chekhov.
I love everything that is Anton Chekhov.
Wasn't he the phrase-king,
The subtle-passion-king and
The intriguing prose-king?

And, then there was Garcia Marquez
Who I don't want to ignore.
What a giant of words he was.
What a master of
Juxtaposition and inflection.

But, were any of them better than
Richard Wright, John Steinbeck,
Joseph Conrad, Stephen Crane,
F. Scott Fitzgerald, Edgar Allan Poe,
James Joyce, or Franz Kafka?

Were they better than
Guy De Maupassant, Leo Tolstoy,
Walter Mosley, Herman Melville
And all the others lodged in my head?

Were they superior to Hermann Hesse,
Eugene O'Neill, Langston Hughes,
D.H. Lawrence, Ernest Hemingway,
Dante Alighieri, Miguel De Cervantes,
Christopher Marlowe, Homer, Sophocles, Ovid?

If some noted or un-noted scholar asked
Probingly about any of these authors,
I will spend hours and even days and weeks
Explaining Until LouSill tells me to stop.

11

It was 1938, October 21, they tell me all the time,
Thinking I might have forgotten the date.
The records, according to all that have read them –
And I have no reason to doubt what they tell me -
I was ten-years-old when I was found in dump pile,

Next to a dead little girl who had a busted head.
Sometimes later. I was brought from
That pile of trash, where that dead girl was.
It was a place not too far from here.

This means I was born in 1928, the same year
Lots of famous people were born;
Like that man from Scotland,
Doctor Fleming, discovered penicillin.

That was also the time of the Roaring Twenties;
Yet, I've never roared and don't
Plan on starting to roar.
And, I've never had a roaring thought, either.

12

It is nighttime
And I'm starting to hear these darn crickets
Chirping and talking, laughing,
And fussing with each other.

Male crickets looking for female companions
To spend the night with while
Making me more confused.
Making me want to run out into the darkness
With a long and hard stick and strike them all dead.

13

About twenty-five years ago,
When I was much younger
And less wise, and when things
Didn't turnout like they should have
Or didn't happen on time,
I would scream and shout really, really loud

Until they would bring me a book.

In those early years
I could only make out a few simple words
But all those simple word were pretty words.
Got so good at learning to read the pretty words,
That after a while,
I could read all the words and I started
Reading a book, a day, every day.

So, they kept bringing me books.
Brought me books so big and confusing
They thought I would never understand
The pretty words, the ugly words, and
The symbols and the inferences.

Once while Brandon was out walking with me
And telling me what he thought were scary stories,
I asked him what he knew about a Russian man
By the name of Fyodor Dostoevsky
Who I wanted someday to write like –
Like Mister Fyodor Dostoevsky.

Then, later I told Brandon
I had dreams of becoming
A Russian or a Chinaman or a German
Or a fighter from any of the Arab speaking
Countries or other type foreign countries.

Told him I dreamed I was running through sand
And over mountains and through snow,
Through shallow rivers and into villages
And into towns and inside of buildings.

Told him I had dreams of firing at airplanes

And shooting at ships,
And attacking other people who
Believed differently than I did.

Because of my questions and my rants,
I was hurriedly taken by
Brandon to the head office.
It was in that horrible place Brandon took me,
I was treated like a criminal.
They called me a traitor.
I was made to feel like I hated America.

A female-looking doctor said Brandon had
Mentioned many authors I had spoken of
But failed to tell them about any women
Writers I said I might be fond of.
She asked me if there were any women writers
I could recite like I claimed
I could recite Pushkin, Faulkner,
Henry James, and of course, Chekhov?
She asked if I was afraid of women writers,
That women writers might make me
Remember things that happened years ago.

I told her – looking directly and deeply into
Her brown eyes, that I found Shirley Jackson's,
The Lottery, poorly written
And not worthy of remembrance.

She then, with a sardonic
Smile creasing her face –
I suppose it was a "her" –
Asked me what I thought of Doris Lessing
And Pearl Buck and Emily Dickinson
And Joyce Carol Oates and Edith Wharton

And Flannery O'Connor and Harper Lee
And Sylvia Plath and Harriet Beecher Stowe
And Virginia Wolfe and Shirley Jackson
And Amy Tan and Jane Austen
and Harriet Tubman?

I balled up my fist,
Put a whole lot of spit in my mouth
And then, with all my might,
I spat that spit on the floor right
Next to one of her shoes.

She, all quick-like,
Jumped from her chair and
Told the rest of the doctors
That I was one crazy sonofabitch.
Then she left the room.
I think it was a "she."

Right then and there, I wanted to do
What I had never thought of doing
Since I was a small child:
Kill another human.

Doctor Kindred, with his long,
Braided, white hair, smiled all the time,
Allowed me to explain, as he always did,
How I did not know any real
Russians or Islamists or Chinese
Or anyone other than good ole,
Patriotic, church going,
And gun-carrying Americans.

It was only through books,
He told the gathering,

That I knew so many of these other kinds
Of people that I always dreamed about.
He told them,
Like they didn't already know,
That I had no place for
Communism or any of
The other isms.

The good doctor, smiled like he knew most
Of my deepest secrets,
Said maybe they would have to reduce
The number of books I received each week.

I studied him for a short while, then,
I asked him if he ever heard
The crickets crying?

They put the treacherous Brandon
On another floor, in another ward.

14

That's how I got to be with LouSill
Who turned out to be
A most wonderful person.
She would tell me things about
The nearby small town
And the far away big city.
About how there were very few jobs,
Lots of hungry people, and too much violence.
She explained how she was married,
With two sons and a six-year-old daughter.
Said they attended church services
On the Sundays she didn't have to be with me.
But, being with me, she said,

Made up for the times she
Was away from her church.

15

Some people, I've read,
Can't tell the difference between
A cricket and a katydid.
Sometimes this confuses me, too;
Especially, when the chirping never stops
Until my head is pounding
Like a jackhammer pounding
On a hard-clay road.
Makes me end up, because of the confusion,
Not knowing what insects to curse,
Which ones to fear.

16

I never have like using the word *fear*.
Strange, wouldn't you say?
Fear, I mean. It is an unusual emotion.
Why would someone of my ilk fear anything?

Is *fear* the same as *Being Afraid*?
Is *Being Afraid* the same as *Being Scared*?
What about *Frightened*?" is it the same as *fear*?

Just because I've been angry with these crickets
Since the day I arrived at this place,
Does not mean I'm getting
To the point where
They don't bother me as
Much as they used to.

What they have done is

Make me want to change:
To become brave, to stop
Letting them terrify me.
Is *Terrify* the same as *fear*?

So, to hell with the katydid.
My enemy will always remain
The darn cricket
Who is always hopping,
And moving sly-like though forests,
Backyards, and outside windows.
Keeping tired minds from resting.
Disturbing people like me who
Anxiously desire quiet.

17

A visiting stranger,
Steeped in knowledge of insects,
Talked for hours but never
Mentioned the cricket.
Mostly, he just wanted to prove his brilliance.
I almost raised my hand
To ask a question about this little thing
That keeps me awake
But LouSill anticipated my anxiety
and squeezed my shoulder, gave me a signal.
This caused me to just sit and wonder
What song would the crickets sing that night.

Chester Alfonso is a pseudonym for Percy Brazier. A product of the Deep South, during a period when racial segregation was the norm, he was determined to rid himself of whatever ails such an environment imposed on people, Black and Non-Black. He has been writing for most of his adult life. He has lived throughout the world. Currently, he, with his family reside in Virginia.